The Sweetest Dark

The Sweetest Dark

Shana Abé

BANTAM BOOKS 🐓 NEW YORK

Copyright © 2013 by Five Rabbits, Inc.

Published in the United States by Bantam Books,
an imprint of The Random House Publishing Group,
a division of Random House, Inc., New York.

BANTAM BOOKS and the rooster colophon are registered trademarks of Random House, Inc.

Library of Congress Cataloging-in-Publication Data

Abé, Shana.
The sweetest dark: a novel / Shana Abé.
   p. cm.
ISBN 978-0-345-53170-4 (acid-free paper)—
ISBN 978-0-345-53171-1 (ebook)
[1. Supernatural—Fiction. 2. Magic—Fiction. 3. Boarding schools—Fiction. 4. Schools—Fiction. 5. Great Britain—History—George V, 1910–1936—Fiction.] I. Title.
PZ7.A158935Sw 2012
[Fic]—dc23   2011050411

Printed in the United States of America on acid-free paper

www.bantamdell.com

9 8 7 6 5 4 3 2 1

First Edition

Book design by Liz Cosgrove

For all my readers—Thank you for taking this journey with me

Prologue

Are your eyes truly open?

Are you one of the few who have truly *seen*?

Then perhaps you already know about the hidden realm tucked inside your own.

It shares the same sky as yours, the same mountains and creeks and hills. It has the same constellations slanting across the heavens, the same roads cutting across the earth. The same towns and nations. Food, drink, fashion, language: everything seemingly the same.

But it's not.

The hidden realm presents a false front to fool you, to make you trust what you never should. Because there—right there living beside you—are monsters of ferocious beauty, ribbony creatures formed of smoke and color and claws. Monsters you've been taught to think are only myth.

They are not.

They stroll your streets, and dine in your restaurants, and wrap themselves in furs and silk and jewels. When they wish it, their faces resemble yours. Their lips smile as yours do; their skin gleams ebony or russet or milky white.

They use wings to slice through the stars at night. They'll murmur your name and shake your hand and you can't look away, because once they hold your eyes and touch your flesh, you belong to them, whether you like it or not.

They are the *drákon*.

And this is the story of one of the last of them.

The Sweetest Dark

Chapter 1

These are a few of the secrets kept from me until my sixteenth year:

That planets had spun and turned themselves out of their orbits to aid in my conception. That magma from the heart of the earth had speared through choking rock channels, stealing carbon and diamonds for me, jetting high to fall and die upon the surface of the world in a celebration of lava and flame.

That the moon had slowed for my birth, and the sun had blinked, and the stars had created a celestial new chorus from my name.

When I was a child, everyone believed that I was an ordinary human girl. Even I believed it, which shows you how little I knew.

I looked almost like a regular girl, though. Maybe one who was paler than normal, a little thinner, a touch more swift to react to sudden sounds or bright lights.

My eyes are gray. Not the gray of a sullen sky or sea but the unlikely lavender-gray of a nimbus surrounding a winter moon, colors both opaque and translucent at once.

My hair seems brown. It's such a light brown that it's almost the color of nothing, but that's a trick, one I can't control. Depending upon the hour of the day and the aspect of the clouds, my hair shines any color from fawn to pale pink to gold.

In the month of February, in the year 1909, I had been found wandering aimlessly along the streets of one of the most massive cities ever built by man: London. I was starving, alone, and ten years of age.

I'd been noticed first by a team of pickpockets—but there was nothing on me to steal, not a farthing or even a modest silver chain—then by a pair of prostitutes, who only eyed me up and down. Finally a tinker showed me some mercy, guiding me toward a constable before melting off down an alleyway.

I could not speak. I had no words to describe my situation, only my stare, which most of the grown men at the station avoided within seconds. I think they found it far less uncomfortable to study the barren walls of the station house or gaze out the grimy windows.

They gave me a blanket, an eel pie from a vendor, and a mug of gin. I claimed a spot on the floor behind the main desk and fell asleep.

Eleven hours later, since no one in the parish of St. Giles had come forward to claim me, I was handed over to the local orphanage, a miserable well of scrubbed faces and forsaken souls.

St. Giles was a knot of blighted streets and crumbling buildings. The relentless odor of gin and beer mingled with the constant stench of rotting garbage, and the unwelcome offspring there were as common as dirt. As the fifth anonymous child abandoned to the Blisshaven Foundling Home so far that year, I was assigned the name Eleanore, surname Jones. Gradually—no one even noticed when or how—Eleanore evolved into Lora, which became the name I answered to.

Lora Jones.

Speech returned in stages. Little words first, popping past my lips. *Pie. Blood. Comet.*

Then bigger ones. *Steamship. Regina. Aria, gemstone, field gun, museum.*

To the astonishment of the proprietors of Blisshaven, I shaped every word with the sort of precise, lilting intonation that indicated I might have just stepped foot from the king's court—or so I overheard them mutter. I couldn't explain it; I couldn't prevent it. That was simply how I spoke. And for all my elegant words, I never once told anyone where I'd come from or mentioned any second of my life before the day the tinker had found me.

I didn't remember. I really didn't.

Yet there were some things that *did* come back to me, a few basic things. Arithmetic, reading, writing—someone from the misty veil of my past had taught me that much. I would chase the discarded sheets of the dailies that blew into the courtyard of the orphanage, clutching each page close to my face, devouring the printed words as eagerly as if they were that delicious hot pie and cold gin I'd once consumed on the floor of the constables' station.

Like all the orphans crowding the Home, I felt certain that I did not belong where I was. That someone, somewhere, was surely searching for me, because I was special.

Unlike all the rest of the orphans, I was right.

. . .

I began to hear things.

Elusive noises, pretty sounds no one else seemed to perceive. As I grew older, they blossomed into full melodies. Snippets of song followed me about, trailing my every step. Even when I cupped my hands hard over my ears, I couldn't stop the notes from seeping around my fingers, tickling the inside of my head.

That would drive anyone barmy, wouldn't it?

At the age of twelve, I realized the songs were coming from the high stone wall surrounding the Home. From the metal rings and keys of the matrons who walked the halls with their nightsticks. From the pale, blazing diamond fixed in the stickpin the Home's director, Mr. H. W. Forrester, wore in his necktie every single day.

From even the distant stars.

They weren't the worst of it, though. The worst was the voice. The one that seemed centered not inside my head but instead just exactly inside my heart.

It was cunning and fiendish, whispering the maddest things: That it was natural that gemstones would sing to me. That it was good to hate the Home, with its dull walls and dull boiled turnips and dull spiteful girls who openly scorned me, who tripped me in the hallways and dipped my plaits into ink pots during our few hours of schooling.

The heart-voice would say things like, *Smite them. Tear them apart. I won't let you alone until you are who you are.*

And I wanted to. I was trapped and friendless, and if I'd had the slightest notion of how to smite *anything,* I bloody well might have.

I grew up considered by one and all to be peculiar at best, aloof at least, and most likely destined for the streets the day I turned seventeen, since even the factories had standards for hiring.

None of them knew that each black night, long after they themselves had curled into their dreams, I would steal from my bed to perch upon the sill of the window close by, my no-color hair a slippery curtain against my back. I would press my palms flat against the glass and gaze down at the cobblestone courtyard below, four long stories below, and puzzle over the fiend in my heart.

Every night, the fiend would whisper, *Open the window. Jump.*

So finally I did.

Chapter 2

The Moor Gate Institute for Socially Afflicted Youth
Case File No. 039985–27b
Subject: Eleanore Jones, Aged 16 years (approx.; actual DOB unknown)
Date: August 28, 1914
Date Admitted: October 21, 1913
Assoc. Dr. Julius M. Sotheby, assigned.

Subject is physically hale child of unknown descent, average height, underweight. Complexion, hair color, eye color: Fair.

Subject admitted Moor Gate via Blisshaven Foundling Home. See: Mr. Henry Forrester (director). Subject physically, verbally combative in Home; Melancholy; Antisocial; Complained of constant, nonexistent songs/voices; Unusual sensitivity to tastes, colors, smells.

Diagnosis: Behavior consistent with adolescent Feminine Hysteria.

"Tell me, Eleanore. How are we feeling this morning?"

"I'm well."

"I'm pleased to hear it. How was breakfast?"

"It was fine."

"Mrs. Pearl informs me you finished all your eggs."

"Yes."

"And . . . how did they taste?"

"They were fine."

"Powdered, were they?"

"I . . . suppose."

"You couldn't tell?"

"No."

Appetite showed marked improvement in past six months. No weight gain as yet. Subject no longer leaves meals unfinished.

"And how did you sleep?"

"Well."

"Any dreams?"

"No."

"Really, Eleanore? None?"

"I . . ."

"Mrs. McLeod left a note here for me. It says she heard you moaning last night on her rounds. Tossing about. You don't remember that?"

"I—I might have dreamed. I'm sorry, I really don't recall."

"That's all right. That's just fine. We don't remember every single dream, do we?"

Subject initiates and maintains eye contact. Visible trembling of hands first witnessed in October '13 vanished. Hair combed and plaited. Shirtwaist neat.

"I understand you've been paying particular attention to another girl here. Hattie Boyd. Eleanore? Is that right?"

"Yes, sir. Hattie's nice."

"She certainly doesn't seem to enjoy the company of anyone else. Intentionally speechless. Afflicted with unpredictable spells of rage or sudden screaming. Does she ever speak to you?"

"No."

"No words whatsoever?"

"No."

"Why, then, are you kind to her? What is it precisely that makes her nice?"

"Hattie . . . needs a friend. I understand that. So I try to be her friend."

"I see."

Subject demonstrates evidence of reemerging Feminine Virtues: Compassion. Docility. Tenderness.

"Tell me about the songs, Eleanore."

"I beg your pardon?"

"The songs you hear. Are they still haunting you?"

"No, sir. I don't hear them any longer."

"Truly? That seems peculiar, don't you think? When you first arrived here, you insisted they were everywhere. In the stones of the walls, in the nails in the doors. The iron bars of the cells. Do you recall that?"

"Yes. But . . ."

"Yes, Eleanore?"

"I'm sorry. They simply aren't here any longer."

"Are you quite sure about that?"

"Yes. Quite sure. I suppose it was rather as if . . . they grew fainter and fainter during my time here. During the treatments. And now they're no longer here at all, Doctor."

"Excellent."

Subject's marked improvement in all Areas of Concern indicates treatment course successful. Recommend discharge in one month back to Blisshaven Home. In the interim, continue treatment course: Daily ice bath submergence, mercury tonics, biweekly harnessing/electrical shock.

"Doctor Sotheby?"

"Yes?"

"Is it true, what the nurses are saying? About the war?"

"What is it you think they're saying?"

"That now that we've declared against the kaiser, we'll be under attack. That he'll send his aeroplanes straight to London, and his armies right after."

"It's really none of your concern. You need only concentrate on getting well."

"But—a war—"

"This war, child, will be concluded in a matter of months. His Majesty will see to that. The Germans will never have a chance to reach us here, neither by air nor land nor sea. We are safe as can be. I assure you, there is absolutely nothing for you to worry about."

Eight Months Later

Victoria station was cavernous, a fairy-work construction of wrought iron and steel and great canopies of glass, with locomotives that heaved and puffed into their slots by the platforms like groaning, overstuffed beasts. I'd never been in a place so big before. I'd never seen so many people amassed together at once.

I stood with my single suitcase clutched in one hand and my ticket in the other. Men and women in fine coats and hats pushed by me as if I was invisible—which, in a way, I was.

I had a coat, but it was rather obviously too small. Once it had been a decent black worsted, but that was several owners past. By the time it had been given to me, the dye had faded to more of a drabby charcoal, and the cuffs were frankly tattered. Sometimes, were I caught in the rain with it without an oilskin, my skirts would darken and my wrists would end up stained with bracelets of gray.

I had a hat, too, plucked straight from the donation bin. It was straw, a summer hat even though summer was very much done, and so plain that it couldn't be termed in fashion or out. A hairpin stabbed through it into the thickness of my chignon, a pin that never stopped humming against my scalp. The buffed steel ribs stretching across the glass ceiling above me sang a deeper bass, great reverberating *ba-ba-BUM-bum* sounds that were nearly drowned out by—

Stop. We don't think of that.

The canopy revealed a murky sky. It was not yet noon, but the sun had been swallowed by London's ever-present miasma of fog and soot. A sheet of paper pasted to a pillar nearby declared in hasty lettering that the gas lines had been damaged in last night's bombing, and there was no gas to burn in the jets along the walls. Every-one around me was wrapped in shadow. We were ghosts in the steamy stink of the station.

The East Smithfield Ladies' Society for Relief—that's what their banner read—had set up a table of free biscuits and hot tea for all the departing soldiers jamming the platforms. A quartet of pink-cheeked women was pouring cups as quickly as possible from the urns. Tommies surrounded them, laughing and shifting their rifles awkwardly from shoulder to shoulder as they drank.

The tea smelled stale. The biscuits, however—oh, the biscuits were nearly still warm and iced with maple sugar. I wished devoutly that one of the Tommies would offer me one, but not a single man returned my stare.

A young boy to my left was sobbing. He had hugged both arms around his mother's knees, refusing to let go.

"Now, Bobby," she was pleading with him over and over, her hat dribbling faux blackberries and her skirts all bunched up by his grip. "Now, Bobby, *please.*"

He wasn't the only child in tears. There were scores of them, probably hundreds, all over the station, everyone wan and snif-fling and red-eyed, their parents—if they'd come; sometimes it was clearly only the nannies—forcing smiles and making promises that no one in their right mind would believe, no matter how young.

"It's just for a while, sweetheart. Just a short while. You remem-ber your auntie's farm, don't you? All the fine ponies and sheep? Of course you remember—"

"—and I'll come get you soon. As soon as I can, me and your grandmum both. Soon as I can—"

"—Because you'll be *safest* there, that's why. I've made up my mind about this, Sally, you know that I have, so do stop arguing with me about it; you've given me the migraine. I need you to get *on* that train this *instant—*"

"—it'll be over in no time. Right? Right? We know that. Buck up, son, there you are! Milk a few cows for a few weeks, and there you are. Home again quick as a wink, m'boy, I swear."

There was no one accompanying me to offer any lies about returning to the city soon. I'd left the foundling house alone, astonished enough that they'd paid for the hansom cab to get me to the station. It would have been a very long walk.

I turned my gaze to the ceiling once more, inhaling the scent of damp wool and biscuits and tea, watching the billowing steam from the trains wind upward in corkscrews, condense into rows of silvery tears strung along the steel ribs.

Then I moved past Bobby and his mum, shouldering my way through the crowds to the train that would take me away from this place.

What with the dismally methodical determination of the Germans to blow us all to smithereens, it seemed a strange miracle none of the glass above me had yet cracked.

. . .

"Ticket, luv?"

The ticket agent stood over me, his gloved hand flat out in front of my nose. I'd been daydreaming, gazing out the window at the last looming shadows of the city whipping by. With my eyes half closed, with my breath clouding the pane, the outlying dregs of London became one long, lovely smear of mist.

The agent startled me out of my reverie; my head jerked back and my hat mashed against my seat.

"Er—sorry—"

"Righto," he said cheerfully enough, but his hand didn't move.

Ticket, ticket—I straightened my hat and patted my empty coat pockets. Where had it gone? I'd begun to run both hands rather desperately down my skirt before I recalled I'd stuck it in the suitcase at my feet.

I bent over to snap open my case. The stout woman crammed next to me shifted irritably. The third-class compartments had rows of narrow wooden benches and too many passengers and precious little else. My bench mate had been pushing her boot against my bag for the last half hour, as if she could shove it through the wall of the train to get it out of her way.

She reeked of days-old sweat and chickens. I wished I could shove *her* out of the train.

"All the way to Wessex, then?" the agent inquired, still jovial, his hand punch biting holes in my ticket with a series of rapid *click-click-click*s.

I nodded.

He cocked his head and gave me a dubious squint. "Land Girl, izzit?"

I knew I looked young; I was small and angular in all the wrong places, something the too-tight coat seemed to emphasize. But the Land Girls, those strapping city girls headed out to England's farms to finish the work all our fighting young men could not do, were usually at least eighteen. However old I actually was, I knew I was nowhere near that.

"School," I said, and the man's face cleared. He gave me back my ticket.

"Aye. Wessex, then. Good luck, luv."

"Thank you."

He walked on. As the train rocked back and forth, the chicken-woman began to brush at the wrinkles in her dress, using the movement as an excuse to force me harder to the wall. She spread her legs and jammed her foot up against my case again.

I had not grown up in the halls of Blisshaven for nothing. I freed my own foot and kicked down against her instep. For someone my size, I was surprisingly strong.

"Oh, I'm *awfully* sorry," I said sweetly, meeting her outraged look. "Was that your foot? I had no idea. It's so dreadfully tight in here, don't you agree? I swear, I can hardly breathe."

I had to do that twice more before she got up and left.

. . .

The hours crept by. As the sky beyond my window grew glummer and darker and the stops more frequent, the train began to empty. Around four I rummaged in my case and found the meal that had been packed for me back at the Home: an apple, a thick slice of buttered bread, and an actual, amazing seared pork sausage.

The Home had never been overly generous with food, and meat was already becoming scarce. I stared down at the sausage in its waxed-paper packet, genuinely shocked that someone in the kitchens had thought to give it to me. Perhaps it was meant as a final farewell.

The air raids were taking their toll, and the government had recommended sending as many children out of London as possible. Blisshaven itself had been hit nearly right off. No one had been killed, but the entire northern section, a decrepit labyrinth of leaky pipes and peeling paint that had served as our schooling arena, was now rubble. Most of us considered it an improvement.

So the Home had been emptied. I was, in fact, the very last orphan to leave, and I knew this was not because I was the eldest or the youngest or the least or most attractive, or any of the other rumored criteria that had been whispered about the dormitory in the days after the hit.

I knew I was the last because I was tainted. I had been sent to Moor Gate.

All the other wards had been scattered to the four corners of the kingdom, sent to whichever other foundling homes had room to take in more of the unwanted.

But for me. I hadn't been assigned to another orphanage.

"The Iverson School for Girls," Mr. H. W. Forrester had informed me, examining me like a nearsighted owl from over the tops of his spectacles. "It enjoys a sterling reputation. You are fortunate indeed they had an unexpected opening for a new charity student."

"Yes, sir," I had replied. I had been summoned to the hallowed office of the director, seated with well-mannered precision at the edge of the chair before his desk. The room was cramped with bookcases and cabinets and the lace curtains behind him were caked with dust; it was a little surprising more of it hadn't flaked off from the air strikes.

Mr. H. W. Forrester had fleshy jowls and salt-and-pepper hair greased with pomade and veiny, restless fingers that tended to tap across the scattered sheets of paper before him. I was very careful never to look even once at the diamond stickpin in his tie.

"It's on the southern coast, set near Idylling. Seat of the dukes of Idylling. The Louis family, you know."

"Oh," I said.

"Lovely area. I myself spent a holiday there once." He leaned back in his chair, his gaze taking on a faraway cast. "Sandy beaches. Balmy breezes. One may sea-bathe in utter comfort. . . ."

I counted silently to twenty, then cleared my throat. "What happened to her, sir?"

Mr. Forrester lowered his gaze back to me. "To whom?"

"To the other girl? The one who left the opening for a new student?"

"Why, I'm certain nothing *happened* to her, Eleanore. Really, what a question. I trust you will manage to curb that macabre bent of yours once at Iverson. You won't make many friends that way."

"No, sir," I agreed, and pressed my lips shut.

London wasn't the only part of the country being attacked. The dailies were full of articles about how the Germans were beginning to bomb the coasts, as well, as far as they could go in their massive zeppelin airships.

Wessex. I'd bet the sterling school of Iverson had found itself with a sudden slew of student openings.

"The headmistress, Mrs. Westcliffe, has been made aware of your particular . . . personal history and has decided to take you in anyway. Provisionally, I might add. The duke himself sponsors the school, you know, and has granted it a very generous endowment for a select few impoverished students. You are an extremely lucky young woman, Eleanore."

"Yes, sir."

"I expect you to make the most of this opportunity."

"I shall, sir."

"Indeed. Not many patients from Moor Gate will ever be offered such a reprieve. You must always remember them and your months spent there. Strive to succeed for their sakes, as well as your own."

I wondered, very seriously, if Mr. H. W. Forrester had ever noticed the curtain cord hanging down the wall just behind him or considered how easy it might be to wrap it around and around his neck.

He leaned forward again, his jowls swelling over his collar, and frowned at me with his owlish disapproval. The diamond securing his tie flared.

"You seem much improved from your first years here, child, but do not give me reason to regret this arrangement. Obey the head-mistress without question, and fulfill all your duties to the duke and to the school."

"Yes, sir."

He frowned at me for a moment more, then sighed. "That will be all, Miss Jones."

And it was. That had been my last evening in the Home.

Idylling, Iverson, dukes and bombs and sea-bathing . . .

I didn't care if the Huns shelled it every night, if the duke wanted me to dance a jig for my suppers, or if the school itself was situated smack in the middle of the South Pole. It would be better than Blisshaven, I told myself, savoring each chewy bite of that cold sausage on the train. Better than Moor Gate.

Better than anything, really. How could it not be?

Of course, that last, hopeful thought occurred to me only hours before I would meet Jesse and Armand, those two savagely different and yet dangerously similar creatures who were destined to dig their talons into me and change my life forever.

Chapter 3

Mine was the final stop of the line. By then there were only two of us left in the compartment, me and a slouched, elderly man with a tweed cap pulled down low over his ears, a cane and valise propped by his feet. He'd been snoring for the past two hours, even through the lurching stops and starts.

Beyond the glass of my window the night was now amethyst. Infinite amethyst, deep and dark with a ripple of stars winking over the obsidian break of the forest paralleling the tracks. I found that depth of purple sky mesmerizing. Nights in the city were always gray or black or the color of the streetlights. Always. So I wasn't sure why this particular hue—those stars, the jagged line of trees—was so familiar. I must have imagined it this way, I decided. I read so much. I must have read of amethyst nights and imagined it.

"*Bourne*mouth, *end* o' the line," called the stationmaster from past my window, clumping along the wooden platform as the train hissed to a halt.

I stood, stretching the ache from my shoulders, and found my suitcase. A glance back at the snoring man showed he was already up and shuffling out, so I followed him, my case bumping against my knees.

A waft of damp air hit me as I exited, stirring the loose strands of hair that had pulled free of my chignon. It wasn't balmy precisely. It was April, so it wouldn't be, even here. But it carried the promise of warmth, smelling strongly of the salty channel and of the coming summer that only waited to bloom.

I took it in with wonder. I could *taste* the sea, I realized. I could taste it.

"Last stop, miss," barked the stationmaster, now paused before me. "Everyone off. Even little girls, eh?"

I had lingered too long on the steps leading down to the platform. In my chagrin, I jumped over the last two rungs, landing smartly on both feet, but the man was already pacing off.

I walked slowly away from the train, looking around the platform.

Someone was supposed to meet me. Director Forrester hadn't known who, but he had been reasonably certain—those had been his exact words, *reasonably certain,* mumbling to himself as he'd ruffled through all the papers on his desk, *because surely they could not expect you to find it on your own, no, indeed; I cannot seem to locate the telegram that says so, but*—that someone from the school would meet me here and take me on the rest of the way to Iverson, which apparently involved traveling by foot and carriage and maybe even a ferry. I was as unclear on the exact location of the school as the director had been.

I prayed he was right, that someone would come. I didn't have enough money left for another cab.

But . . . the station itself seemed closed, its curtains shut, its windows dark. That by itself wasn't too surprising; in London the streetlamps were extinguished at six and windows were papered in black to block any little leaks of light. No one wanted to guide the Germans' nighttime bombs. Yet the train station's windows weren't papered. There was simply no one left inside to turn on the lights.

I did hear music playing from somewhere, lovely and haunting, muted. Perhaps the stationmaster had left on a phonograph in his office.

The platform was virtually empty. There was no one at all to my left, toward the end of the train, and only a pair of porters unloading a stack of luggage far up by the front, near the first-class compartments, threading in and out of a single pool of light cast from a lamppost nearby.

The stationmaster had aimed their way. After a few more minutes of glancing nervously around the deserted platform, I did the same.

Before I'd gotten far, a new cluster of people approached the growing wall of trunks. There were four of them plus the stationmaster, their hats and shoulders stroked with gold from above. One of the newcomers was a man of about forty in a long taupe coat. The other three were younger people more my age, two boys and a girl.

Or not quite my age, I amended to myself, as the nearest of the boys noticed my approach. They were all taller, probably a few years older. And much, much better dressed than I.

The boy who'd seen me had sandy hair and heavy-lidded hazel eyes; they looked me up and down without interest before he turned his attention back to his companions.

". . . to Idylling," the second boy was saying to the long-coated man. "Is it really just you, George? I mean, look at all this. Chloe alone brought enough trunks to fill three autos."

"Armand!" protested the girl, with a sort of trilling little laugh. "Honestly!"

"Not to mention Laurence's and mine," the boy went on, speaking over her. "No, there's no hope for it. There's not room for all of us. We'll have to motor there without you."

"My lord, I don't believe His Grace will—"

"Right, well, what Reginald doesn't know won't hurt the rest of us, will it, old chap? I'll send Thomas back for you with the auto as soon as I can. You can wait here with the baggage."

"Sir," broke in the stationmaster from behind them, just outside their ring of light. The other four angled as one to see him, still brushed in buttery gold. The stationmaster rocked back on his heels. "We closed for the night five minutes past, sir."

"Ah," said the second boy. He had longish chestnut hair that touched the top of his starched collar; much of his face was obscured by the brim of his hat, but I saw him tug at his lower lip in thought. Even to me, it looked utterly contrived. "I see. Perhaps, though, you might make an exception tonight? For the duke?"

"The duke, sir?"

"Well, the duke's *son*," said the hazel-eyed boy, sounding impatient. "Lord Armand, of course."

"Station closes at ten sharp," said the stationmaster. "Rules, sir."

"Now, *really*," began the boy named Laurence, and in his clipped voice he was speaking very quickly, but curiously enough I no longer heard what he was saying, because just then the other one—the Duke of Idylling's son himself, I supposed—had caught sight of me hanging back in the shadows.

He had been reaching into his inner coat pocket for something. I saw dimly and without surprise that it was a wallet, and while still holding it he pushed up his hat, staring at me intently. His skin was pale as ivory, his eyes were blue and heavily lashed, quite as striking as a girl's.

The line of his lips began to flatten into an expression that might have been pain or irritation or perhaps pure distaste.

"Who are you?" he demanded.

Laurence and the stationmaster, who had been working themselves into an actual argument, fell silent. The trilling girl leaned past the duke's son to get a better look at me, the lace wrap around her neck and shoulders prickled with light. She was as stunning as I'd expected, dark hair, dark eyes, a rosebud mouth puffed into a pout. An overripe scent of jasmine and sugar surrounded her like a cloud.

"Oh, Mandy, do send her off," I heard her plead under her breath. "Tell her we haven't any pennies to spare."

I spoke to the dark-haired lord. "I'm going to Iverson. To the school. Can you give me a lift?"

Laurence snorted and the girl looked truly appalled, but Lord Armand only stared at me harder.

"What's your name?"

"Eleanore."

This bit of information didn't seem to satisfy him. He took off his hat with his free hand, and for one wild and unlikely moment I thought he was going to offer me a bow, but instead he pushed his fingers through the shiny brown hair that had been mashed to his forehead.

"I haven't got a trunk," I said into the silence. "Only this." I tapped the toe of my shoe against my suitcase. "So I won't take up much room."

Chloe raised a hand to her mouth; her snicker was still loud enough to hear.

Yet I held on to that steady blue gaze. From the cut of his clothes to the angle of his chin, Lord Armand of Idylling was every inch an aristocrat and no doubt used to people of my class scraping low whenever he passed by. I wasn't going to be one of them. There was something about this young man, some indefinable thing that felt like—like a living snake poised taut between us. A real, electric, dangerous thing, and if I dropped my gaze, it would turn on me, and I would lose more than just this moment.

"How about it?" I said, trying to sound confident but instead managing something barely above a whisper.

The pressed shape of his lips began to loosen. He opened his mouth, maybe to speak, but before he could, a new voice chimed in.

"No need, m'lord."

I didn't have to look away first; Lord Armand did. His gaze cut to someone behind me.

"Hastings," greeted the boy, strangely flat, and when I turned around fully I saw that the new person who'd spoken was my fellow passenger from the train, the snoring old man, standing now motionless beneath the awning of the station roof. "How . . . nice to see you again."

"Aye. I'm here for the gel." The man curled an arm toward me. "Come along, miss. Haven't got all night."

I flicked a last glance at Armand, who was scowling faintly. None of the others were looking at me at all.

I picked up my case again and walked away.

The elderly man didn't wait for me to reach him. He limped off into the amethyst-and-star night without another word, his cane tapping emphatically with every other step.

I was feeling my way down the platform stairs when I heard the imperious tones of Lord Armand lift sharp behind me.

"Eleanore who?" he called.

Bugger him and his gorgeous eyes and his snide friends and his chauffeured motorcar. I kept walking.

"Eleanore *who*?" he called again, much louder.

"Jones," yelled back the man ahead of me; he'd paused at last to let me catch up. "Eleanore Rose Jones!"

A carriage with a pair of horses and a driver waited at the end of a graveled lot. It was a big carriage, the old-fashioned kind that was entirely enclosed, a bit like a fairy-tale pumpkin transformed into a coach. Which was fortunate, because horses always hated me. No matter how gently I spoke or how quietly I passed by, to a one they hated me, and venturing too close meant nearly always a bolt or a lunging bite.

We crunched along the lot, countless little stones grinding beneath the soles of my feet. A long, gleaming automobile had been parked at an angle in the exact middle, clearly waiting for trunks and lords.

"Mr. Hastings?" I said after a moment.

"Aye."

"My middle name isn't Rose."

Funny that I couldn't see him smile, but I thought I sensed it anyway. "No? What's it, then?"

"I haven't got one," I admitted.

"Well, I'd say Rose is as fine a name as any, ain't it?"

I saw his point.

. . .

The interior of the carriage was not nearly as musty as I'd feared it'd be. In fact, it was luxurious, far nicer than the London hansom I'd been in so many hours past. The seat cushions were plush and newly padded, the walls had been papered in silk, and a pair of folded fleece blankets had been left out for me to ward off the chill.

Since Mr. Hastings had climbed up outside to sit beside the driver on his perch, I drew one blanket over my shoulders and the other across my lap. I wasn't terribly cold, but they were so soft. As the carriage rolled away from the station, I rubbed a velvety edge slowly over and over the back of my hand.

For each tiny, merciful gift from life, I was grateful.

The blankets at the Home had been of boiled wool. There was a fleece coverlet at the nurse's station, but you had to be white-knuckled, wishing-you-were-dead sick for her to offer it, and usually it smelled like iodine.

I'd kept the curtains opened and the window cracked. I craved that outside air, which still tasted of wonderful salt to me.

A motorcar roared up behind us, its reflective lanterns splashing a feeble illumination along the fence posts lining the bend in the road. The horn bugled twice before the car sped past, spitting pebbles in its wake. Chloe's laughter was full and loud as they vanished into the dark ahead.

The dust settled, and the horses pulling our carriage only plodded on.

I didn't feel sleepy. I should have; I should have been exhausted, actually. In my excitement over leaving the Home I hadn't slept much the night before, and certainly today had dragged on long enough. I removed my hat and rested my head against the seat's back, closing my eyes, listening to the sounds of the shore and the horses and the country night.

We bumped over a bridge spanning a river, waking wooden thunder from each and every plank.

I'm not sure when I began to grasp that I was hearing more than just those ordinary noises. Ten minutes later? Thirty? It came upon me gradually, the awareness that the phonograph music from the station was still playing, even though we were no longer anywhere near it.

I opened my eyes. I sat up. Was I dreaming?

It was still playing.

I slapped my cheeks with both hands, pinched my arms. I was *asleep,* this was a *dream,* I needed to wake up, because this *was not happening.*

But it was.

"No," I muttered, caught somewhere between anger and disbelief. "Not again."

I searched the carriage, pulling up the cushions, running my hands along the smooth walls, the door latch, the window frames, the floorboards. I found nothing new, nothing to explain the slow, sweet music that was playing very markedly all around me.

And it *was* around me, not merely inside my head. I was not imagining it. I'd never heard this composition before, this wistful combination of notes that swelled and subsided but never fully ended. It was not entirely unlike the music emanating from metals or stones but was far more complex than that. More a symphony than a single song.

I dropped my head into my hands, squeezing my eyes closed, trying to find some peace. I'd been doing so well. I'd been recovering. I hardly ever noticed the silent stone-music any longer, and

when I did I was able to shut it out, distract myself with other matters until it went away.

I could do this, I thought grimly, looking up again. *I can do
this.*

Oh, really? mocked the whispery fiend in my heart.

In the frigid depths of Moor Gate, strapped to their drowning
chair, I'd made a vow to myself never to speak of the music or the
voice again. Never to acknowledge anything that made me any different from anyone else.

Ever.

"I will do this," I said out loud, my jaw clenched so tight it
ached.

This time my heart made no reply.

For the rest of the ride I stared straight ahead into the dark, a
fold of fleece pressed to my lips. I thought about rivers, and I
thought about sheep, and I thought about the kaiser and the smell
of London and how the Home had looked after the bomb had detonated inside its rotting walls, the red-brick dust coating everything and the water line spewing and all the rubble of the desks
and chairs and the scorched books flung every which way like
burning paper birds. That initial shock of displaced air. All the
screaming children and then the dreadful calm afterward, when
we realized we couldn't flee anyway because there was nowhere
else for us to go.

When the carriage finally rolled to a halt, I fancied I had things
in hand. The symphony had not ceased, but I was ignoring it. It
wasn't really there, and if it was, it was the result of someone else's
madness, not my own.

One of the horses let out an unhappy whicker, and the carriage
rolled back some. I heard for the first time the driver's low voice,

not so much words but a soothing string of sounds, and the horse subsided.

Mr. Hastings was talking now, but I didn't bother to try to make it out, nor did I bother to wait for him or the driver to climb down and open the door for me. I grabbed my case and had my other hand on the latch as soon as the wheels stopped moving. I was hungry and on edge and more than ready to be free; I leapt out onto fresh gravel, into the purple dense dark.

For a horrible instant I thought they had played a joke on me and we had driven in a great circle, because it seemed I was standing where I had been when I first entered the carriage, right back outside the station with its phonograph after all.

Amethyst sky, silver stars. A ragged black line of trees stretched beyond me.

Then the horses began to snort and stomp. When I turned about, I saw the castle.

Iverson.

It actually *was* a castle, high and wide and utterly ominous, a series of narrow windows glowing amber against the stone. It had round towers with peaked roofs, heavy arches set deep into the sides, and a notched edging along the top just visible from where I stood. It loomed over me, over all of us, eating up the stars.

The horses whickered again, one louder than the other. It turned into a squeal, climbing higher and higher, and over it rose Mr. Hastings's voice.

"Get back there, will you, girl? You there! Eleanore Jones! Get back, I say!"

I retreated hurriedly into a hedge, then stumbled around it; I'd thought he was addressing the horse.

From behind the hedge I heard the driver once more, still speaking so soft, but it worked, because the squealing stopped and within a minute the snorting, too. I peered cautiously past the foliage to see Mr. Hastings limping my way, his white hair poking out from under his cap and his hands knotted into fists.

"I'm sorry," I blurted, an instinctive reaction to being caught in the wrong by an adult. Old lessons, scored deep into my bones: *Duck your head, apologize at once, perhaps they'll let you skulk by.*

But Mr. Hastings only paused, looking at me there six feet away with my side pressed against the thorns of the prickly hedge. I had nowhere to skulk.

"Gah," he said, or something that sounded like that. He shook his head, and his voice seemed to gentle. "She's a good 'un, the old mare, but every living thing has its limits. You'll need to learn better, city girl. Keep clear of the beasts, you hear?"

"Yes."

He nodded, as if that had settled things between us, and jerked his chin toward the castle doors.

"Ready?"

"Yes," I said again, which was an absolute lie.

He stumped off. I began reluctantly to follow.

"Wait," called the driver from behind us.

I swiveled, hearing footfalls approaching lightly. Against the stars all I could see was that he was blond and broad-shouldered, moving with the kind of grace that bespoke a natural athlete, someone who probably ran and rode horses and swam leagues in the ocean every bloody day.

In two breaths he was before me, still in shadow, lifting something round between us.

"Your hat," the driver said.

I took it from him, and our fingertips brushed.

With that mere glancing touch, the music I'd been attempting so hard to repress flared to life, a brilliant, beautiful explosion of sound that filled my body and flooded my senses, wiping away everything else like chalk from a slate board. I was suffused with a pleasure so profound, it robbed me of sight and speech; I was only blind aching bliss, and for all I knew I was moaning with it, just like the whores on the street corners back in St. Giles, and, God help me, I didn't even care.

Hello, screamed the fiend inside my heart. *Hear me, hear me at last, hello!*

"Hello," said the driver, his voice reaching through the notes to pull me back down into the trembling, stunned husk that was my flesh. "I'm Jesse."

Chapter 4

Lora.

That was her name. He'd caught her choked murmur just before she'd darted away, bolting like a rabbit after Hastings. She actually overtook the old man, only hesitating by the main doors until he could open them for her.

The image of her turning around that one last time, throwing that swift, frozen look back at him, with the atrium light spilling a dull tarnish behind her and her hat crushed in one hand—

He'd frightened her. He'd not meant to.

Jesse propped his elbows on the sill of his open window and regarded the tangle of woods that whispered to him to *come out, come out now.* He wouldn't be able to spend the rest of the night here in his cottage, he knew that already. But in his hands he held one of the fleece blankets he'd put in the carriage for her, and he was unwilling to relinquish it quite yet. After a few long minutes more of watching the dark, he brought it up to his face.

Loosestrife, he thought. Delicate spiky flowers, sweet and spice.

Lora.

A pretty name, even if it wasn't her true one.

He stood, draped the blanket over the chair behind him. With a single practiced vault he was out the window and out of the confines of roof and walls, bare feet in moss, fresh air on his face. An easy run that sank him deep and quiet into the dark.

Chapter 5

The walls of the castle closed in around me with a gray cold sameness, broken only by flickering shadow and flame from an oil lamp burning in an alcove by the doors. I followed the lumpy shape of Mr. Hastings without really seeing him, without taking in the fine paintings that began to appear along the corridor or the wool runner that unfurled like a long woven tongue into the gloom ahead.

Jesse. Jesse of the blissful touch. Jesse of the silent song.

I remembered the starlit contours of his face and felt a shivery echo of that pleasure begin its way through me, from the top of my scalp to my toes.

Oh, God. There was definitely something wrong with me.

"Keep up, gel." Mr. Hastings had stopped before a new door, a much more modern one than the ancient iron-and-oak pair blockading the main entrance. He waited until I crept closer, nodded, then knocked hard twice against the painted wood.

"Enter," came a female voice from the room beyond.

Hastings opened the door, motioned for me to go ahead.

It was clearly the headmistress's chamber. I'd seen enough of

Director Forrester's office to recognize the subtle signals of adult power, although it was accomplished much more elegantly here: the bookcases filled with important tomes, their lettering a gilded gleam along flawless spines. Long, creamy lace curtains framing the windows—no dust on these—beautiful enough to be bridal veils. Vases of lilies perfuming the air, a low crackling fire in the hearth. A chandelier of brass and wax candles throwing glints of honeyed illumination. A ticking clock.

A wide polished desk of cherrywood with two wing chairs before it and a more imposing one behind with a woman seated in it, her head bent, writing.

"Thank you, Mr. Hastings," she murmured, without glancing up from her work.

I heard the door close behind me. I stood where I was without moving, without even loosening my grip on my hat and case.

The clock continued to tick. The woman continued to write. Her hair was confined to a strict ebony twist, not a strand out of place, something I never managed to accomplish with my own.

A ring flashed on her hand. Instinctively I knew—and hated that I knew—that it was a green sapphire, one-and-one-quarter carats, with a band of platinum.

I realized then that I felt queasy. The light was too slick, the scent of the lilies nearly overwhelming. I swayed a bit on my feet and dug my fingers deeper into the straw of my hat.

It's all a mistake, I thought. *She'll look up, she'll look at me and tell me it's all been a mistake, I'm too peculiar, I'm not wanted here after all. I'll have to find my way back to the station. I'll have to speak to Jesse again and hear that music, and what if he touches me—*

The woman's head lifted. She was older than the absolute black of her hair had implied. Her features were finely lined; the corners of her lips had wrinkled into puckers.

"Miss Jones. You are quite late."

"I beg your pardon," I replied automatically, although a spot of resentment began a sudden burn in my chest, dispelling some of the nausea. What was I supposed to have done? Pushed at the train with my bare hands to force it faster?

Perhaps she noticed my instant of rebellion. Perhaps not. Her eyes seemed to narrow, but it might have been merely the poor light.

"You may be seated."

I moved to the wing chair nearest me, sinking like a child deep into the leather.

"I am Mrs. Westcliffe, the headmistress of Iverson."

I tried to inch up higher in the chair. "How do you do?"

"How do you do. I'd like to commence our relationship by speaking with you plainly. I trust you won't mind. You're a rather different sort of student than we typically host here at the school. Your records indicate that you are not without intelligence, so you will perceive this fact for yourself soon enough. I have no wish to alarm you or to shame you, but, apart from the servants, you will not find a peer here at Iverson."

I thought of the divine Chloe and her less-than-divine laughter.

"Oh," I said, sinking back again.

"The Iverson School for Girls attracts young women from the most elite families across the empire. We are considered the foremost educational opportunity for such young women, and hence it is imperative our reputation remains unsullied. I want to assure you that I will personally do whatever I must to protect my students and this school from any hint of impropriety."

She paused, gazing at me. It was pretty clear where she thought any hints of impropriety would be coming from.

"I understand," I said.

"We are also fortunate enough to enjoy the patronage of the Duke of Idylling himself, whose own social connections are, of course, unimpeachable."

"Of course."

Mrs. Westcliffe shot me an abruptly beady look. "It is due to the duke that you are here before me now. His allowance for the castle and its grounds includes the proviso that, for any given semester, at least one scholarship student must be in attendance, preferably one from out of the area so as to lessen tensions among the locals. Whatever my misgivings about your previous circumstances, I find myself perfectly in accord with the duke's wishes. Honest charity is never to be frowned upon, nor are intentions of the purest nature."

She paused again, waiting, so I added another, "Of course."

It seemed to mollify her; the beady look softened. "Your classes will be identical to those of every other pupil in your year. In this respect, at least, you *will* be equal. What you learn here will be up to you, Miss Jones. But I will add frankly that graduation and a magnanimous letter of recommendation from this school will place you at the top of any governess list in proper British society, and with good reason."

"Thank you," I said, because I was not without intelligence, and by then I'd learned my cue.

Mrs. Westcliffe inclined her head, a gracious queen in her gilded realm.

Governess. I wanted to sigh out loud, but it was an enormous boon, I knew. Most girls from Blisshaven went straight to the workhouses when they were too old for schooling. They became the necessary hands populating the vast city factories: ropemaking, sewing machines, beer.

Or they became willing bodies for the streets. More money, less time. Less life expectancy, too, usually.

"On to more-practical matters. A schedule of your courses awaits you in your room, along with any required texts. You have been allocated six uniforms, five for everyday classes and one for more-formal school functions. I presume you have the sum of your belongings in that case? And that you have presentable garments for the weekends?"

"Yes, ma'am." *If you wish to call a pair of threadbare skirts and darned stockings* presentable.

"Students are permitted a single item of personal jewelry with the uniform. Something discreet, naturally. A cameo brooch. A filigree pin, a pearl. Possibly a small watch, should the chain drape well enough. Some of the girls have taken to wearing gold bangles. It's a slightly vulgar fashion, I feel, but as long as it is only *one* bangle and you show it to me first so that I may be certain it is appropriate, that may suffice, as well."

"Yes, Mrs. Westcliffe," I said gravely. "I shall show you any bangle I wish to wear first."

"Excellent. As tomorrow is Sunday, all that will be required of you is to attend services in the chapel. After that, you may explore the grounds at your leisure. It will give you time to learn the castle, as well." She rose to her feet, and I did the same. "I feel we are to get on, Miss Jones. I hope I am not mistaken."

She stuck out her hand, surprising me—I thought I'd just get a royal dismissal. Her grip on my fingers was both chill and firm.

"Almeda will show you to your room. Allow me to be the first to say welcome to you, Eleanore Jones. Welcome to Iverson,"

. . .

I learned that night that the loveliest, most lonely sound in the world is that of the sea striking the shore. It rocked me into slumber, echoing my drowsing pulse.

The room assigned to me had clearly never been meant to serve as a bedchamber. It consisted of the upper floor of one of the towers, with a high ceiling and curved walls that made the bed jut out awkwardly no matter where I moved. There was no rug and no fireplace. Come winter, the tower would be an icebox, but at least there was a pile of quilts at the foot of the bed.

I didn't care. I could not recall a time in my life when I had slept in a room of my own; the cell at Moor Gate did not count. That I didn't have to scrap for a better pillow or drawer space or a clean chamber pot seemed an indescribable luxury. Princesses, I thought, running my hand over a quilt, lived sovereign like this.

The solitary window of my room once was probably little more than an arrow slit but at some point had been widened and glazed. The glass shone in a thousand diamond-bitty pieces, many of them splintered but all still in place. I'd shoved at the rusted hinges to open it, peering out at the view, and that was when I realized that the castle was on an island.

We had crossed so many bridges in the carriage, I'd stopped counting them. Plus, I'd been fiercely focused on blocking Jesse's music from my mind. But from my window I could see the bridge that connected us to the mainland, a slinky wooden track braced with pillars that sank into the waves, foam bursting silver against them. It looked to be nearly a mile long.

A mile of sea from here to there. I don't know why that thought seemed so pleasant.

I was a princess in a very dark tower. I banged my shin twice against the bedpost, trying to maneuver to the bureau, and my hip once against the bureau, attempting to grope my way back to the bed. There was an armoire, too, but I didn't feel up to wrangling with anything pointy like hangers or hooks.

I'd found two candles but no matches, and knew better than to look for a light switch.

"Castle's not wired for the electrical," Almeda had informed me as we climbed the tower stairs. She was heavyset and huffing for breath by the second landing, tackling each stair with a substantial stamp of her foot. By her apron and cap, I'd guessed she was the head maid or chatelaine, but she'd not volunteered the information, and I had not asked.

"We make do with good old-fashioned means here," she'd panted. "Coal and the like. Fine, traditional ways. You'll get a filled lamp for your room and two candles per month. Don't waste 'em, and don't go asking for more than that, because you won't get more, eh?"

Eh, indeed.

It happened that the lamp was missing—perhaps one of the less frugal girls had pinched it—and the candles, without matches, were useless. But after I had unpacked my case by touch and found my way into my nightgown and settled into the bed, the moon had risen just enough to pearl the window, and the diamond panes began a slow, dazzling show of light that made the darkness no longer matter.

I fell asleep with my stomach growling and the sea beyond my tower striking the land, striking, striking, a giant's hand against a huge hollow drum.

But for a single passing dream of a caress to my forehead—a whisper of sensation, safe and gentle and then gone—I slept deep.

Chapter 6

Here is the list of weapons I counted in the headmistress's serene golden chamber:

The candles from the chandelier.

The poker and its stand by the fireplace.

The pink-daisied porcelain lamps, which had been unlit,
    on the secrétaire and side cabinet and reading table.

Every single oil painting, remarkably flammable.

The curtains.

The crystal vases.

The bronze-framed mirror.

The glass face of the clock.

The inkwell.

And, of course, the letter opener on her desk, made of hard,
    sharp bone.

Hattie Boyd once held a letter opener she'd snatched from a nurse's hand to the jugular vein of Mrs. Buckler, the most vicious matron in Moor Gate. She held it there until she was promised one of the beef-and-potato pasties being served to the staff for supper. It cost her a blackened eye and two entire months in the isolation cell in the basement.

A few days before they managed to kill her for good, Hattie confided to me that that pasty was the most delicious thing she'd ever tasted.

Chapter 7

My eyes opened the next morning to a prism of sunlight stretched across my face and down my pillow. I groaned and rolled away from it, smelling feathers and brine. And . . . something fruity. Oranges?

I sat up, caught in that hazy state of not-yet-ready-to-be-awake, but the sun was bright, and about a second later there was a tapping on my door, which creaked open to reveal a housemaid.

"Good morning, miss. I'm Gladys. I've brought your fresh water."

And so she had, carrying a filled pitcher up what had to be at least three flights of stairs. She moved to the bureau and set it there by the basin, then turned to me, still bundled in my quilt.

I swiped a mess of hair from my lashes and smiled at her tentatively. No one had ever brought me an entire pitcher of water before.

She was older than I, about twenty I would guess, with a skinny, angular frame and an apron so severely starched it looked like the edges could slice cheese. She did not smile back.

"Food's not allowed in the students' rooms, miss." Gladys aimed her gaze pointedly at something by my side.

I looked down. There *was* an orange—a real one, fat and colorful—nestled right up against my pillow.

It had not been there last night. It had not. I would have felt it, smelled it. Certainly it hadn't come with me from Blisshaven. I'd emptied my case down to the stitches.

Yet in an act of inexplicable sorcery, the orange was here now.

I remembered abruptly my dream, that touch to my face, how it had seemed so pleasurable and so real . . . like a gift.

"I—" I glanced up again at the maid; there was no mistaking now the rancor behind her eyes. Here was someone who was not especially pleased to consider me her peer. "I must have unpacked it last night and forgotten about it," I lied. "So sorry. It won't happen again."

She returned to the door. "Breakfast begins in a half hour. I'm to show you the way, so I'll be back before then."

"Right. Thank you."

The door clicked shut without a response.

I sat there for a moment, then picked up the orange, rolling it between my palms. Never once had any form of my madness produced food from empty air; someone had given me this. Last night. As I slept. And even though I hadn't dreamed of music, there was no question in my mind about who it had been.

The tower door had no lock, no bolt. If Jesse worked for the school, as I suspected, he probably knew the castle like the back of his hand. But why would he risk such a thing? I could only imagine what Mrs. Westcliffe would do were she to come across her coachman sneaking into pupils' rooms.

My room, rather. I'd likely set an Iverson record for Most Hastily Arranged Expulsion.

If it *had* been Jesse. If my mind hadn't snapped, and I hadn't carried the orange with me from London after all. In the clear light of day, it was difficult to envision even the mysterious Jesse venturing all the way up here just to leave me fruit.

An odd bit of folklore rose to the surface of my thoughts, something I'd read years ago in a battered, dusty book I discovered tucked in a cupboard at the Home. I'd always read every book I could find, and this one was about monsters, so old the pages had crumbled against my fingers:

Do not Eat the Food of the Fay. Do not Drink their Wine. You give Yourself to Them with every Sip, every Swallow. They shall Darken your Blood until you Desire only Dark. Only what Pleasures They may Bestow.

I shivered in the morning sunlight. I brought the orange to my lips in a deliberate hard kiss, meant to hurt. The rind hinted of bitter but the scent was still sweet.

"What am I to make of you?" I muttered into it. "Are you Dark?"

I will be delicious, was all the orange seemed to reply.

Dark or not, I was starving. But I didn't own a clock or a watch, and I didn't know how long a half hour might truly be. Gladys seemed like the kind of person who'd be delighted to tell anyone she could about how she'd discovered the new scholarship girl half dressed, with orange juice dribbling down her chin.

I stored the orange in the depths of the bureau, then opened the drawers containing my two clean outfits brought from the orphanage and sighed, wondering which would embarrass me less.

I decided on the one *without* the rip in its skirt. It was Sunday, after all.

There was a small looking glass upon the bureau, pushed off to the side by the stack of textbooks and papers I hadn't yet examined. I was accustomed to slipping in and out my clothes without being able to see myself. We'd had a standing mirror in the dorm of the Home, but with fifty girls to a room, all of us bound to the same schedule, good ruddy luck getting in front of it to dress.

I honestly wasn't used to seeing my own reflection. It was with a little jolt of surprise that, when I bent my neck to stick another pin into my hair, I saw a corner of a girl doing the same nearby.

I dropped my hands, curious, and picked up the frame. Yes, there I was. Hair of indeterminate color—but at least I'd gotten it up into its roll—eyes of indeterminate color. Eyelashes, eyebrows, reddish lips. Complexion, not the perfect peachy silk of a debutante but something more like . . . like stone, really. I tipped my head this way and that, critical. My complexion was probably my best feature, I decided, mostly because my skin was unblemished and uniformly marble pale.

I returned the glass to its place. I looked exactly like what I was, a slum girl from the city, where hearty meals were rare and the sun was a stranger.

I was ready when Gladys gave her next knock. I smoothed my hands along my hair one last time and followed her down the stairs.

. . .

I heard them before I saw them: high, chattering voices swelling and fading above the unmistakable clatter of flatware against china. The doors to the dining hall were open as we approached. I glimpsed a space deep and wide with pastel plastered walls and yellow spears of sunlight falling in precise angles from windows unseen. Chandeliers glittered with crystal. Tables gleamed with food. And girls in gowns of every hue were seated in chairs along the tables, rows and rows of rainbow girls, some beaded, some ruffled, gobs of lace.

As Gladys led me closer to the entrance, the vivid colors and

increasing noise reminded me of nothing so much as a flock of par-
rots, swept into the castle to dine upon kippers and tea.

I would learn later that this confusion of colors was unique to
the weekends at Iverson. For every other day of the week, we all
wore the same uniform in the same style, crisp white shirtwaists
paired with long, straight, dark-plum skirts and black-buttoned
shoes. No doubt then we resembled a rather stilted colony of pen-
guins, milling here and there in our ladylike shortened steps.

Gladys paused by the doors, and so did I. She seemed disin-
clined to take me forward, and as I wasn't particularly inclined to *go*
forward I merely stood there, allowing the voices and the delirious
aroma of hot fresh breakfast to wash over me, looking at all those
elite-of-the-empire girls and wishing I was anywhere, *anywhere,*
else on earth. Even Moor Gate.

I dropped my gaze to the folds of my skirt. I'd accidently chosen
the one with the rip in it, after all. They were both plain brown
twill; we'd all worn brown at the orphanage, because it didn't show
dirt.

The toes of my boots stuck out, light and dark with scuffs.

"Miss Jones," said a voice right in front of me.

Mrs. Westcliffe. No tear in her gown. The tips of her black
leather pumps shone like glass against a discreet pleated hem.

I lifted my eyes.

"Late again," the headmistress noted, with that pinch to her
mouth.

I glanced back quickly at Gladys, but she'd vanished without a
word.

Thanks ever so much. You bony cow.

"I beg your pardon," I mumbled. I had the dismal feeling I was
going to be using that phrase quite a lot in my time here.

"Breakfast begins at precisely eight-thirty every morning. Do make a note of it."

"Yes, ma'am."

Mrs. Westcliffe sighed. "Very well. Let's find your table, shall we? Seating is assigned for all meals, barring teas. Follow me."

I did. And as soon as I took my very first step into the hall, all the girlish, parroty chatter choked into absolute silence. I suppose that was the moment the other students realized I wasn't merely some disgraced scullery maid popped out of uniform, but instead someone who was *going to be seated at a table,* which meant— horrors!—one of them.

By my fifth step, a new sound had taken over the hall: the hiss of a hundred whispers escaping cupped hands, punctuated with giggles. It rose with every group we passed, heads turning, and by then Mrs. Westcliffe had apparently recognized her mistake, for her back grew very stiff and her heels began to strike the floor as hard as castanets.

I weighed at least three tons. Three tons of sluggish lead and shame clunking step by step in my scruffy orphan boots into the sumptuously decorated hell that was this dining hall, and what a terrible wonder that the ground did not crack apart and swallow me whole.

We ended up before a table that had a conspicuously empty chair at the far end. The students filling all the other seats gazed up at us with sparkling, hungry eyes.

"Good morning, ladies. May I introduce to you Miss Eleanore Jones, late of London. She will be in your tenth-year classes with you. I trust you will all bid her a very gracious Iverson welcome and will do your best to ensure that she feels quite at home with us."

"Yes, Mrs. Westcliffe," they chorused as one, sweet as sugar.

There were seven of them. They smiled seven identical smiles, and the message behind each was identical, as well. It read: *blood-bath.*

The giggling at a table of younger girls across the chamber sharpened into laughter. The headmistress threw them a frowning look.

"Lady Sophia. I will leave it to you to make the round of introductions."

"Yes, Mrs. Westcliffe," responded a flaxen-haired, glacier-eyed young woman who clearly was used to being cast in the lead. She stood, revealing a frock of rose chiffon that matched the color in her cheeks to an uncanny degree. She aimed her frightening smile straight at me. I bared my teeth back at her.

Lady Sophia knew her game. Her lashes lowered, demure. "You may rely on me, Headmistress."

"So I presumed. Enjoy your breakfasts. Oh, and, Lady Sophia, may I ask also that you escort Miss Jones to the chapel when the meal is concluded? She is unfamiliar as yet with the school grounds."

"Of course, Mrs. Westcliffe."

"Thank you." She gave a nod to the table. "Ladies."

"Good-bye, Mrs. Westcliffe," chirped the chorus, precisely on cue.

We all watched as she clipped toward the laughing table. As soon as she was out of hearing range, I felt Sophia's ice-blue gaze return to me.

"Eleanore, is it? That's quite a mouthful of a name for someone so . . ."

"Plain," sniggered the girl in the chair next to her, round-faced and bug-eyed, with oily, wavy black hair escaping its bun.

"I was going to say *penniless,*" countered Lady Sophia smoothly. "But as you like, Mittie. Oh, Eleanore, this is the Honourable Mittie Bashier, of the Doyden Bashiers, of course. And on down the table we have Lady Caroline Chiswick, Lillian St. Clair, Beatrice Hart-Stewart—the Hart-Stewarts, undoubtedly you've heard of *them*—Stella Campbell, and Malinda Ashland. Ladies, Eleanore . . . dear me. It appears I've forgotten your surname already. Smith, or something like that?"

"Call me anything you like," I answered, pulling out my chair. "I certainly understand how someone with such an abnormally tiny head would struggle to remember even the most undemanding facts. It must be quite a burden for you."

There was a collective intake of breath. I reached for the platter of bacon and toast nearest me. My fingers trembled only a little as I picked up the silver serving tongs.

Bitch, snarled the beast in my heart, and it might have meant me.

"My," breathed Lady Sophia, after only the barest moment of suspension. She sank gracefully back into her seat. "How nearly effortlessly you managed that. Hardly any spittle! Let us beware, girls. It appears the mudlark has claws."

I swallowed my bite of buttery toast. "Claws, and more."

"Indeed. I'm sure all the passing sailors and whatnot admired your pluck, Eleanore, but *here,*" she lifted her teacup and took a sip, staring straight ahead, "we abide by rules you will find quite unfamiliar. We are, after all, daughters of the *civilized* class, nothing like your own."

"What an interesting definition you must have of the word *civilized.*"

Lady Sophia's lips formed a derisive curl, but before she could respond, a handbell was rung from the teachers' dais. Girls began pushing back their chairs.

"Time, ladies," called out Mrs. Westcliffe, still holding the bell. Her tone stretched high and thin; she knew she was attempting to herd cats. "Off to services! Miss Faraday! Miss Turner! Put down your spoons, thank you very much. Yes, Miss MacMillan, I see you there. Walk on. *Walk,* I said. We are gentlewomen, one and all. We do not rush, but let us not keep the good reverend waiting!"

My tablemates had nearly all left. Mittie smirked at me before moving off; Sophia paused to dab her mouth with her napkin, then offered me her shark's smile. "A pity you arrived so late. I do hope you had enough to eat."

"Yes, quite." I smiled back at her.

. . .

The lovely thing about brown, and about brown twill in particular, isn't merely that it doesn't show dirt. It also disguises grease spots quite well.

Although I admit the pockets of my skirt did smell suspiciously like bacon until I thought to rinse them out again.

. . .

The morning sky had brightened into blue velveteen, and, surely only because a pair of teachers strolled behind us, Sophia and her minions let me tag at their heels out of the school and across the green to the chapel.

The sun felt warm on my head, a pleasing heat after the stony-cool inside air. My shadow strode long and rippling over the grass, lapping at the edges of the others, never quite cutting in.

I was deliberately lagging behind. I could not seem to stop gawking up at the castle.

I supposed us to be now on the opposite side from my tower; nothing around me looked familiar. I couldn't see the bridge to the mainland or anything of the sea. In fact, I could no longer even hear it and wondered how large the island could be.

There was no question that Iverson itself was truly massive, enormous dun stones scrubbed pale near the top and blotted with lichen and moss along the base. It went on and on, a big squatting hulk of limestone, gripping its solitary fist of land fast against all comers.

The grounds seemed velveteen, too, perfect as a painting, with clean-cut grass angled sharply around flower beds, tidy shrubs and roses and fruit trees, all precisely arranged. Even the hedges bore the brunt of human design: I realized that they were shaped as animals, all of them, giant rabbits and lions and unicorns scattered about. Everything contained, everything pruned and clever, until the rough woods took over, real nature at last, encircling us.

I caught sight of Mr. Hastings on his knees by one of the beds, a spade in hand. Then the winds turned, fingering through my hair, and that was when I heard Jesse. His music.

I missed a step, glancing all around me. One of the girls a few paces ahead—Malinda? Caroline?—gave the girl next to her a poke with her elbow.

"Oh, my," she said, loud enough to carry. "Look *there,* Mal."

So the elbower was Caroline. Malinda slapped her back with a slim hand.

"Stop it!"

"You know you're *desperate* to see him!"

The entire cluster of girls slowed, allowing me closer. Past their shoulders I glimpsed him at the distant brink of the woods, loose-shirted and fluent. He breached a hill and strode toward Mr. Hastings without glancing over at the bunching mass of us. Sunlight kissed him from head to toe; he was a figure of splendid radiance.

"Jesse's your *beau*, Malinda!" crowed Lillian.

"Yes!" That was Beatrice, bright and malicious. "Come to pay a call!"

"Stop it, I say! Stop it, all of you!" Malinda's voice had taken on an edge of panic. "He's not deaf *and* mute! He'll hear!"

"If only he could speak to you! He'd tell you about how he wants to whisk you away to his horrible little cottage!"

"And have his way with you!"

"And marry you and have lots and lots of little mute babies, just like him!"

"Jesse's not mute," I said, before I could stop myself.

I had put my foot in it, it seemed. All the girls paused and turned to me. Malinda's cheeks were red as apples; Sophia arched a single plucked brow.

"What did you say?"

I decided to plunge on. "He's not mute." It occurred to me belatedly that *mute* might be their private code for something else—*dirty* or *forbidden* or *so savory for a stable boy*—but Lady Sophia only raised the other brow.

"And you know this because, what, in your sole night here, he's already spoken to you?"

"Yes," I said.

Sophia released a melodic laugh, one that everyone but Malinda immediately copied.

"Impoverished *and* a liar," Sophia said to them, and shook her head. "Dear me. Not a propitious start for you, Eleanore."

"I'm not—"

"Jesse Holms doesn't *speak*," interrupted Lillian. "Not to you or to anyone else. It's why he can't sign up for the war. Even the Tommies won't have him. He's *simple*. Don't you understand?"

"Perhaps she's simple, too," suggested Mittie.

Sophia turned around, linking arms with Malinda. "A perfect couple, then! Cheers to them!"

I stood there and let them leave. I moved again only when the teachers behind me caught up and shooed me onward.

Before I entered the chapel, I threw a look over my shoulder at Jesse. He was seated alone on the grass where Hastings had been, watching me with a hand held to his eyes to block out the sun.

. . .

Sunday services were cold. Later on, that was mostly what I remembered. The pews were hard; the chapel was cold. The vicar was roughly two hundred years of age and he spoke slowly—*slowly,* with biting clear elocution—about warfare and chastity and virtue, somehow eventually entangling the three. By the time we were dismissed, the tips of my fingers felt numb.

I wanted outside again. I wanted to feel the sun again.

I wanted to see if Jesse was still there by the bed of flowers, free of Sunday lectures, illumed with light.

He wasn't. Only students dotted the green now, girls spreading out in spokes from the chapel door. Most seemed headed back to the main entrance of the castle. A few wandered in groups the other way, toward the gardens.

I thought of the orange in my room and trailed after the castle girls. Perhaps I could sneak it out in my blouse. There had to be a private place somewhere out here where I could sit in the sun and eat in peace. Maybe an arbor or a meadow in the woods.

The graveled driveway curving near the double doors was clogged with students, everyone surrounding a very familiar automobile loaded with trunks. A pair of menservants was struggling to unbind the luggage cords.

My feet stopped moving before my mind had fully processed what lay ahead. All those schoolgirls, and Chloe in cherry stripes and a huge, scarf-fluttering picture hat. Lord Armand standing beside her with a fist on his hip, driving goggles dangling from the other hand, his long-paneled coat flaring with the breeze.

I was held in place, unable to go forward, unwilling to go back. Chloe tilted her head and said something up to him, and he smiled at her, but it was a cold smile, cold as the chapel air. I wondered that she couldn't sense it . . . or maybe she did and it didn't matter. She was the shining star of the moment and she reveled in it, more beautiful and more important than any of the other girls, even Lady Sophia, now a rosy-pink sylph shunted off beside the auto's spare tyre.

Because Chloe evidently had what no other girl at Iverson did. She had *him.*

There was no question Lord Armand was handsome. I'd seen that last night, right up close. Yet I thought now that *handsome* wasn't truly the best word to describe him. Behind the wind-disheveled hair and burning blue gaze lurked a complexity not easily captured by words. Even from a distance, he struck me as deeper, darker, than those obvious good looks suggested. Like the hidden red glint inside a clouded ruby, visible only by holding the stone just right; if you didn't know the trick, all you ever saw was deceptive shadow. And I wondered if Chloe sensed that, too.

Feral, whispered my inner fiend, plucking the word from my black, black thoughts. *Alpha.*

The skin along the back of my neck prickled, and not in a good way.

The breeze shifted. I was upwind and he was down and I swear I saw him lift his face to it, breathe it in deep—then turn at once to find me.

No one else noticed. Our eyes locked.

He didn't offer me his icy smile. He hesitated, then gave a nod instead.

It was enough to cause Chloe to tuck back her scarf and look my way. She *definitely* didn't smile.

Move, I thought. *Turn around. Go back to the chapel, to the woods, hurry.*

But it was too late. Armand leaned close to speak to Chloe, walking off before she could reply. All the girls within earshot turned amazed faces toward me as he angled through them. Straight in my direction.

I managed one step backward. That was as far as I got.

He hadn't run. He hadn't even hurried. But he was there before I could take that second step.

"Miss Jones," Lord Armand greeted me, with another nod. "You made it, I see."

No thanks to you.

"I did," I replied. My mouth had gone inexplicably dry.

"I realized we never finished our introduction last night. I'm Armand Louis."

He gave it the French pronunciation, *Lew-eee,* which wasn't how Director Forrester had said it at all. It didn't make me like him any better.

He held out his hand. I didn't take it.

If I'm rude, he'll go. If I make it clear I don't like him, he'll go.

"Hmm." His hand dropped, but he didn't leave. "Well. How is it?"

"How is what?"

He made a vague, circular motion with the goggles. "The school. Mrs. Westcliffe. Everything."

"Satisfactory." I took that second step back.

"Have you seen the conservatory yet?"

"No."

"The grotto?"

"No."

"How about—"

"I've been at Iverson approximately twelve hours, my lord. I have been to my room and to church, and very briefly to dine. That is all."

Now he smiled at me, sharp and alluring, and it was just as unsettling up close as it had been from afar.

"Call me Mandy."

"I don't believe I will," I said, with another step.

"It's quite all right. Lots of the girls do."

I summoned my own chilly smile. "How lovely for you. Why don't you go chat with them? I'm sure they miss you already."

"Eleanore, look." He matched my retreating step with a forward one. "About last night. You'll have to forgive me if I—if matters didn't turn out as you liked. It's just that, you know, Chloe. She's—"

"Coming this way," I finished for him.

And she was, striped skirts lifted with both hands, long coils of chocolaty hair blowing past her shoulders. She didn't raise her voice, not quite, but the look she shot me could have melted steel.

"Mandy, darling! They've nearly finished unloading the motor-car, and I promised Lucille you'd take us for a spin along the coast. She's got her hat and gloves and we're all set to go."

Lord Armand didn't even turn around.

"Tea's at four," he said to me. "It's decent enough. Will you be there?"

"I don't know," I answered, honestly.

Chloe had reached us. She placed a hand on his arm, fingers curving into his sleeve. The filmy tail of her scarf whisked up between them to tap against his coat.

"Ready?" she asked, almost a purr.

Armand looked from me to her, then back to me. I saw the change come over him, an invisible shield that dropped across his eyes, no warning, no retreat. He resurrected that icy smile, then escorted Chloe back to their waiting group of safely adoring schoolgirls.

. . .

It was impossible to hold a conversation while driving. That was one of the things he loved best about it, Armand decided. The raucous roar of the engine. The thick smell of grease and oil mixed with dust from the road, coating his face and the inside of his mouth.

And the speed. It was speed without the pure galloping smoothness of a horse, true. Driving as fast as he liked meant jolts that could rattle apart bones. But it *was* speed, and control, and the knowledge that the speed was dangerous and the control a mere fine-edged illusion. A ruse of shiny knobs and grinding gears.

He'd nicked the auto from the motor stable before Reginald had recovered enough from last night's claret to notice. Armand wasn't technically permitted to drive—it was one thing on a very long list of perilous things he wasn't permitted to do—and so, when he could, he enjoyed driving very, very fast. He enjoyed that the Atalanta's engine was so rough that neither girl next to him could politely shout over it. Chloe and her friend rode with their lips squeezed shut and their eyes narrowed and a hand each to their hats.

He'd told Chloe repeatedly to wear something with less of a brim if she wanted to go out motoring with him. She never listened.

What there was of road along this part of the mainland was dirt. Sometimes rocks and dirt. Sometimes ruts and rocks and dirt.

He saw a deep groove in the way ahead and hit the accelerator for all he could. They smacked over it high and bumped back down hard. Both girls screamed: shrill, birdlike peeps.

A pair of ewes stared at them, startled, from a patch of clover growing close to the road. The auto tore past them before the sheep even began their first running hops away.

Under other circumstances, on another day, Armand would have steered right for the next rut. But his mind kept drifting elsewhere.

To *her*.

He'd had the worst night. If he'd slept at all, he couldn't remember it. His memory had run like a mouse on a wheel, the same scene, the same face, over and over and over until he was exhausted with it, and still he'd not been able to block her from his thoughts.

Perhaps he'd simply been too tired to sleep. Seeing Reginald again; dealing with the consequences of being sent home midterm from Eton. Again. It was all a right bloody mess. He'd been stewing, secretly sick with dread, the entire trip back, although Laurence and Chloe had eased matters somewhat.

Well, Laurence had. He was out of school, likely forever, so why wouldn't he be cheerful? But Lady Chloe Pemington, joining them at the last moment after attending some royal wedding or another in Norfolk, had been less than her usual carefully charming self.

The water served aboard the train was not chilled enough. The wine was not French enough. The staff was not prompt enough. She'd desired roasted lamb for supper and was served ham croquettes instead, and she had been coolly and surgically tearing apart the sweating steward until at last she'd noticed Armand's steady, interested gaze upon her.

Then she'd shut right up. And smiled.

They'd all dined upon the ham and frankly he'd thought it damned delicious. Or possibly he'd just been giddy with relief at her sudden lack of complaints.

If her parents hadn't already wired the duke to confirm she was to spend the night at the manor house, he would have taken her straight back to the school and been done with it.

Yes. That was why he'd been so eager to get to Iverson. Not just to see if that girl, that girl with the remarkable gray eyes, was there yet. Not just that.

She had been the specter haunting his night. Hers was the face that had burned behind his eyelids until the sun had risen, and cursed if Armand could figure out why. She wasn't even pretty. Not really.

From somewhere inside him, sly and surprising, came a response to that thought.

Not yet. Wait.

The Atalanta jounced over a fresh rut. Like clockwork, Chloe and Lucille let out their little peep screams.

Then a tyre blew. He felt it, heard it, and held hard to the steering wheel as the automobile snarled into a spin, fighting to flip. The world blurred into a whirlwind of sunlight and grit and the girls screamed again, really screamed, full-throated. Armand himself might have been screaming. Or laughing. Both.

And for just an instant—with his lips peeled back and his knuckles clenched white and Chloe's voice a high, keening cry in his left ear—that sly thing within him welled up strong and demented, compelling his hands to *let go*.

But he didn't.

They came to rest not two inches from an ancient rowan tree growing bent in a meadow, one that surely would have smashed the chassis and maybe them as well into shiny tinfoil had they spun any farther.

It took more than three hours to change the tyre. He'd discovered the jack broken and had to push the Atalanta across the meadow and over to a drainage ditch so that the wheel might hang free, but without anyone to help—his lady guests had withdrawn to the shade of the tree to dab at their foreheads with handkerchiefs—it was slow going.

It took nearly another hour to drive back; the girls insisted upon stopping at the nearest farmhouse to tidy up before returning to school. The farmer's wife had offered water and cider, and they'd all accepted both.

By the time they reached Iverson again, tea was done.

He found out later from the housekeeper that Miss Eleanore Jones had attended after all.

Nuts.

Chapter 8

Letter dictated and signed by Rue, M. of L., dated August 3, 1808

My darling girl,

You're sixteen. I've counted the years until this day, felt them pass in my marrow, each minute creeping, each second a fresh bleeding ache. How I long to be with you during this time. You've no idea what's to come, and those with you now have no real way to prepare you. Not as I could. I knew the moment I first cradled you in my arms how strong you were going to be. How different. Our blood is thinning, and there are not many born such as you. Per-chance that's a blessing; I truly don't know. But what I do want you to know, the very first thing, is that it's going to hurt. It's going to hurt so very much that you will wish you could die.

You must not die. Not yet.

When it first begins, you'll feel a sense of tearing within; I can think of no better word to describe it. Tearing. Renting, your skin from muscles, your muscles from bone. It will be a pain at once so exquisite and so horrifying that it will devour you whole. And it will be swift. You won't even have the dubious relief of opening your mouth to scream.

You will no longer have a mouth.

Nor eyes, nor face, nor limbs. You will no longer have a human body. You will exist as nothing but smoke and pain.

I require that you hold on to one single, final thought during this agony: *I will live.*

Without it, every bit of you, every last lingering essence, will merely evaporate. Your parents will have nothing left to bury.

I wish I might be there for you when it happens. I wish I might be a better guide for you, my beloved girl. You are my great-great-grandchild. You have my husband's eyes. And yet I remain trapped, old and blind, at this miserable distance, countries away, mired in my worry.

The first Turn has destroyed so many of our kind. Do not become one more early death.

All my love,
—Rue

Chapter 9

I walked along the outer walls of Iverson, looking for other doors, a cracked window, anything that might let me slip back inside without having to brave the flock of girls that still jostled about the main entrance. I walked at first without really seeing where I was going. I just needed to get away. The memory of Armand's cold, empty eyes followed me like a cloud above my head.

There were no other unsecured entrances, but I found several windows out of reach and four oddly elfin wooden doors set back deep in stone arches. These were so small I'd have to stoop through them and so old the wood had blackened. They were also locked.

By then I was very much alone. I no longer heard anything but a solitary blackbird way off, testing out the notes of an amorous invitation. And the wind through the branches of the oaks and elms, a low rustling sibilance that swirled around me in a language I almost understood.

Still no drumbeat of the sea.

I discovered why soon enough. I'd been walking and walking, and even though the day was brisk, I'd begun to perspire. I reckoned I'd covered about a half mile of wall by then, or so it seemed.

When I looked up, I saw the tip-top of what might have been my tower past the crenellations; the diamond window was still open. I was squinting up at that, wondering idly if anyone had ever thought to scale that high—a medieval prince, perhaps, determined to steal through the window to claim his princess—when I rounded another corner and found myself at the end of the isle.

The forest cut short. The sea was visible but far away, a sparkling smudge against the horizon, dusky flecks of boats sprinkled upon it. The ground I'd been treading tapered from grass to rocks, lots of rocks, until that was all there was. Huge tan and cream boulders sloughed down a cliff, strewn along a beach far below.

The bridge to the mainland stood on dry, spindly legs. There was no seawater beneath it, only sand laid out in ripples.

I stopped, confused. I closed my eyes and opened them again.

No water.

The brownish-gold sand surrounding the island gleamed with isolated puddles. Silvery shimmers bent the air above each, fairy air, dancing in mirage.

I edged closer to the rim of the cliff. The scent of earth and brine washed up and over me, raw in my lungs. My first step upon the nearest of the boulders roused it into a growling hum.

I set my teeth. I would ignore it. I'd come all this way, and I wanted to see the beach. I wanted to climb down there and dig my fingers into that sand, because it looked damp to me. And I *had* seen the water last night. It was *not* another delusion.

My boots were sturdy but not especially meant for climbing; the soles had worn slick. As I crept down, long strands of hair blew across my eyes, stuck in my lashes. My fingers groped for purchase among the pits and crags.

Still, I was halfway down before I fell. It was simple, stupid. I had my weight on a loose stone and then I didn't. The stone pushed free of the pile and I was careening backward and downward with a hand still clenched in my skirt, too astonished even to shriek.

There was a second of suspension, that tiny fraction of time when you're weightless and doomed and you know that everything is about to crash down hard and *hurt*—but then an unyielding force cinched around my shoulders. I was yanked back to the rocks, arms and legs flying.

I landed against something soft, something that gave a grunt as we hit the boulders. I heard the stone that had slipped smacking end over end down the pile, loosening others, a showery rainfall sound that ended with wet thuds against the beach below. But even all that was nearly drowned beneath the song of Jesse, who held me fast against his chest.

I didn't have to twist around to confirm it. The strange bliss of his touch was already spreading through me, so sweet and acute I might dissolve with it. I tried to jerk free, and his arm cinched tighter, a stranglehold at the base of my neck.

"Don't be daft, Lora. Unless you're ready to fly."

Not mute. I tugged at his arm with both hands until it relaxed slightly.

"Let go," I choked out.

He did, slowly, his palm dragging flat along my collarbone until he gripped my shoulder—*oh, heavens, so sweet*—holding me steady as I wobbled upright and inched around to face him.

As soon as his hand fell away, the bliss subsided. I was aching without it, angry without it. Our shadows mingled down the rocks like lovers still entwined.

So, this was Jesse:

Colors, brilliant and glimmering. Music. A good height, and a country boy's tan and muscled strength. An easy, inviting smile and eyes long-lashed and green as sultry summer. He was probably just seventeen or eighteen but already beautiful in that severe way men sometimes could be, and I knew exactly why Malinda and the rest followed him with their eyes even while they disparaged him with their words. If Armand was the darkened ruby, then Jesse was pure, vibrant gold. His hair was gold, and his skin was gold, and his touch lit gold inside me, a torch that burned still in places I'd never considered.

The fiend in my heart had come awake, as well, basking in his song. It radiated hunger, keen as a bayonet blade.

What *I* felt was rather more like . . . agitation. Or fear.

"It's a long fall," Jesse said. "Worse at low tide."

"Thank you," I managed, begrudging. Then his words sank in. "Is that what this is?" I motioned to the beach. "The tide is out?"

"The tide rides high, and we're an island. The tide pulls low, and we're one with the mainland again. You could walk there from here, if you wanted. But you've only got a few hours. Then you'd have to take the bridge back, or else swim."

"You *do* speak." It came out as an accusation.

"When there's someone around worth speaking to." He turned about, began to scale the boulders behind us. Big hands, callused hands, going from rock to rock. "It's too dangerous here, Lora. Come with me."

I stood for a moment, debating, but even as I thought about climbing down instead of up, a new shower of rubble broke free below. The combined song of the boulders rose in pitch, sounding remarkably like an alarm.

I followed Jesse. I wanted to avoid the hand he held out to me for those last few vertical feet, but he said, impatient, "Grab on," so I did. The scrubby grass growing at the top of the cliff felt like a godsend, wonderfully firm.

Again, I pulled free as soon as I could. Again, every part of me tingled, and that made me defensive.

"What were you doing here? Were you following me?"

"Yes," he said.

No denial, no excuses. I blinked up at him, and his smile widened.

"Why?"

He didn't answer, not at first. The green of his eyes seemed to shift, growing darker, a summer storm rolling in. It was pulling me with it, too, spellbinding. I stared up at him and felt a fresh heat wash over me, dry lightning charging the atmosphere. Everything around us glowed brighter and brighter, as if we ourselves were caught in an electric strand. I smelled cinnamon and vanilla and rain, a combination so delicious I nearly licked my lips.

I took a sustained breath instead. I looked away to the unclouded sky, and the spell unraveled.

"I wanted to make sure you'd be safe," Jesse was saying, but something in his tone was tinged with a lie.

"Was it you who left the orange in my room last night?"

"You were hungry. And I thought you'd be up before Gladys arrived."

Hungry, echoed the fiend, almost a moan.

"I wasn't!" I barked, wanting to stifle them both—and then the shock of his admission hit. I'd thought about it but hadn't truly *thought* about it: the moonlight spread along the blankets on the bed, the thin flannel of my nightgown pulled tight against my breasts. The small rounded room, the sensation of a caress. He'd *been* there, *with* me—

Jesse lifted his open palms, a gesture of surrender.

"I meant no harm. You're a deep sleeper, Lora, heavy dreams that carry you deep. Beyond memory, I'd guess. I'll wake you next time."

My cheeks began to burn. "Are you *insane*?" I hissed. "You're not to go into my room, not at night or any other time! Do you think I don't know how to defend myself? I'm from bloody St. Giles! Do you think I've never been in a fight before?"

"No," he said, unsmiling. "I don't think any of that."

"Look," I said, and now my anger was a fine weapon zinging through me, putting power behind the finger I jabbed into his chest. "I don't know what you're about, and I don't care. I've dealt with boys like you for as long as I can remember, and I'm *not* interested. Just because I'm poor doesn't mean I'm weak. The next time you try something like that, I swear to God I'll make you sorry." I had no idea what I could do to make him sorry that wouldn't also land me in the soup, so I gave him another jab for good measure. "Got it?"

"I apologize," Jesse said. He'd made no move to defend himself, although he was taller than I. And older. And a boy. His hands remained lax at his sides. "I just . . . didn't want you to be hungry."

And there was something in his tone again, something unsaid, only this time I swore I nearly heard it. The beast in me heard it, gathered it near.

It became: *beloved.*

I closed my mouth with a snap. I backed away from him, letting the wind push me sideways until I met the cool, scoured wall of Iverson. Then I turned around and ran.

I never heard him follow.

. . .

Sunday was Visitors' Day at the school. It was the one day of the week outsiders were permitted inside the halls . . . but only some of the halls. And only *some* outsiders. I doubted that anyone I knew from the Home, for example, would have made it as far as the prickly hedges, much less found themselves escorted into the shining sophistication of the castle's front parlor.

Most of the girls had families that lived too far away for regular visits. For all its bucolic charm, this part of Wessex wasn't in any danger of becoming a serious social destination. It seemed no one of any real consequence—barring the Duke of Idylling and his irritating son, of course—lived nearby.

But a few girls did have guests on my first Sunday at Iverson: mothers and fathers, a scattering of boys in jackets and tight collars who might have been brothers. Or beaux. The rest of the students sat in softly chattering circles, ankles crossed, drinking tea and eating tiny morsels of food without spilling a drop or a crumb. Without even, I noticed, seeming to part their lips.

I sat alone, naturally. I hadn't wanted to come, but the scent of cold smoked salmon and dill wafting from the doorway had been too much to resist. After everything that happened that afternoon, I'd missed lunch entirely.

I'd claimed a solitary chair wedged into a corner. It was horsehair, old, wretchedly uncomfortable. I sat with my plate of finger sandwiches balanced on my knees and tried to chew as the other girls did, teensy bites followed by short, dainty sips of liquid, a process that could easily consume ten minutes for a single sand-wich. Perhaps that was why no one had sprigs of dill in their teeth.

At the orphanage we'd had one meal a day, plus tea. Tea at Bliss-haven was old chipped teapots filled with twice-used leaves and a platter of stale sliced bread. If yours wasn't one of the first hands groping for the bread, all you got was tea.

The pots here were of silver. The china had cherubs and gilded trim. The tea was flawlessly steeped, possibly my first ever from vir-gin leaves. And there were enough salvers of miniature sandwiches and iced cakes to satisfy even me—although after I had served my-self thirds, Mrs. Westcliffe sent me a fixed, frigid smile from across the room that had me slinking back to my chair.

Lady Sophia held court in the corner opposite mine, reclining on a chaise longue, letting her jackals do all the talking. I pretended not to hear, but the parlor sported mirrors on all the walls. Every-thing reflected.

". . . so ridiculous. I mean, of course she has no money, but does that mean she has to dress like some woeful matchstick girl? You know the ones I mean, Stella, those deplorable little rags one sees at Drury Lane, bleating for coins after the shows."

"Quite."

"And her *hair*. Gracious."

"Perhaps someone might lend her a proper comb. You've got an old one, Caro, don't you? That ugly one your auntie gave you, carved from a camel bone or something?"

"I'd rather throw it away, really. I doubt she'd even know what to do with it. Look at her. Did no one tell her this was Sunday tea?"

Chew, chew, chew, chew. Swallow. Sip.

"Is that a *hole* in her skirt? Look, look—oh, Mittie, don't be such a fishwife! With your *eyes,* not your entire torso! But just there, at her knee."

"It is!"

"Yes!"

"Now, that is truly pathetic. Truly."

"Pathetic!"

Chew, chew, chew, chew. The salmon turned to mush in my mouth.

"What on earth do you suppose Lord Armand had to say to her?"

That was from Lillian, sounding genuinely baffled. I took my sip of tea in the midst of their silence, washing down the mush.

"Well, she's the new charity girl, isn't she?" said Mittie. "So most likely he was merely saying hello. All the charity girls have to meet the duke. To make certain they're appropriate and everything. He was probably only saying hello. For his father."

"He never did before," said Lillian, still baffled.

"Of course he did. You just never knew."

"It didn't seem *Chloe* thought it a mere hello."

"No," agreed Sophia thoughtfully, speaking at last. "It didn't."

My cup and plate were empty. I rose, placed them on the sideboard with the other lovely dirty things, and walked off. The mirrors all around showed me images of a phantom girl, shadowy and gray.

I left her behind me. I was careful not to look too closely at her face.

. . .

And that was the sum of my first day at Iverson.

The worst part of it all was that Jesse was right. I *was* hungry. I was definitely too hungry not to eat his orange.

If it was Dark, it didn't matter. I was already doomed, because every Dark cell of my being already hungered to see him again.

I stood by my window that night and dropped the peeling through bit by bit, flickers of white and orange that tumbled down to the grass, became swallowed by the moonlit green.

Chapter 10

Proper young ladies of the British Empire were, apparently, expected to know how to dance, to organize a supper of up to twenty courses, to embroider, to speak a foreign language—not German—to play the piano, and to paint.

We were not expected to wrestle with mathematics, beyond what might be required for common household management. We need not bother with horticulture but were encouraged to learn to arrange cut flowers artfully in vases. We studied history because, I supposed, it was dry and full of the dead and therefore mostly harmless. But science was a subject fixed absolutely within the realm of men. So was literature of the darker sort; no Dante or John Ford for us. We read books about moral forbearance. Or else poems, the fluffy sort that rhapsodized over windmills and kings and kittens and good girls who liked to sit by the fire and knit.

I could not dance. I could not reliably position forks on a dinner table for a prince. When I embroidered, the needle buzzed so loudly in my hand that I pricked myself with it, and my first attempt at a sampler ended up stippled with blood.

I understood no other language but my own and that of the metals and stones.

I'd never held a paintbrush.

But something happened on my first day of piano class.

Something magical.

"Middle C, if you please, Miss Jones."

Monsieur Vachon lurked behind me, unseen, but I knew exactly how he would appear, anyway: tall and lanky, with a spine bent at the neck like a shepherd's crook, his eyes sharp behind his spectacles, his hands clasped together at the small of his back. He wore a black jacket and waistcoat and pristine spats over his shoes. He looked like an undertaker but for his hair. It was tawny and unruly, a lion's mane framing his face.

And he fully expected that I, seated for the very first time in my life before a piano, would know what middle C might be. Perhaps all the girls in France were born with sonatas bubbling through their veins.

The sheet music in front of me swam with dots and lines. It might as well have been penned in ancient Etruscan.

"Miss Jones," Monsieur Vachon prompted, only with his accent it became *Meez Jonzzz.*

"I . . ." My hands hovered above the keys. Was middle C one of the ones in the middle? Wouldn't that make sense? Was it ivory or ebony?

I'd tried to explain to him before the class began that I couldn't do this, that I had no notion of how to play, but he'd brushed me off. "Everyone must play," he'd pronounced. "This is Iverson."

I supposed now he understood I wasn't really *everyone.*

I heard Mittie heave a sigh from her chair against the ballroom wall. She'd already had her turn, pecking out a tune that had reminded me of one of the kitten poems. Perky, insipid pap.

Monsieur's patience began to fray.

"Here." A finger reached past me, pointing to one of the ivory keys. From my seat of mortification I noticed that he had hair all over his knuckles, too.

"C," he enunciated in my ear, and I quickly mashed my own finger down against the key.

The note hit the air slightly muffled. I hadn't done anything with the pedals, as I'd seen the other girls do, and it died its solitary death without a fuss.

But then the magic came. Another note, another C, lifted around me, soft at first and then louder, exquisitely pure. I raised my head, searching for its source, but no one else was holding an instrument. In fact, the only other instrument in the entire chamber was a harp, and it was still shrouded in its sheet.

The ballroom had wooden floors and long, decorative tapestries, a frescoed ceiling painted into a cloudy heaven. The chandeliers suspended above us were also covered in sheets; only the bottom curving loops of crystal beading showed, swaying gently with a draft.

All the rest of my class gazed back at me from their line against the wall. Their expressions ranged from boredom to impatience to happy spite.

Sophia turned her head to whisper something to Lillian, who giggled. Mittie crossed her legs to swing her foot from side to side.

C, sang the silent music. My finger pressed the key again, and then C changed to another note, and my finger found that one, too. And another. And another.

I needed both hands. I was using both hands to play the song that saturated the chamber. My head felt clear and my heart felt at peace for the first time in so long. I heard the song as it happened, and it was as if it sank into me, became part of me. The piano was now part of me, too, the voice I did not have otherwise. Melody, harmony, my hands moving faster and faster along the keyboard, creating sounds I'd never imagined.

I wasn't thinking about any of it. I just let it be, and the music came.

Then it ended. The song finished and the ballroom fell into silence. I echoed the final passage and let my fingertips rest atop the keys, relishing their sleek warmth.

"*Mon Dieu,*" said the monsieur. At some point he had come to stand right beside me; I hadn't noticed at all. He gazed down at me with wondering eyes. "You told me you could not play."

"No, I—" I pulled my hands back to my lap. "I never have before."

"*Never* before?" he repeated, with an incredulous arch of his bushy lion's brows. "What is the name of that piece? Who is the composer?"

"I don't know," I said, nervous. "I . . . made it up."

I hadn't, though. *I* hadn't made it up. It had been the song of the ballroom. The song sung by the stone walls and rock-crystal drops of this room.

I swallowed. Monsieur Vachon had brought a hand to his chin. He was rubbing it, scowling, trying to decide if I was attempting to make a fool of him.

One of my fellow students coughed the word *cheat*.

"At the—where I came from," I said, "we had no piano. We had nothing. Not even books of music. I've never touched a piano before today."

"You cannot read this?" He indicated the sheet music.

I shook my head.

"And you just now created what we heard? All at once, *sans répé-tition*?"

I nodded.

"Can you play for us something else, Miss Jones?"

I swallowed again and looked helplessly at the far wall. I heard music still, but it was so dim. My pounding heart was so much louder.

"I feel a little ill," I whispered.

"Try," he ordered, dropping his hand.

Please, I thought, a plea to the ballroom, to anyone, anything. *Please, please help me.*

I pressed a key, but it was the wrong one. I closed my eyes and listened harder, waiting, breathing through my mouth. Someone—*Mittie,* said the fiend, *bloody fishwife Mittie*—let out a stifled snort.

My index finger found a new note, one of the ebonies. That one was right.

Soon it was happening again. I had to strain for some of it, and this song seemed sadder than the first, more ethereal. But when it finished I opened my eyes and there was my piano instructor star-ing down at the floor instead of at me, and I would have sworn there was a gloss of tears behind his spectacles.

"*Brava,*" he said to the floor, then lifted his head and made it louder, so that everyone heard. "*Brava.*"

I sat back on the bench and folded my hands over my stomach. The piano gleamed huge and black and white in front of me, a grin-ning, separate thing once more, an opportunity I'd barely begun to comprehend.

. . .

A jungle existed within the castle. It was an upper-crust sort of jungle, concocted entirely by upper-crust imaginations—and funds. There were no wild, messy monkeys or screaming macaws, no piranha in sight but for my classmates. Even the vines clinging to their lattices seemed too polite to stretch their tendrils beyond their allotted space.

But there were trees in oversize bronze pots: palms spreading fronds in wide, emerald fans; pomegranates and mangoes and figs, all jeweled with luscious fruit. Orchids opened fleshy petals of magenta and saffron from hanging baskets and urns. Statues stared from unexpected corners. Bamboo grew in a tended thicket, leaves sighing each time someone walked past.

A pond filled with koi and lotus plants marked the center of the jungle world, an octagon of liquid hemmed with stone. Orange and red fish, purple flowers, dark waters. A domed glass ceiling shone like a pearl overhead.

This was the castle conservatory. It was a more recent addition to Iverson, only about eighty years old, according to our teacher, Miss Swanston.

"And the light," she said, lifting her cupped hands upward in benediction to the dome. "The *light,* children. We could not ask for more."

I thought privately that we could. We could ask for a window to be opened, for instance, to release some of the heavy air that moistened every bit of my skin and stank faintly like rotting compost.

Lovely hushed music played from within the bamboo, music I knew no one else heard. Jesse was part of the jungle, as well, moving leisurely through the stalks, trimming errant stems. And if I'd had the power to ask for more of anything, really, it wouldn't have been for an open window. It would have been for more of him. For him to come out from the thicket, so that I could see his face.

But he didn't.

Art instruction was a combined class, meaning that two separate years of girls took it at once. There were twenty of us standing before our easels today, circling the pond. Since my class had been combined with the year ahead, one of the other nineteen students was Chloe Pemington.

She managed to ignore me magnificently. I thought Sophia might take a lesson from her. I was a gnat, a speck, an absolute nothing that required no greeting, no eye contact. Not even a sidelong sniff.

I simply did not exist, and I was standing right beside her.

I squared my shoulders and tried to do as good a job shutting out the rustling of the bamboo. Another older girl stood at my other side; I knew I existed to her, because she kept sneaking looks at my painting.

Hers, I noticed, literally dripped with color. Our assignment was to depict the lotus blossoms. Our medium was watercolor. There would be no undoing any mistakes.

"Good, good." Miss Swanston was walking from girl to girl. "Excellent use of perspective, Sophia. Most ingenious. Fine shadow work, Florence. Perhaps a touch more . . . there. Yes. Beatrice. What is that? A fish? I see."

Jesse moved nearer. Beautiful music, alluring music, sifting through green leaves.

I was listening to it despite myself, drawing languid brush-strokes along the section of my painting that was the surface of the water.

"Eleanore."

I stepped back, glancing up at my teacher. Miss Swanston wasn't what anyone would call fetching, but she was handsome, and far younger than most of the rest of the staff. I wanted to like her for that alone. She had hazel-gray eyes and a long nose and wide lips. In close quarters she always smelled of charcoal; I finally realized it was from the sketching pencils she carried in the pockets of her skirts.

Her head tilted; she was studying the line I'd just added. "Very nice. Very nice, indeed. You've captured the illusion of depth in the water quite well. Chloe," she said, turning in place. "Do come here and have a look. Do you see what I mean?"

"I'm afraid I don't," said Chloe, indifferent.

"I'm referring to our previous conversation. You asked about the use of transparency for depth. Eleanore has provided us with an example of a wash of separate colors to achieve her desired effect. Notice the dark beneath the light?"

Chloe pretended to care. "I suppose."

Jesse moved nearer still. From the corner of my eye, I glimpsed the beige of his shirt through the shoots.

"Blue under ocher, violet under green. Opposing colors that, when joined, create a perfect illusion of a shimmering whole."

"But isn't that only a trick, Miss Swanston?" asked Beatrice, from across the circle. "I mean, there isn't really any special *skill* involved in putting two colors together, is there?"

Miss Swanston smiled. "One might argue that all of art is trickery. A landscape is not merely a representation of what one sees but also how one sees it. Using pigment and paper, Eleanore has suggested quite nicely the idea of water and of what exists beneath the water. But her vision is unique."

"Rather," muttered Chloe.

"As is yours," said Miss Swanston, turning back to Chloe. "And yours, and yours, and all of yours. That is what makes art both perfect and imperfect."

"But a fish should look like a fish," insisted Beatrice.

"In your world, then, yes. But to someone else, a splash of red might be a fish, and that is fine, too."

"I hardly think splashing color about is *art*," Beatrice griped, just loud enough to be heard.

"Art," replied Miss Swanston, "may take its form however we wish. That is its joy."

A throat was cleared behind us. We all looked; Mrs. Westcliffe stood at the doorway, a taller figure in the gloom behind her.

"And that will be all for today," concluded Miss Swanston smoothly. "Leave your brushes and trays where they are for Mr. Holms to clean; thank you, ladies. We shall save the fish for our next lesson. Kindly place your smocks in the hamper there by the fig tree."

Jesse had ventured to the edge of the bamboo, clippers in hand. He was looking at the doorway, at Mrs. Westcliffe walking toward me, Armand Louis in a dapper tweed suit at her side.

I quickly checked the rest of the circle; none of the other girls seemed in a great hurry to leave. Most of them were watching either Armand or me, folding their smocks into squares, lingering around the hamper. Whispering.

The smocks were of rough cotton and tied in the back. I yanked at the bow of mine and felt it contract into a knot.

I yanked harder, swiveling back to my easel, closing my eyes as my fingers fumbled with the cloth.

I am invisible. Invisible. If I can't see them, they can't see me.

Surely they weren't here for me. Surely Armand was here to visit

Chloe. She was still standing right there beside me, practically licking her lips with anticipation. She'd removed her smock already and had it arranged elegantly over one arm.

I pulled at the knot again and heard threads begin to pop.

"Allow me, Miss Jones," said Armand, right at my back.

There was no gracious way to refuse him. Not with Mrs. Westcliffe there, too.

I exhaled and dropped my arms. I stared at the lotus petals in my painting as the new small twists and tugs of Armand's hands rocked me back and forth.

Jesse's music began to reverberate somewhat more sharply than before.

"There," Armand said, soft near my ear. "Nearly got it."

"Most kind of you, my lord." Mrs. Westcliffe's voice was far more carrying. "Do you not agree, Miss Jones?"

Her tone said I'd better.

"Most kind," I repeated. For some reason I felt him as a solid warmth behind me, behind all of me, even though only his knuckles made a gentle bumping against my spine.

How blasted long could it take to unravel a knot?

"Yes," said Chloe unexpectedly. "Lord Armand is always a perfect gentleman, no matter who or *what* demands his attention."

"There," the gentleman said, and at last his hands fell away. The front of the smock sagged loose. I shrugged out of it as fast as I could, wadding it up into a ball.

"Excuse me." I ducked a curtsy and began my escape to the hamper, but Mrs. Westcliffe cut me short.

"A moment, Miss Jones. We require your presence."

I turned to face them. Armand was smiling his faint, cool smile. Mrs. Westcliffe looked as if she wished to fix me in some way. I raised a hand instinctively to my hair, trying to press it properly into place.

"You have the honor of being invited to tea at the manor house," the headmistress said. "To formally meet His Grace."

"Oh," I said. "How marvelous."

I'd rather have a tooth pulled out.

"Indeed. Lord Armand came himself to deliver the invitation."

"Least I could I do," said Armand. "It wasn't far. This Saturday, if that's all right."

"Um . . ."

"I am certain Miss Jones will be pleased to cancel any other plans," said Mrs. Westcliffe.

"*This* Saturday?" Unlike me, Chloe had not conceded an inch of ground. "Why, Mandy! That's the day you promised we'd play lawn tennis."

He cocked a brow at her, and I knew right then that she was lying and that she knew that he knew. She sent him a melting smile.

"Isn't it, my lord?"

"I must have forgotten," he said. "Well, but we cannot disappoint the duke, can we?"

"No, indeed," interjected Mrs. Westcliffe.

"So I suppose you'll have to come along to the tea instead, Chloe."

"Very well. If you insist."

He didn't insist. He did, however, sweep her a very deep bow and then another to the headmistress. "And you, too, Mrs. Westcliffe. Naturally. The duke always remarks upon your excellent company."

"Most kind," she said again, and actually blushed.

Armand looked dead at me. There was that challenge behind his gaze, that one I'd first glimpsed at the train station.

"We find ourselves in harmony, then. I shall see you in a few days, Miss Jones."

I tightened my fingers into the wad of the smock and forced my lips into an upward curve. He smiled back at me, that cold smile that said plainly he wasn't duped for a moment.

I did not get a bow.

. . .

Jesse was at the hamper when I went to toss in the smock. Before I could, he took it from me, eyes cast downward, no words. Our fingers brushed beneath the cloth.

That fleeting glide of his skin against mine. The sensation of hardened calluses stroking me, tender and rough at once. The sweet, strong pleasure that spiked through me, brief as it was.

That had been on purpose. I was sure of it.

Chapter 11

I was dreaming. It was a good dream, one I'd had nearly every night since coming to Iverson, and I liked it.

In my dream I was heavy at first, heavy as one of the massive rocks that made their rough stair steps down the cliffs of the island to the sea. I felt the weight of me sinking into the earth, and it was as if I would sink forevermore.

But then I changed. I became buoyant—immediately, fantastically buoyant, without any weight at all. I rose in a mist, in smoke, silvery curls that shone translucent in the moonlight, rising, rising. Free to flow beyond windows and walls. Free to descend into the unknown depths of a very dark woods.

I was in flight. The air pushed by an owl's wings, the breeze off the sea that ruffled bracken and oak leaves. I could go anywhere, high or low or as far as I wished, but what I wished was to float through the open door of a cottage nestled in those woods, a place that was also dark. Also unknown.

In the cottage was a bed, and in the bed was Jesse.

His eyes were closed; his lips were parted. I sank closer to him, to the heated contours of his uncovered skin, his chest, his shoulders, up to his peaceful face. I touched him, and his hands lifted to touch me back. He inhaled deep and I became the oxygen that nourished him. I was inside him. I was outside him. My lips were on his and our kiss pulled me back into weight, but not as a stone.

As me. As Lora with Jesse in his bed.

Our arms locked, our bodies pressed into one. His hair a golden sift against my throat, his unshaven cheek on mine, deliciously, wonderfully rough. The sheets knotted around us. Our kisses. His tongue. His hands stroking my back and arms and down, following the curves of me, cupping me, cradling.

I was empty and full at once. I was the opening flower, the ripe berry ready to burst. I wanted more of him and could not get more; we were already so close our bodies slipped slick together.

Beloved, murmured the voice that lived inside me, tender as I'd never heard it before. *I've missed you. I've waited so long.*

His eyes opened and he smiled at me: a green summer storm, a shadowed eternity there in his gaze.

You already know that I love you, Jesse said, and in that instant I awoke.

Alone in my own bed, plain Lora again.

Every bit of me aching and aflame.

. . .

Saturday edged nearer. I tried not to think about it but it ate away at me anyway, ever gnawing at the back of my thoughts.

I endured my classes. Monsieur Vachon had decided that since I was something of a prodigy, it would be his duty to deconstruct me, to take apart my talent piece by piece until he could reassemble it into a whole that better reflected him.

In other words, he was forcing me to learn scales, to read music.

I was as clumsy at it as the ten-year-olds in his beginners' class, but at least it required something most of my other lessons did not: absolute concentration.

Otherwise, my thoughts were flurried. An unpleasant tightness had lodged in my chest and it would not leave. Even the fiend could not make it leave.

History, art, French. I'd stare at my textbooks and see nothing; I'd stare at my teachers and see nothing. At the walls. At my supper.

Saturday tea was looming. Judgment Day, four days away. God knew what would happen to me if the duke didn't like me. If Chloe decided to openly shame me. If Armand kept up his focused, uncomfortable attentions.

If I used the wrong spoon for the sugar, or sneezed on the scones, or knocked over a priceless vase—

Three days. Two.

One.

"I *said,* pass the butter."

Malinda was the unfortunate soul assigned to the seat next to mine for meals. She bore up under this regrettable burden as well as she could, which was to say not well.

"Are you earless, Eleanore? The rest of us might enjoy butter on our potatoes, too. If you're *quite* done with it."

I'd been clutching the butter bowl for who knew how long, staring at the ribbed yellow curls and seeing . . . nothing. I handed it over to Malinda without looking at her, glanced down, and realized I'd forgotten to take a curl.

"*Thank* you," she sneered. "So *very* kind of you."

"Now, Miss Ashland," scolded Caroline, in a spot-on imitation of Mrs. Westcliffe. "One must always show charity to a charity case!"

The other girls erupted into laughter.

"It's true." Mittie was sawing through her portion of tonight's beefsteak, which had been boiled to the consistency of shoe leather. "No matter how pathetic some girls may be, there is always the possibility they will sink lower without proper guidance. So, in _that_ spirit: I say, Eleanore. Did you plan to comb out your hair for the duke's tea?"

"Or mend your skirt?" snickered Stella.

"Oh, _do_ wear the brown one! That one the color of mud. _So_ fashionable!"

"It truly compliments your lack of a figure!"

Malinda was closest. I suppose that's why it happened to her. She was the one at my elbow, stuffing her mouth with a cube of potato while glancing down the table at Sophia, eager for reassurance that she was in on the fun.

I bent toward her and said quietly, "Choke on it."

Her eyes went round. Her hands flew to her neck. She began to cough and then to wheeze, her face turning red. Bits of food flecked her lips, and her fork clattered to the floor.

Everyone stopped eating to stare. Lillian, at her other side, began hitting her vigorously on the back. Malinda lifted her arms straight out in front of her, waving them frantically. She was probably trying to get Lillian to stop.

"Stop," I said to them both, and at once Malinda sucked in an enormous gulp of air.

Lovely, whispered my fiend, dancing with glee. _Lovely, lovely power._

Lillian hovered, a hand raised, ready to clout Malinda again.

"Great heavens," drawled Lady Sophia, rolling her eyes. "Such a fuss. Someone give her a drink of water."

"Perhaps you shouldn't toss down your food so," I said to Malinda. "Not very dignified, is it? You've potato all over your face," I added.

She seemed too out of breath to reply. She swiped her napkin along her mouth and glared at me. I smiled at her.

My entire body buzzed with an energy I'd never felt before. It spread through me, marrow to blood to flesh, sinister and strong.

I had done that to Malinda. I didn't know how. But I had.

I stared down at the food on my plate, the blanched meat and potatoes and asparagus tips sprinkled with pepper, and suddenly it all looked luscious.

Beside me, Malinda was surreptitiously flicking food from her lap.

"What *are* you planning to wear, Eleanore?" asked Sophia.

"What do you care?"

"I don't, much. I was merely curious. I thought you might like to take a look at my wardrobe to see if something fits."

"What?" gasped Mittie and Lillian together, perfectly timed.

Sophia shrugged. "Well, why not? She's going to represent Iverson. Our class more than the rest. I'd rather she make a better impression on His Grace than not."

Beatrice laughed uncertainly.

"Why don't you come by my room after supper?" Sophia was ignoring all the other girls to hold me in her flat gaze. "And we'll see what's what."

"All right," I said, lifting my chin. My newfound power buzzed through my veins like caffeine, like potent gin.

Let her try to humiliate me with an ugly frock. Let her try.

"Splendid." She looked away once more and took a bite of the leathery steak, chewing and chewing and chewing.

. . .

I had not ventured into the section of the castle that housed the other students. I knew that they had their own wing and that it was adjacent to my tower. Sometimes late at night, when the wind stilled, I heard their whisperings, secret confidences exchanged. Sometimes when I looked down the connecting corridor, I saw the dull orangey glow of their lamps shining beneath door slits or silhouettes of girls slipping from room to room in their robes.

But I'd not been invited into that realm, so I had not gone.

Sophia walked ahead of me without looking back once, obviously certain I'd do nothing but follow. It was what all her other acolytes did.

They marched behind us in a clot of purple skirts and disbelieving head shakes.

Every door in this hallway looked alike to me, white paint with sharp black trim. I wondered if the other girls had to count them just to remember which one was their own.

I suppose it was inevitable that I would enter one sooner or later. It was actually surprising that none of my classmates had thought to torment me this way before tonight.

I might have been a princess in a tower, but Lady Sophia was an empress in a palace, one complete with a fireplace, fancy paintings, and a rug of lavender posies on cream so thick I sank with every step. All the furniture was rosewood, slick with wax. The windows had been hung with sheer, billowing curtains—bridal lace, just like in Mrs. Westcliffe's office.

My only consolation was that there were two beds in this room, not one, each pushed against a wall. So at least the empress had to share.

Mittie went and flopped across the far one, eyeing me with out-right hostility. She looked like an angry pug ready to mark its territory.

The other girls positioned themselves silently along various settees and chairs. No one sat near Mittie.

"Let's see," said Sophia calmly, still ignoring everyone but me. "I'd say we're nearly the same size. If you're a tad smaller, it won't matter. Everything this season drapes so loose. I have a few things that might do."

She opened an armoire so huge it reached nearly to the ceiling. I glimpsed the same white and plum uniforms that hung in mine. She pushed those aside on the rod ruthlessly with one hand.

"Here. And here. Perhaps this. This . . . this . . ."

Colors began to spill forth, delicate creations of taffeta and organdy, serge and chiffon, pitched to the unoccupied bed like dirty rags, a few slithering to the floor. I remained near the doorway as she worked. I was waiting for the punch line of her jest.

"Tea with His Grace, but not Sunday tea," Sophia mused aloud, examining the pile of frocks. "So . . . I think not anything too bright." She plucked free two of the gowns, handing them off to Lillian nearby. "And nothing too long." Another gown gone.

Her fingers traced the sheen of a blue satin tunic. "Too bold for an introduction to a duke? What do you think, Caro?"

"I . . ." Caroline clearly didn't know what to think. "I imagine so?"

"Agreed." The tunic was tossed to Lillian. "Ah, wait. I have it. Yes. Here we are."

She used both hands to free a new gown from the mess, shaking away all the rest in a tumble of unwanted glimmer. She turned around to me with it held up in front of her, a smile at last breaking through the calm.

The dress was beautiful. Of course it was; all of them had been. This one was floaty and silvery gray, the color of the moonlit mist of my dreams. It had a silver sash and a dash of silver sequins along the bodice. I knew straightaway it was worth more than I'd make in a year as a governess.

Probably more than five years.

"Try it on," Sophia said.

I didn't move.

"Oh." She looked around the room, sighing. "Right, everyone out. Give her some privacy. Go on."

Lillian went first, still mindlessly clutching the discarded dresses. The others filed out in an unenthusiastic line.

"You, as well," Sophia said pointedly to Mittie, who'd stayed on the bed.

"Why should I? It's my room, too."

Lady Sophia only stared at her. Mittie's mouth tightened into a downward curve, her pug face gone sour. She was no match for Sophia's ranking in the pack, and she knew it.

"Fine," she huffed, and went. The door slammed hard behind her.

Sophia looked back at me. "You needn't be concerned about undressing in front of me. I don't care a whit about your body or your modesty." She walked over, shoved the dress into my arms. Layers of gauzy silk puffed against my chest. "Try it on."

"Why?" I demanded. "So you can tell me to take it off and then kick me out in my knickers? Or, better yet, tell me I may borrow it and then accuse me of stealing it?"

"No," she said, flat again. "I want you to wear it to the tea."

"Why?" I wasn't going to play her game, not without proper answers.

"Because Chloe will be there. And I want to make her as miserable as I possibly can."

My arms dropped. The silver dress felt light as paper in my grip.

"She's my sister," Sophia said. "Didn't you know? Stepsister, actually. Her mother wed my father four years ago."

"You hate her," I said. It wasn't a question.

"You've no idea."

"How will me in *this* make Chloe miserable?"

"Anything that drags attention away from Chloe makes Chloe miserable."

The lamplight flickering on Sophia's desk behind her burned a halo around her pale hair. She gazed at me bright and hard, an unlikely angel in a schoolgirl's shape.

I lifted a shoulder. "Fair enough. I'll wear the dress."

Her distant smile returned. "Good."

. . .

The route back to my tower lay thick with night. I knew the way well enough now not to need illumination. My feet took me where I needed to go.

Sophia's dress was a silken veil across my arms. It tugged at the shadows behind me, murmuring to the dark as I climbed.

My door was closed, as I'd left it. But there was something at the base of it. Something new.

It was a box. A small one, cardboard, unadorned. I picked it up and felt a weight sliding around inside, singing as it moved.

By the light of my window I pried open the box to find a circlet of tiny roses made of solid gold, perfect as true life, attached to a pin.

It was a brooch.

A message had been written on the inside lid. It read: *For your tea. And I didn't come in.*

Chapter 12

Tranquility at Idylling was surely the largest, oddest house ever graced with the word *tranquil* in its name. It was much newer than the usual aristocratic manor homes that dotted the English countryside; a sprawling, five-story wonder of limestone and stained glass and spires commissioned by the present Duke of Idylling after he'd decided to remove his family from Iverson Castle fifteen years before.

In fifteen years, it had not been finished.

Walking through its halls, it was easy to imagine that it never would be.

Even on that day, the day of my first visit to the house, I was struck by its strange and awful beauty. It seemed a construction of elaborate nonsense, of inspiration and madness combined. Rounding each new corner was a lesson in surprise; it was always wise to glance both up and down before committing to the next step.

Up, to see if you were about to be concussed by a stray bit of pipe or scaffolding.

Down, to make certain the floor didn't suddenly end.

In time, however, I grew to learn the folly of Tranquility very well.

Warrens of elaborately paneled hallways led to nowhere. Luxurious rooms of pressed copper and imported wood were left dusty and half complete. Sometimes there was a roof overhead, sometimes only the sky. A gorgeous grand staircase in the atrium curved sinuously up the wall before ending in open space. The very last step would drop you like a stone two floors down.

As we motored up the drive, I noticed that the entire south wing tapered off in what looked like the middle of a window, tarps covering the roof and walls, a rubble of bricks and planks exposed to the elements, already dissolving in the salty wind. A solitary old man was stooped low over a retaining wall, slowly troweling mortar along a section at the top.

"Astonishing, isn't it?" Mrs. Westcliffe was my companion in the chauffeured automobile the duke had sent for us, both of us hanging on for dear life to the straps fixed to the doors.

"Very," I replied.

Perhaps it was the silken dress on my body or the golden roses at my shoulder, but I had determined that I was going to be the most perfect, delightful charity student the duke had ever encountered. I was going to stand correctly, speak correctly, smile correctly, listen attentively. I was going to make him positively reel with my perfection, so I added another "Very," with a trace more of awe. Mrs. Westcliffe granted me a glance of approval.

"The duke designed it himself, every corner. When completed, Tranquility will feature some of the most modern and superb workmanship in the kingdom. Of course, with this dreadful war dragging on, finding enough laborers to finish it all has become something of a chore."

I wanted to ask about the fourteen years before that, but today I was the perfect charity student. So I merely nodded in sympathy.

How do you do, Your Grace? So sorry to hear about your lack of peasant workers. What a rather large bother this war with the kaiser has turned out to be!

A butler stood at the front doors to welcome us. Our little party from Iverson had taken up two of the duke's automobiles; Chloe and two of her friends had crowded into the second.

Apparently, when Armand had invited her to tea to make up for her fictitious game of lawn tennis, she'd taken it to mean she could bring along the other fictitious players. And neither of them, I noticed, was nearly as pretty as she. Not by half. One had a weak chin, and the other badly frizzed hair and a red runny nose.

Clever Chloe.

We all five stepped out of the autos and into a brisk spring wind. The girl with the bad hair gave a squeal as her dress flipped up, revealing her knees. She slapped it down again as if she were smashing a bug with both hands, still squealing.

"Come, ladies." Mrs. Westcliffe brooked no such nonsense from her own garments. Her skirts were firmly in hand as she led the way up the stairs into the house.

I was the last one in. I paused for a moment to look back at the untilled field before the mansion, the crushed-shell drive and the azure sky. Past the slope of the field and a notched break of trees, the channel glinted, pebbles of light broken only by the shadow island that was the duke's former home, and now my own.

"Miss?" The butler was waiting, watching me with a patience that might have disguised something deeper. Like pity.

I scurried inside.

Tea was to be held in one of the few chambers that had been fully completed. It wasn't quite a parlor, at least not in the traditional sense. It resembled more an auditorium. There was no stage, but I was sure entire theatrical productions could take place within its walls. It was that huge.

And everything—everything—was black and white.

The marble checkered floor. The silk-papered walls. Clusters of tables and chairs of every size and shape, all black woods and spotless white velvets.

Black-and-white rugs. Black-and-white drapery.

A black grand piano stood ponderously in the middle of it all, a circle of chairs surrounding it like a noose.

Uh-oh.

And there were other people here, as well, about two dozen men and women standing in pockets and speaking in small, civilized voices. I saw no sunburned arms or faces, so they might have been the local gentry. Formal suits and starched-lace dresses and ostrich plumes in the ladies' hair; everyone serious, no one smiling.

Tea with His Grace looked to be a torturously grim affair.

Mrs. Westcliffe was addressing a man who was leaning against the piano with one hand. I wasn't surprised to see that he was dressed to match the chamber. Only the ring on his finger shone with color.

He wore a ruby, a big one. I knew at once it would be clouded.

". . . and—ah, here she is." With her back to the man, Mrs. Westcliffe threw me her pinched *do-hurry-up* look. "Come, Miss Jones. Come at once, if you please."

I did. I glided past the others and stood with my lovely, absolute obedience before the man and his ruby.

"Your Grace, may I present Miss Eleanore Jones, the latest happy beneficiary of your great goodwill. Miss Jones, I have the honor of introducing His Grace, the Duke of Idylling."

I sank into a curtsy so low it made my knees ache, my gaze fixed to the floor.

"A true pleasure to meet you, sir," I murmured, rising as slowly as I could.

"And you," the duke said back to me in a plummy, bored tone.

I took it as permission to look up at him.

I saw Armand before me and not. The duke was both taller and thinner than his son, with sallow skin and startlingly concave cheeks. I recognized that combination too well; it was the look of unhurried starvation. It seemed impossible to conceive, though, that a man with this house and a gemstone nearly the size of a robin's egg on his hand would live starved.

He did share the same wavy chestnut hair as Armand, but the Duke of Idylling's face was, at best, intriguing instead of handsome, and his eyes were brown instead of blue.

He was freshly shaved and pomaded, smelling of a lemony soap. When he removed his hand from the piano it quivered noticeably, and he tucked it into his jacket pocket to disguise it.

I moved on to my next scripted phrase. "Thank you so very much for inviting me into your home."

But the duke had no interest in my script. He was staring at me, staring at me hard, just as his son had done when we'd first met.

"Good God" was what he said.

I froze, my gaze flying to Mrs. Westcliffe. She looked from him to me, her eyes narrowed.

"You . . ." the duke began, and pressed a fist to his chest, still staring.

"Sir?" I whispered.

"Your Grace." Mrs. Westcliffe was abruptly professional. "Do forgive Miss Jones. She's unused to such exalted company, you may be sure, but we—"

"No, no." The duke began to laugh, strangely high-pitched. "It's not that, Irene. I thought I'd seen a ghost. Good God," he said again. He turned away from us all, collapsing into a chair. "Armand!" he called. "Have you met her, boy? Have you?"

"I have."

I don't think any of us noticed that Armand had entered the chamber. He strode toward us, mannered and composed as his father was not.

"It's the eyes," Lord Armand said, looking square at me. "That's all it is, Reginald."

"Yes, yes. You're right. Her eyes. Of course."

It seemed everyone around us exhaled; the gentry felt it safe to begin to breathe again.

"You have something of the look of my mother," Armand explained. "It's quite subtle, really. Hardly noticeable."

His father gave another laugh, but this one seemed despairing.

Mrs. Westcliffe came to the rescue.

"I hadn't realized," she said, beaming. "Well! How interesting! You've been given quite a compliment, Eleanore. Her Grace was said to be a true beauty."

"Oh, yes," agreed His Grace, sounding leaden. "Yes, she was."

I hesitated, then curtsied again. "Thank you."

Chloe drew breath to speak. "Mandy, I—"

"Shall we pick a table?" Armand offered me his arm.

Perfect student.

I took it and smiled. I hoped it wasn't too insincere.

. . .

I did not sit with the duke for his tea, nor with any of his other guests. Armand and I had our own smallish table next to the larger one that hosted the rest of the group from Iverson. There was space at ours for His Grace, a vacant chair next to mine; I saw him look at it, look at me, and turn away.

He sat between Chloe and Mrs. Westcliffe. The whole time he neither ate nor drank, only shot me those odd, uneasy glances when I supposed he thought I couldn't see. Only Chloe glared at me more.

My, yes. This was going *so* well.

Maids came; food appeared; refreshment was poured. I noticed that *tea* for the adults evidently meant *wine,* as well. The chatter in the room began to climb steadily. A few bold souls even told jokes, those indoors gentlemen chortling into their sleeves. Someone— one of the wives—eventually went to the piano. A ripple of ragtime filled the room.

Lord Armand and I sat without conversation; everything I'd practiced to say was for the duke. I picked at the jeweled bits of pe- tits fours on my plate, wishing I was alone and had a thousand more. Armand merely pushed his around with his fork. Neither of us looked at the other.

I had to salvage this somehow. I had to at least make an effort.

I searched through the mental pages of my script. "You have a lovely home."

His dark lashes lifted; his eyes held mine. "Do you think so?"

"Of course."

"Then you haven't seen enough of it."

He went back to pushing around his food. Chocolate was get- ting smeared all over the tines of his fork.

"Where is your friend?" I tried. "That boy from the train station?"

"Laurence? Exeter, I imagine. He was only here for a night. Had a pass to go home before shipping out. So Exeter. Or maybe even France by now." He stabbed viciously at a fresh petit four, impaling it all the way through.

"Oh? He signed up?"

"That's what I said, wasn't it?"

"Not really."

Armand sighed, clearly put upon. "Yes, Eleanore. He signed up. He signed up and *his* father allowed it. There. All sorted now?"

"You seem different here," I said.

He looked up once more, waiting.

I clarified, "Even less charming than usual."

Oh, well. I'd tried enough.

Armand set aside the plate and fork. He reclined back and crossed his legs, perusing me up and down. "Nice frock. Did you steal it?"

"Not yet. Is your mother dead?"

"Yes. Is yours?"

"I've no idea. Is your father mad?"

"Possibly. Is it jolly fun to be an orphan?"

"Absolutely. The most jolly fun ever."

"Poor little waif, desperate for a proper home."

"Poor little lordling. It must be sad to act like such a bastard and have no one actually care."

We regarded each other for a moment in crackling hostility. I was aware, dimly, of a figure suddenly next to us and the spare chair being pulled free.

"Dearest," said Chloe, settling in with her back to me. In this place, before these people, it was a massive, deliberate slight. "I was just regaling your father with all the woes of Sybil's wedding in Norfolk. I saw Leslie there, did I tell you? It's no wonder he hasn't joined up yet, Kitchener probably wouldn't take him, anyway. He looks perfectly *dreadful,* utterly *enormous* since he inherited the title, and he said it was merely the cut of his coat! Can you believe it? It was Parisian if it was anything, a first-rate merino. He's fortunate it wasn't Italian or he'd have looked like a stuffed sausage—"

"Chloe," said Armand. "Why don't you have a go at the Steinway?"

"What?" I couldn't see her face, but I could envision the pout. "But Mrs. Fredericks is already playing. She's doing an acceptable job, for a squire's wife."

"I'd like to hear you sing."

"Oh. Really?"

He sent her his cold, cold smile. "Really, truly."

She wavered, but there was no overcoming that smile. "All right, then."

She left far more reluctantly than she'd arrived.

"You'd better marry her before she reaches eighteen and the spell wears off," I said.

"Spell?"

"Yes. The one that's hiding her fangs and pincers from plain sight."

"I don't find them especially hidden," he said mildly.

"Then perhaps you're a pair."

His brows lifted. "Now, that's the cruelest thing you've said so far."

Mrs. Fredericks cleared off, and Chloe took her place before the piano. A beam of sunlight was just beginning its slide into the chamber, capturing her in light. She was a glowing girl with a glowing face, and Joplin at her fingertips.

"Give me time," I muttered, dropping my gaze to my plate. "I'll come up with something worse."

"No doubt." Armand pulled a flask from his jacket and shook it in front of my nose. "Whiskey. Conveniently the same color as tea. Are you game, waif?"

I glanced around, but no one was looking. I lifted my cup, drained it to the dregs, and set it before him.

He was right. It did look like tea. But it tasted like vile burning fire, all the way down my throat.

"*Sip* it," he hissed, as I began to cough. His voice lifted over my sputtering. "Dear me, Miss Jones, I do beg your pardon. The tea's rather hot; I should have mentioned it."

"Quite all right," I gasped, as the whiskey swirled an evil amber in my teacup.

Chloe's song grew bouncier, with lyrics about a girl with strawberries in a wagon. Several of the men had begun to cluster near, drawn to her soprano or perchance her bosom. Two were vying to turn the pages of her music. She had to crane her head to keep Armand in view.

He sent her another smile from his chair, lifting his cup in salute.

"I'm going to kiss you, Eleanore," he said quietly, still looking at her. "Not now. Later." His eyes cut back to mine. "I thought it fair to tell you first."

I stilled. "If you think you can do so without me biting your lip, feel free to try."

His gaze shone wicked blue. "I don't mind if you bite."

"Biting your lip *off*, I should have said."

"Ah. Let's see how it goes, shall we?"

I felt flushed. I felt scorching hot in Sophia's cool floaty dress, and Jesse's circlet of roses was a sudden heaviness against my collarbone I'd only just noticed. My stomach burned, my eyes itched. I wanted to leave but knew I couldn't. I wanted to vomit and knew I couldn't do that, either.

The duke was still sneaking glances at me and his son was downing his second cup of spirits without even blinking, and then Chloe's song ended and I heard, with a sinking sense of resignation, Mrs. Westcliffe addressing the duke.

". . . thought we might have Miss Jones jump to the fore. It happens that she's a fairly gifted pianist, according to Vachon. A natural talent."

"Indeed," said His Grace.

Mrs. Westcliffe twisted to find me. "Miss Jones?"

I was on my feet. I was moving dutifully—because I was the perfect charity student, one who did not drink or swear or bite—to the grand piano, and the bench was a hard resistance against my thighs, and the keys shone in the sun like the rest of the room, dizzyingly bright and dark, the same pattern repeated over and over, and I knew that if I did not look away I would become lost in it, perhaps just as lost as the black-and-white duke.

The sunbeam shone directly along my arms. It highlighted the silk sleeves of the dress and the scars circling my wrists, paler rings of flesh usually concealed by cuffs.

My audience had gone obediently silent. Beyond the occasional rustle of cloth against the velvet chairs, the scrape of leather soles against marble, I heard nothing.

No stone song. No metal.

There had to be *something.* The wives wore wedding bands, earrings, bracelets. There was a mass of actual gold pinned to my bodice. There had to be *some* music I could steal. But for the first time in forever, I heard nothing. Even the fiend inside me had nothing to say.

"When you're ready, Miss Jones," Mrs. Westcliffe said.

I brought a hand to my forehead, feeling the whiskey heat rolling off my skin. I searched up and around and at last connected with the eyes of Reginald, Duke of Idylling. He rose awkwardly to his feet, the untouched napkin on his lap sliding to the floor. He looked as terrible as I felt.

That's when I heard it. The call of his ruby.

And instantly, simply and sweetly, it was all that I could hear. My fingers searched out its echo on the keyboard; it became less and less an echo until the ruby and I were completely in concert. We shone as one.

I don't recall much of it. I sank into the rapture of the song and did not emerge until my hands hurt, until my hair had loosened from its pins and my breathing was ragged.

One moment I was playing and the next I looked up and found myself back before all those people. My ears rang with the silence.

Then they rang with the applause.

The duke was still standing. So was his son behind him. They were quickly matched by everyone else, though, because the rest of the guests began to push free of their chairs, still applauding. Even Chloe and her ugly underlings joined in, although they didn't look pleased about it.

For some reason, I focused on Reginald and Armand more clearly than on anyone else, one in front of the other, an older wreck of a man and his younger reflection. They looked more alike in that moment than I'd believed they could: both of them white as snow, both of them aghast.

. . .

That finished it with His Grace. He wouldn't even look at me as I curtsied my good-bye. He reared back when I approached as if he might actually flee, but since we were already departing he managed to glue his feet in place and stare desperately at Mrs. Westcliffe beside me instead.

He was afraid of me. I knew it in my heart, even without the fiend telling me so.

It wasn't that he didn't like me or that I had failed in my obligation to be the most grateful street urchin ever.

He was afraid.

I'd say the same of Lord Armand, but he'd vanished right after my turn at the piano. No one even offered his excuses.

"That went very well," Mrs. Westcliffe announced, climbing ahead of me into the backseat of our auto. "Your playing was excellent. Your manners were acceptable. His Grace seemed impressed." She settled in against the squabs, smiling; her new pet had performed its best tricks for the master. "*Most* impressed."

"Poseur," whispered Chloe, walking swiftly past.

Chapter 13

Second letter from Rue, dated January 30, 1809

Darling girl,

Your missive arrived at last. How thrilled I am to have received it. And how your questions have stirred my memories. It has been many, many decades since I worried about my own first Turn.

I'm afraid I cannot tell you precisely when your Gifts will manifest. I can only assure you that they will. And that, in the end, the pain will fade, and you will be magnificent.

I wish that you might have the example of your mother to lead you into your powers, but she was not graced with the Gift of the Turn. Your father, of course, is naught but human. I do not know why the peculiarity in our blood produces, every few generations, a child of your potential. For too many years, it seemed our kind was doomed to extinction no matter how we tried to stave it off.

Then I was born, a girlchild like you: half human, half not. My children were all blessed with my abilities, and theirs less so, and theirs less, and less.

Until you. You, the true heir to my power.

You must continue to be strong in the days ahead. You must think of me, and be strong. Listen to the gemstones; celebrate their music. Imagine how it will feel to stretch your wings for the first time. To taste the clouds. To hunt the moon.

I must rest now, my magical child. I shall write again soon.

All my love,
—Rue

Chapter 14

That night, no matter how I tried, I could not fall asleep.

It seemed to me a far-off thunderstorm roiled the sky, but when I paced to my window to find it, all I saw were stars. The tide had come in, the surf dancing silver along the shore in its own deliberate rhythm, but that wasn't the storm.

I returned to my bed. I got up again. My skin felt too tight; my muscles burned to move. Even my joints burned. I felt as if I could sprint for miles, nimble as a hart.

Instead, I stood at the window and watched heaven turn on its unhurried axis, finally deciding I needed to get outside to the green and then to the woods.

It was an unexpected thought, something I'd never even considered doing before. Curfew was ten o'clock every evening, and breaking it would mean a great deal of trouble should I be caught. Yet once the idea burrowed into me, I couldn't shake it. If Jesse could slink about at night without anyone spotting him, surely I could, too.

Almeda always performed the final check of the evening, usually around eleven. Sometimes she knocked, sometimes she didn't; tonight she'd already been by, so I didn't have to worry about that.

Certainly the forest would be less confining than my little tower. Despite my nagging feeling that there was a thunderstorm—*yes, there is*—there wasn't. The night was clear. I ached to run.

At the very least I'd see more stars.

The tower stairwell ended at my door, so there was no way to slip out but down along the main corridors. I crept along the stony halls of Iverson in my bare feet, boots in hand, grateful once more that Blisshaven had outfitted me in the dullest of colors.

When I got to the hall that led to the wing of the other girls, I stopped to listen. It was very late or very early, depending, but if any of them were up, I wanted to know.

All I heard was muted breathing. A few of them snored.

The suites of the younger students were interspersed with those of the older ones, so a pair of lamps at the end of the hall were kept burning through the night, the better to ward off evil dreams.

As I stole by, they sat cold and dark.

Curious—but not enough to make me turn back.

Eventually I reached the main doors. I fancied they'd be locked, but I'd try them anyway before searching for another way out. If nothing else, the windows of the front parlor had looked promising. . . .

Yet my hand closed on the wrought-iron latch and it gave at once. It seemed a fairly shocking lack of security, but I reminded myself that this wasn't the city or anything remotely resembling the dodgy streets of St. Giles. Who would bother to venture all the way out here for thieving? We were an island of leftover pin money and probably miserly teacher salaries.

If anyone wanted to steal anything, they'd have better luck simply walking straight into the shambles of Tranquility, where they'd have their pick of priceless, neglected things.

I opened the doors a crack and squeezed through.

My hair swished back over my shoulders. My face lifted and I breathed deep, as deep as I could until it hurt, and then let it all out in a rush. I raised my arms above my head and stretched hard, wind whistling through my spread fingers.

Freedom smelled of wild waters; it glimmered in a path of stars above my head. Freedom tasted like sea salt on my tongue.

It was another amethyst night, like the one when I'd first arrived. There was that long streak of Milky Way, bright in its cloudy curve, but the very heart of the sky was a purple so intense it was closer to jet.

The castle and the woods and I—the whole of the earth—lay bathed in its fey, colored beauty. We were soaked in purple night.

I bent to shove my feet into my boots, hitched up my skirt, and ran.

The green had been shaped by human hands, so it was easy to cross. Wide and smooth, it had been designed to showcase lovely young ladies moving sedately into their well-polished futures. Only when I reached the first shaggy trees of the forest did I have to slow, and even then not by much.

The woods felt instantly better, *safer,* than Iverson's lawn. Secrets could live in here, tucked between tree trunks, hidden in the boughs, and no one would ever see. Secret things, secret hearts, could open up wings and thrive.

Shadows swallowed me in slippery black. The air took on a richer, loamy note. The ground crunched with leaves, and ferns slapped at my shins and knees, painless. I splashed through brooks and left footprints in peat. Crickets called in time to my stride, a steady *chee, chee* that never broke.

I was running swifter than a hart, swifter than even the advancing night, because that was outside the forest and everything surrounding me here was enchanted, as I was. I didn't know where I was going, but it didn't matter. Sooner or later I'd run out of land, and then I would turn back.

But I began to slow before that happened. Not because I was tired, but because I realized I was coming close to something, and although I was sure I'd never been here before—I hadn't, not to this part of the isle—I knew I was getting near to where I needed to be.

Where I'd come out tonight to be.

By the time I reached the cottage, I was walking. I was following a path that seemed like a whisper, a bare impression in the earth, the slightest break in woolly grasses bounded by huge, gnarled birches and beeches and mossy logs and flowers that I could smell but not see.

There was a single candle lit in the front window. The door was open and the way stood empty, exactly as it always was in my dreams.

I slowed to a stop, a little winded still, engulfed in the perfume of wildflowers and the fragrance of the candle, paraffin, and smoke.

Go on, urged the fiend, pushing hard from within the cage of my chest. *We're not afraid.*

So I finished the last of the whispering path that led to Jesse's door.

I knew what awaited me beyond. The dreams had shown me so many times before that, when I ran my fingers along the frame of the doorway as I passed, I found the protruding knot that was always there, a cat's-eye shape at the height of my shoulder. When my feet met the rug beyond the entrance, I didn't have to look down to see that it would be red and sage and teal, a design of intertwining vines ending in an ivory fringe.

The cups and plates on the shelves along the kitchen wall would all be arranged largest to smallest.

The cast-iron stove would be sooty and scorched. An oversize mug would be placed nearby, knives and ladles poking out of it in a sharp metal bouquet.

There would be a river-rock fireplace to my left and a dining table with four chairs.

And there would be one other door, the only other one in the house. I knew that, too, because it led to Jesse's bedroom.

Dark Fay, reminded the fiend. *Dark dreams. Dark desires.*

A window—no curtains—was shiny with night, directly across the room. Jesse was seated in one of the two armchairs before it, relaxed, unmoving. He appeared to be gazing out at the trees that slept just beyond the glass.

"Lora," he said. In the reflection of the panes, I might have seen him smile. "I'm glad you came."

The candlelight hardly revealed him; he was more wily shadows than light. It must have danced along me a good deal more clearly as I lingered there by the front door.

"I don't know why I'm here," I said, and it was true. Somewhat.

"That's all right." He nodded toward the chair opposite his. "You still can come in. I won't bite."

I swallowed, abruptly remembering my idiotic threat to Armand—*biting your lip off*—and fighting a bloom of something in my throat that felt perilously close to panic.

"I'm not giving back the brooch," I said.

Jesse Holms turned in place to see me. Even by the solitary candle, even from this small distance, I was near flattened by his beauty: hair, skin, jaw and brow, throat and shoulders, every inch of him golden. Every inch of him perfect, as if he'd been sculpted by the gods from some lovely, impossible stone.

"No, you shouldn't," he said. "That was for you."

I tore my gaze from his and edged a step toward the free chair, then gathered my nerve and made it all the way. I sat down, feeling guilty, flustered. I'd been braced for at least a token argument. After all, I had no idea how he'd gotten it. It might have been his mother's, or his grandmother's, or he might have spent every last penny he'd ever saved on it, just to offer it to a girl he hardly knew. I hadn't actually expected to keep it, but the words had popped out, anyway.

A round piecrust table, surprisingly delicate, separated the armchairs. A jam jar holding a collection of starry white flowers gleamed square in its middle. I pulled free one of the stems, inspecting it as if it held all the answers to every question I'd ever ask.

It sounds peculiar, but touching that stem, feeling the cool smoothness of it in my hand, made me realize that I truly *was* inside Jesse's home, unaccompanied and unchaperoned and far, far from where I was supposed to be. I didn't even have the debatable comfort of knowing that this was another dream.

This is how girls get into trouble, I thought. *This is how charity girls end up shunned and starving on the streets. They venture out alone at night to beautiful boys, silly stupid moths to incandescent flames.*

The crickets outside seemed suddenly, embarrassingly loud.

"I hope it didn't cost much," I said at last. "The brooch, I mean."

"It depends."

"On what?"

"On how you might . . . characterize cost."

"Pardon?" I glanced back up, confused.

This time Jesse's smile was aimed straight at me. "Don't fret, Lora. I can easily afford you that brooch."

"But why?" I blurted. "Why would you just give it to me?"

I knew I sounded ungrateful, but I didn't care. The truth was, the brooch was exquisite. I'd never be able to repay him for it, not with money, and we both knew it.

He tipped his head, thoughtful. "Well, you didn't like the orange I left you. So I tried something else."

"Didn't *like* it?" I began, but had to stop, because my throat had squeezed closed. I pretended to take in the view beyond the window; all I could see was the faint mirrored image of the chamber behind me, broken into rectangles. Jesse and me, fixed in the glass as if we'd been painted there in watercolors, transparent as wraiths.

I closed my eyes and tried again. "It's not that I didn't like it. It wasn't the orange. It was that . . ." *You were there in my room. You saw me sleeping. I think you stroked my face.* I managed, "Food is extremely important to me."

The emotion in my voice discomfited me. I sounded raw, far more pained than I'd meant to. I had to wait to open my eyes again. When I did, he was watching me without expression.

"It's hard, isn't it?" he said.

"What is?"

"Being here. Being around all of them. Knowing that none of them, not one, has ever known what it's like to go without."

I shook my head, which wasn't an answer really but all I could muster.

I did not want his pity. I did not want to evoke that sweet, melting look in his eyes. I didn't want to feel this unexpected sorrow mixed with trepidation and something else—*desire,* insisted the fiend—that grew with every shared glance between us.

Mad, get mad, I thought to myself, but it was no use. I didn't feel angry.

I felt . . . different. Drowsy but wakeful, nervous but lulled, a victim of the soft sliding light and the candle and the calm, patient way this particular beautiful boy, this dangerous flame, was looking at me. As if he was waiting for me to figure out something he already knew.

I wanted to kiss him. I wanted him to kiss *me.*

The thunderstorm chose that moment to save me by rousing again, *boom-boom-boom-boom!* I angled in my chair to find it, but the crickets chirped on, and the woods remained unflustered. No rain, no lightning, no gusts. I glimpsed teasing patches of amethyst through the crowns of the trees but nothing else.

"It's the Germans," Jesse said. "Airships. They're bombing the coast."

That brought me wide awake. I leapt to my feet. "What? Now?"

"They're not near. The channel intensifies the sound. Believe me, no one else around here will even hear them. They won't make it this far west before dawn."

"Oh, I . . ." I blinked at him, replaying his words, "What do you mean, no one else will hear them?"

"Just that. Only you and I hear them tonight. I'd guess they're somewhere over Sussex right now. Brighton, maybe."

Again, I could not speak. Jesse's calm expression never wavered.

"It's all right, Lora. You can relax. You're safe with me, I swear it."

"What do you mean," I asked again evenly, *not* relaxing, "that no one else will hear them?"

His gaze angled away from mine; for the first time, he looked uncomfortable. He leaned forward to pull out some flowers from the jar, just as I had done. Long, tanned fingers began to weave the stems together, making a braid of blooms. Drops of water beaded the wood.

"All the world is like an ocean," he said. "All of it, not only the water part. And nearly everyone skims along on just the surface of that ocean, accepting what their eyes and ears show them as truth, even when it's not. Even when it's merely the bright skin of the ocean covering the truth. Entire lives are spent skimming that skin, person after person bobbing along the surface of things like driftwood, never sensing aught deeper beneath them. To them, real truth remains unfathomable.

"No one else hears the bombs, Lora, because almost everyone else around us is driftwood, basic human. You and I are the only ones right now who break the ocean skin to glimpse the deep. We're the only ones who can hear the bombs because, from here, they're beyond human hearing."

I allowed the crickets to fill the silence, ardent behind the glass. Jesse's fingers wove in and out between the flower petals; he was shaping the braid into a half circle upon the table, smearing the water beads. He did not glance back up at me or smile to let me in on the joke.

"You're not human, Eleanore Jones. I think that somewhere inside you, you must know that. You must always have known. You're not made of ordinary bone or blood but of something else completely."

"Really. What am I of, then? Kelp and jellyfish, I suppose?"

"You are made of magic."

He said it in an absolutely unremarkable way, as if instead he'd just said, *I had coffee this morning* or *the floor needs mopping.*

His hands stilled and finally he looked up at me. No smile. I saw nothing but that infinite patience etched on his face.

He wasn't joking.

Everything seemed to slow down, the seconds dragging out into a creeping crawl. My pulse slowed, and the dance of the candle flame slowed, and the wind outside slowed. I could not move or even swallow.

I wanted to respond with something cutting and urbane, something Sophia might muster at the drop of a pin—*You are stark mad, Mr. Holms*—but my mouth felt frozen shut. My whole body, in fact, had gone ice cold. I had become crystalline, see-through.

I wasn't driftwood but an icicle, and the wrong words, Jesse's next words, might shatter me to pieces.

Whatever they were, I didn't want to hear them. Yet I couldn't move.

Perhaps he understood. He watched me closely but didn't try to approach.

"Think about it. Don't lose your nerve now, just think. Where did you come from? Who is your family? You've known all your life you're not like any of the creatures around you. You hear things, you sense things no one else does. You can *do* things that no one else can. Those weren't the delusions or even the hopeful fantasies of a lonely child. It was the hidden part of you seizing the truth. Using it. An ancient magic created you, a powerful magic. It twines through you, growing stronger with every full moon. This is only the beginning. It's going to consume you eventually. That voice inside you—"

"*What?*" I did lurch back a step then.

"The voice inside you," Jesse repeated, gentle. "It's not truly a *voice,* is it? It's more *feelings* than that. Instinct. Animal. Bestial."

"Are you—did you just call me—"

"A beast, yes. You are. Better than that, though. You're better than all the other beasts in all the rest of the universe." He paused, a smile breaking through at last. And it was a dazzling smile, one to melt hearts and lies and all manner of icy-cold things. He came to his feet and crossed to me, stopping a handbreadth away.

His eyes captured mine, summer green darkened to dusk. His voice became a whisper.

"Lora, beloved. Lora of the moon and sky. *You* are a dragon."

Ah, sighed the fiend, swelling with delight inside me, filled with an awful, awful recognition. *Ah, ah! AH!*

"That is *enough*," I shouted over them both; rather, I tried to shout, but my voice was so strangled it came more as a gasp. "I don't know what you're playing at, but I don't appreciate your games. I—I came here to tell you to stop pestering me, and leaving me gifts, and *smiling* at me—"

"You dream of flying," Jesse said, which cut me off mid-sentence.

"Aye." He nodded, shadows and gold, tall and warm and much too near. "I know all about it. I know all about you. You have wings at night. You lift as smoke. And you come to me, don't you? Always to me."

I could not reply. I could barely take a breath.

This is a dream, this is all still a dream, it's just a new part to the dream, that's all—

"It's why you're here now, tonight. You're drawn to me, as fiercely as I am to you. You didn't even have to follow my song this time. I muted it, didn't you notice? And you came anyway."

For a long, long moment, I gave up on breathing. For a long, long moment, all I heard was my heartbeat and his, and a gull cry-

ing miles away, and the distant thunder of a German bomb explod-
ing on innocent ground.

Jesse lifted a hand and placed it on my arm. His palm felt hot
against the cotton of my sleeve, his fingers felt firm, and that rush
of longing and pleasure that always overtook me at his touch began
to build.

"Lora," he whispered again, so quiet it was barely a sound. "In-
hale."

And when I did, he bent his head to kiss me.

. . .

He tried to be careful about it. He tried to limit himself to a barely
there touch, just his mouth to hers, nothing alarming, nothing assumed. But her lips were even softer than he'd dreamed, and with
their bodies this close her scent wrapped around him in a heady
rush. Jesse felt like he was drowning in flowers and fever and delight.

He *wanted* to drown. This was so much better than he'd . . .
ever . . .

It spun out longer than he'd planned. It was still a joining of
near chastity; the as-yet-contained part of him was afraid to move,
afraid to lift his hands to her face, as he desperately wanted, to discover the contours of her with his fingertips. To feel her bare skin.

But he didn't want to frighten her, and he didn't want the kiss
to end.

When he pulled from her at last, they were both sleepy-eyed
and breathing hard. She looked stunned, so flushed and so beautiful and so very much at the edge of what he knew her to be that he
nearly smiled, which would have been a drastic mistake.

When her gaze met his, her irises were luminous, pooling bright silvery purple, a definitely inhuman glow.

He'd awoken the beast in her.

Good.

"What *are* you?" she whispered.

Jesse took a step back to clear his head, to free himself from the tendrils of her sorcery. It'd be easier for both of them if he could think straight.

Right. He needed to focus. He'd waited his lifetime for this moment, but, even so, the words came with difficulty.

It was never painless to bare a soul.

"I am both less than you and more," he said. "An alchemist, an amalgamation of two opposite realms. I'm the fabric of the stars."

Chapter 15

There are certain moments in life when hard, hot truth shines at you like a spotlight from heaven, like the focused beam from a lighthouse on the shore of yourself, and you find yourself stripped naked in its light. You can't hide from it. You can't close your eyes and wish it away. It's truth; easy truth or unbearable truth, either way, it won't be vanquished. And there you are for all to see, stuck in its merciless glare.

One of those moments for me came that night with Jesse, there in his cottage in the island woods. I was caught in the glare of not one but three impossible truths:

I wasn't human.

Neither was he.

And he had kissed me. On the lips.

One of those truths—I couldn't even tell which—kept me standing in place before him with a hand pressed to my mouth, as if I could hold in the soft, lingering sensation of that kiss, the cinnamon-vanilla-rain taste of him. The last bit of heat from his body, which I was already growing cold without.

My eyes were wide as saucers as I stared up at him, so I shut them, opened them again.

I was a . . . what?

He was *of the stars*?

The candle flame continued its merry little dance, undaunted by anything but the breeze. A cricket hopped close to the door, right up close, and chirped a few bars before leaping back into the dark.

Jesse was looking down at me with that patient expression, a suggestion of worry now mixed in. This time he was clearly waiting for me to say something, so I said, "Oh."

Brilliant. I still couldn't bring myself to lower my hand, so I'd said it around my fingers.

"Are you breathing?" he asked.

I nodded.

"I can prove it," he said. "My part, at least. Not yours."

He didn't need to prove it. I believed him. It was crazy, as wildly insane as anything I'd ever heard at Moor Gate—but I believed him.

Yet the words remained stuck behind my closed lips.

He walked to the piecrust table, threw a glance over his shoulder at me through the fall of his hair to make sure I was still paying attention. As if I'd be looking anywhere else.

He needs a haircut, I thought, my mind clinging to any sliver of rationality. *He needs a haircut, but it looks so good like that.*

"You don't have to come closer," Jesse said. "In fact, you shouldn't. But watch."

His arm stretched out. His hand reached down, index finger pointing, the others slightly tucked, a familiar contour both elegant and timeless, like that Michelangelo painting on the ceiling at the Vatican. He touched a single petal of one of the white flowers that he'd shaped into that half circle on the wood. Touched just the very tip of it.

And *light* poured out of him at the touch. Light, golden as he was but shimmering brilliant, a shower of sparkles, of glittering diamonds or gold-leaf confetti—I was processing what was happening but wasn't; for heaven's sake, he was shooting *light*. In an instant it engulfed not only the flowers but his hand, and then his arm, and then all of him, and Jesse Holms became the spotlight that I could not bear to see, and I had to turn my face away from his brilliance and truth.

Shadows cut crisp and black around me. The table, all the chairs, every tuft of the rug, every wooden plank of the floor, illuminated. I heard the air leave my lungs again. The thin *whoooo* of my breath, hollow as could be.

I sucked it back in, and the golden light faded.

His back was to me. His shoulders were bowed. He stood for a moment without moving, but there was something about him anyway that read *pain*. He stood as if he hurt, his body held smaller, tighter, than it'd been before. His face was a pale mask in the reflection of the window. His eyes were closed.

"Jesse?"

"Yes. I'm all right."

I guess to confirm it he straightened and returned to me, graceful as ever, offering me the flat of his palm.

He had the braid of flowers balanced there, still in their half circle. But they were changed now. They weren't white any longer or even alive.

They were made of gold.

Actual gold, because they sang to me, just like the circlet of roses had. Just like the regular rings and earrings and bracelets and stickpins of all the people I'd ever known.

Jesse had turned the living flowers into metal.

He lifted my arm and slipped them over my wrist. Rigid in their golden death, they hugged the bones of my arm snug like a cuff, like they'd been made specially for me.

Which, I supposed, they had.

I'm not proud of what happened next. In my defense, it had been a long, strange day followed by a sleepless night, and I was more than a little unnerved from—well, from everything. The tea, the duke's ruby song, Armand and Chloe and the bombs and then Jesse and the night and the *kiss* and not being human. *Not being human.*

All I remember is that I was looking down at the cuff, at the perfect composition of the flowers, how they connected petal-to-petal in the most miraculous way, humming warm against my skin. I thought that the king's own jeweler could not have designed a better bracelet and how funny that was because I was surely as opposite the King of England as a person could be.

Anyway, I wasn't anticipating it: The shadows from the floor rose up in a rush and clasped me in opaque arms. They encased me and Jesse and the entire room.

Yes, I fainted.

Even as I fell, I realized how humiliating it was. My very last conscious thought was, *Please let me wake up alone in my own bed.*

And I did.

. . .

You're wondering if I awoke with the cuff.

Because if I didn't, perhaps it had all been nothing but a dream. Or my own particular brand of insanity, my notoriously hysterical imagination. Even before we're out of short pants and pinafores, we're taught to dismiss both dreams and imaginings as if they count for nothing, and without the cuff, I would likely have done just that. With every fiber of my being, I yearned to be normal. To glide through my days at Iverson without incident. The last thing I wanted was to indulge in my differences from everyone else.

But *with* the proof of those braided flowers, I'd have to face the fact that my life was about to unfold in a very, very different way than I'd ever envisioned. *Normal* would become forever out of reach.

The answer, of course, is that I awoke with the cuff.

At first I didn't even feel it. At first, with the light of day creeping over me—a gray light, a cloudy light, because even though the sky last night had stretched so limpid, by morning a rainstorm was rolling in—I felt only grit in my eyes and the gnawing awareness that if I didn't get up soon, I'd miss breakfast. And I was hungry.

I staggered out of bed and over to the bureau, yanking open the drawer that contained my Sunday blouse and skirt. It was only then I understood that the heavy thing about my wrist was Jesse's flowers.

It stopped me cold.

I remembered it all, everything at once in a sickening flood.

I was a . . .

I was . . .

The beast in my heart said nothing. Ever since Jesse's revelation, it had gone still as death. I had to finish the thought all alone.

I was a dragon.

Reflexively, I ran my hands up and down my sides, feeling my ribs, my hips, my legs. Except for my boots, I was still wearing every bit of last night's clothing—*thank you, Jesse*—and it didn't take long to tear it all off entirely so I could examine my skin.

No scales, no plated spine or new, hideous claws where my toenails used to be. No hint of anything dragonish at all. Even when I twisted around practically in half, using the looking glass to try to glimpse my backside, I still looked . . . ordinary. I still looked just like me.

But there was the cuff on my wrist, singing a soft, soft melody. And what had happened with the piano. And how I'd made Malinda choke. And all those years of all those silent songs.

This is only the beginning.

There was only one person who could explain it all to me. I had to find Jesse again, had to find him right now—

Downstairs a door slammed, followed by startled laughter. The exodus to breakfast was well under way.

Damn. It killed me, but Jesse would have to wait. If I didn't show up for breakfast, Mrs. Westcliffe would send Gladys or Almeda looking for me. I'd heard that the only excuse for missing chapel or meals was illness, and if you were ill, you could expect a sizable dose of cod-liver oil and bloody little else.

I tugged on my clothes and hurried down the tower stairs, only just managing to join the final stragglers darting past the dining hall doors. I made my way to the tenth-year table, hardly registering the customary tittering that churned in my wake.

"*Lovely* coiffure," commented someone beside me. "Was the price of a few hairpins *really* too dear?"

I glanced to my right, where Chloe stood with a hand atop the back of her chair. The runny-nosed girl slouched beside her. Both of them were smiling small, malevolent smiles.

"Excuse me?" I said.

"Your *hair*." Chloe pulled out her chair, turning away. Her ladyship was already bored. "Quite the rat's nest, isn't it? Either you can't afford even cheap pins or else you simply don't care how you look. Either way, it's an obvious indication of inferior blood."

"Obvious," echoed Runny-Nose, pulling out her chair, too.

I had forgotten. I'd gotten dressed and even ensured I'd picked the skirt without the rip, but I had forgotten all about my hair. It hung loose and tangled down my back, and in my haste I hadn't noticed it at all.

Chloe was shaking out her napkin, her back to me. Snug against the laden table, snug amid her bootlicking friends, she had all the power and she knew it. "Run along, guttersnipe. Your stench is truly overwhelming. I swear, you're already curdling the milk."

Blood rushed to my cheeks. I came closer. I placed my hand on her arm.

"Listen—" I began.

I don't know what I might have done just then. What I might have said. I was angry and mortified and angry that I was mortified, and the darkness in me—magic or dragon or whatever it was— was rising in my throat like a black vicious bubble. It was *my* power and I was going to use it. But then two separate things happened, and I never got the chance to finish my sentence.

Mrs. Westcliffe walked by, so near her skirts brushed mine.

And Chloe spotted my cuff.

"Why, what a cunning *bangle*!" she said, in a far louder voice than any of the nastiness before. "Didn't you think so, Mrs. Westcliffe?"

The headmistress dutifully stopped and turned around.

I made myself still. I made myself swallow the black bubble and keep my hand at my side instead of jerking it behind my back, as I wished to do. It wouldn't matter that it wasn't technically a bangle;

it was precious and I was poor, and that would be reason enough to raise suspicion.

Yesterday's brooch might well have been borrowed. Yesterday I had been Cinderella, and the roses pinned to Lady Sophia's dress hadn't raised an eyebrow.

Today I was plain cinders again.

"A bangle?" Mrs. Westcliffe moved her hawk-sharp gaze to me.

"I only just noticed it myself," Chloe said, all innocence. "Rather interesting piece, so *modern,* especially for an Iverson girl. Of course, since *you* approved it, Headmistress, I'm sure it's fine."

I didn't wait to be asked. I lifted my hand and allowed the flowers to show against my wrist, gleaming their delicate gold. Mrs. Westcliffe bent down for a better look.

"I was going to bring it to you after chapel," I improvised. "I didn't want to bother you before breakfast."

"Ah," was all she replied. And then, "Where did you get it?"

"It was a gift." I turned my gaze to Chloe. "From Lord Armand."

The effect of this little burst of brilliance was truly gratifying. Her eyes bulged. Her mouth fell open. No sound emerged.

"Oh?" said Mrs. Westcliffe, in a very different tone.

"Yes."

"Liar!" exclaimed Chloe, apparently unable to stop herself.

"Lady Chloe," said Mrs. Westcliffe at once, "I'll thank you to remember who and where you are and maintain a civil discourse."

"But—he . . ." She trailed off, biting her lip, her face growing brighter and brighter.

"Ask him," I said to both of them, to everyone listening—which by now was everyone within earshot. I wasn't thinking about the consequences of pulling Armand into it or of a single moment to come beyond this one. I was brimming with the confidence of my lie, skating fast and happy on Chloe's bitter chagrin.

Who's curdling the milk now?

"He gave it to me during the tea yesterday. I tried to refuse it, of course, but Lord Armand insisted, saying it was a welcome gift and that he would be insulted should I not accept it. And I thought, well, as a guest of the duke, as a student of the school, I could not graciously continue to decline." I looked straight into Mrs. Westcliffe's eyes. "Was it the wrong thing to do, ma'am?"

Her head tilted, just slightly. I was mightily aware of being judged, of my words, my sincerity, being weighed. I was a nonentity compared to Chloe Pemington; all the sincerity and credibility in the world be damned, she was a member of the peerage and I a nameless orphan, and nothing would ever change that. *But* throw in the backing of the school's noble patron and his son . . .

"No," Mrs. Westcliffe concluded at last. "From your description, it appears you behaved correctly, Miss Jones."

"But—" Chloe clenched her hand into her napkin.

"Yes, Lady Chloe?"

"She didn't even show it to you before wearing it! She broke the rules."

"That specific rule applies to jewelry worn with the school uniform. As it is Sunday, and Miss Jones is not in uniform, the spirit of the rule remains intact." Mrs. Westcliffe gave a nod. "Good morning, girls. Oh, and, Miss Jones. Kindly do put up your hair before chapel."

"Yes, ma'am."

Another nod, and she was gone.

All through the meal, the girls at my table kept pretending not to stare at the cuff. I didn't attempt to hide it, nor did I attempt to flaunt it. I acted just as I imagined any of them would, allowing it to slide oh so casually along my wrist as I ate my food, as I sipped from my cup. When a short-lived sunbeam slipped across the table and I reached into it for the sugar, a spray of light dappled my skin and the china bowl like sparks from a bonfire.

All the girls appeared curious, but none of them appeared either especially pleased or dismayed, except for Lady Sophia.

From her place down the table, Sophia looked from the cuff up into my eyes, making certain I noticed. Then she smiled, smugly satisfied, like the cat that'd gotten the cream.

. . .

Whatever else Chloe cared to insinuate, I did have hairpins. In fact, as luck would have it, I had two in my pocket that I'd stuck in there last weekend, because I'd been bored and restless in chapel and they'd been digging into my nape.

Two were sufficient to hold up my hair—perhaps not as neatly as the other students', but then again, none of them were of my particularly inferior blood. So who cared?

I had Jesse's gold and Jesse's attention, and they didn't, so who cared?

The found pins saved me a trip to my room and granted me an extra fifteen minutes of delicious breakfast, which is why it was after chapel and well after noon when I finally made my way back to the tower. The clouds were shedding their promised rain, decreasing the temperature by a good ten degrees and tinting any light that seeped into the castle the shade of murky steel. Raindrops peppered every window, as if the wind could not decide in which direction to blow.

I would need my oilskin for the trip through the woods. Magical or not, I'd caught colds before.

Shadows lapped the tower stairs, charcoal over gray. My door was ajar, but I thought nothing of it. Gladys would have been in and out by now, making my bed, straightening my things, likely spitting in my water.

The bed *had* been made, but the quilts were all rumpled. That's what happened when someone sprawled atop them, as Lord Armand was when I opened my door. Armand, in a wrinkled shirt and trousers and black woolen socks, his coat and tie and shoes dumped in a soggy heap on the floor. It looked for all the world like he'd been napping.

I stood for a moment without moving, my fingers tight and cold on the knob.

"Hullo," he said sleepily, rubbing a hand along his jaw.

He's here in my room, right in the middle of the afternoon. Great God, there's a boy in my bed in my room—

I came to life. "Get out!"

He yawned, a lazy yawn, a yawn that clearly indicated he had no intention of leaving. In the moody gray light his body seemed a mere suggestion against the covers, his hair a shaded smudge against the paler lines of his collar and face.

"But I've been waiting for you for over an hour up here, and bloody boring it's been, too. I've never known a girl who didn't keep even *mildly* wicked reading material hidden *somewhere* in her bedchamber. I've had to pass the time watching the spiders crawl across your ceiling."

Voices floated up from downstairs, a maids' conversation about rags and soapy water sounding horribly loud, and horribly close.

I shut the door as gently as I could and pressed my back against it, my mind racing. No lock, no bolt, no key, no way to keep them out if they decided to come up. . . .

Armand shifted a bit, rearranging the pillows behind his shoulders.

I wet my lips. "If this is about the kiss—"

"No." He gave a slight shrug. "I mean, it wasn't meant to be. But if you'd like—"

"You *can't* be in here!"

"And yet, Eleanore, here I am. You know, I remember this room from when I used to live in the castle as a boy. It was a storage chamber, I believe. All the shabby, cast-off things tossed up here where no one had to look at them." He stretched out long and lazy again, arms overhead, his shirt pulling tight across his chest. "This mattress really isn't very comfortable, is it? Hard as a rock. No wonder you're so ill-tempered."

Dark power. Compel him to leave.

I was desperate enough to try.

"You must go," I said. Miraculously, I felt it working. I willed it and it happened, the magic threading through my tone as sly as silk, deceptively subtle. "Now. If anyone sees you, you were never here. You never saw me. Go downstairs, and do *not* mention my name."

Armand sat up, his gaze abruptly intent. One of the pillows plopped to the floor.

"That was interesting, how your voice just changed. Got all smooth and eerie. I think I have goose bumps. Was that some sort of technique they taught you at the orphanage? Is it useful for begging?"

Blast. I tipped my head back against the wood of the door and clenched my teeth.

"Do you have any idea the trouble I'll be in if they should find you here? What people will think?"

"Oh, yes. It rather gives me the advantage, doesn't it?"

"Mrs. Westcliffe will expel me!"

"Nonsense." He smiled. "All right, probably she will."

"Just tell me what you want, then!"

His lashes dropped; his smile grew more dry. He ran a hand slowly along a crease of quilt by his thigh.

"All I want," he said quietly, "is to talk."

"Then pay a call on me later this afternoon," I hissed.

"No."

"What, you don't have the time to tear yourself away from your precious Chloe?"

I hadn't meant to say that, and, believe me, as soon as the words left my lips I regretted them. They made me sound petty and jealous, and I was certain I was neither.

Reasonably certain.

Armand's smile briefly grew wider, then vanished. His fingers moved back and forth, playing with the dips and peaks of the crease.

"Where did you learn that piece?" he asked. "The one you played on the piano yesterday?"

And there it was again expanding between us, that electric, ill-defined challenge that felt like danger. Or excitement. I knew his question wasn't casual. He might have been a selfish wretch, but I wasn't the only one who'd get in trouble if we were discovered. It was Visitors' Day, after all, and he could have easily cornered me at the tea. If he'd felt it necessary to sneak all the way up to my room to ask me about the song, it meant he didn't want anyone to overhear.

Perhaps that might give *me* the advantage.

I remembered how his face had looked when I was finished playing. How white. How shocked.

"Why do you want to know?"

The shrug again. "Just wondering."

"Really. You've skipped your lawn tennis or duck hunting or whiskey drinking or whatever else people of your sort do all day, only to come all the way out to the island to ask me about the piano piece. Because you were *just wondering*." I pushed away from the door. "Coming here to kiss me would have been more believable."

"Well, it *was* second on my list."

"I'm not intimidated by you," I said, blunt. "If you're hoping I'll turn out to be some pathetic, blubbering little rag-girl who begs you not to ruin her, you're in for a surprise."

"That's good." Lord Armand met my eyes. "I like surprises."

We gazed at each other, he on the bed and me by the door, neither of us giving quarter. It seemed to me that the room was growing even more dim, that time was repeating the same ploy it had pulled in Jesse's cottage, drawing out long and slow. The storm outside railed against the castle walls, drowning the air within. It layered darkness through Armand's eyes, the once-vivid blue now deep as the ocean at night.

Beyond my window the rain fell and fell, fat clouds weeping as if they'd never stop.

"Nice bracelet," Armand said softly. "Did you steal it?"

I shook my head. "You gave it to me."

"Did I?"

"As far as everyone else is concerned, yes. You did."

"Hmm. And what do I get in return for agreeing to be your . . . benefactor?"

"The answer to your question."

"No kiss?" he asked, even softer.

"No."

His lips quirked. "All right, then, waif. I accept your terms. We'll try the kiss later."

I sighed. "I made up the piece at the piano."

He said nothing, only stared at me.

"Truly," I said. "I made it up. Right then. It's . . ." Now I shrugged. "It's just something I do."

Armand cleared his throat. "You'd never heard it before?"

"No." I took a step closer to him, frowning. There was something odd going on here; the power between us had shifted. I felt it, that danger feeling fading and something new growing in its place.

Something like fear.

"Had *you* heard it before?" I asked, startled.

"Of course not. How could I have, if you just invented it?"

"Yes," I murmured, not taking my eyes off him, exploring that odd new energy between us. "How could you have?"

He came to his feet. "It's only that my mother used to do that sort of thing. Invent songs like that. It was her Steinway, in fact, a wedding gift from my father. Yesterday you—you gave him a start, I suppose. Gave us both a bit of a start. Bent over the keys like that, your hair all tumbling down. You really resembled her."

"How old were you when she died?"

He pulled on his coat, spattering water on us both. "Around three."

"Oh," I said carefully. "But you remember her playing?"

"I s'pose so." Shoes on, the tie shoved into his pocket—Armand turned to face me and, just like that, I knew I'd lost him. His gaze had gone cool and his smile faint. He was entirely a lord once more.

"It's been most delightful, Miss Jones. Let's do it again sometime, shall we?"

I let him walk past me, swing open the door. He peered into the gloom of the stairwell before slipping down the first few steps. At the fourth step he paused, looked back up at me, and lowered his voice.

"Where *did* you get the bracelet?"

"Good-bye, Lord Armand," I whispered. "Try not to get caught."

I closed my door. I pressed my ear to the wood and remained there another whole minute until I heard him moving off, quick footfalls that faded into the more constant patter of the rain.

. . .

Jesse was not at home. I knew that without venturing even an inch into the sodden woods.

After Armand had left, I paused only long enough to remake the bed and blot up the water his coat had left on the floor. It was while I was doing that—on my hands and knees, my hair popped free of the measly two pins to tickle my neck—that I realized I was being surrounded by a new song.

Jesse's song.

It rose around me in a lilting cadence, became a caress along my body, an invitation, our own secret code that echoed and repeated, and every single note meant *come find me.*

I stood and pushed the hair from my face. I crossed to my window to gaze down at the rainlit green, searching the fingers of fog that curled against the animal hedges and flower beds. The long, wet span of grass bereft of students or staff or too-early Sunday guests.

He definitely wasn't down there. He didn't seem to be outside at all. So . . . he must be somewhere within the castle.

Come find me.

My heart began a harder beat; I felt tingly, almost anxious.

Come.

Very well. I would.

I put on my oilskin, just in case. Then I went to answer Jesse's call, sliding as carefully into the stairwell shadows as Armand had done a quarter hour before.

Downstairs, the maids were kindling batches of light, moving from lamp to lamp with their waxed-paper tapers to ward off the day's dull chill. We'd entered that numbed, dragging stretch of hours before Sunday tea and after church, when Iverson's genteel young ladies tended to wander off in their individual clusters to genteelly shred the characters of anyone beyond their circle.

Each year had claimed its own location, I'd learned. The older girls usually headed outdoors to brave the tame wilderness—and relative privacy—of the gardens, while the younger ones liked to remain ensconced safely inside, closer to the promise of biscuits and cake. On days such as today, however, all the girls in all the years recognized that they were made of spun sugar: Rain would surely melt them into puddles. Everyone was forced indoors.

The front parlor was out-of-bounds until four, so they'd draped themselves throughout the other common rooms instead. As I passed the library, I glimpsed Chloe and Sophia standing and chatting by the fire with every evidence of civility. But Sophia still had her cat's smile, and Chloe's cheeks were still red.

Perhaps it wasn't so unpleasant to be without a family, after all.

I moved past the doorway without either of them noticing.

Jesse wasn't with any of the other girls, anyway. He wasn't in any part of the castle that I'd yet explored. The more I walked, the more I understood that even though I had gone all the way down to the ground floor, he was still below me somewhere, in the bowels of the keep.

I didn't think students were allowed below the main floor. I knew the kitchens were there, as were most of the servants' quarters; the professors and Mrs. Westcliffe had their own aboveground wing on the other side of the castle. No one had ever specifically told me *not* to go below stairs, however—probably because a true Iverson girl would never, ever dream of mingling with the help.

I could always say I'd gotten lost. The pillars of the world would hardly collapse. The sky would not shatter. I was barely a hairbreadth away from being the help myself.

The only entrance to the lower level I knew of was down at the far end of the main hallway. I lurked by the sole painting there, gazing up in apparent fascination at the portrait of a man in a tatty fur coat with what seemed to be a dead weasel wrapped around his head. He stared back at me with a cold smile I recognized very well.

Olin, read the little plate screwed into the frame, *5th dk Idylling.*

Like brown hair and lunacy, it seemed hauteur was passed down the family line. At least the current duke was a finer dresser.

A pair of maids holding spent tapers swished past. The servants' door opened; the maids went through; light and voices and the blue-smoke sting of lit cigarettes boiled up into the hall until the door shut behind them, and it was just me and the dead-weasel duke once more.

Jesse's song sparkled louder, so beautiful and wanting, it felt like an ache in my bones.

Come, love.

I glanced up and down the passageway: I was alone. I inched toward the door and put my hand on the latch.

"No, not that way," murmured Jesse, close enough that I felt his breath on my temple.

Chapter 16

"A francba!"

I jumped back, smacking the wall, and knocked into the portrait, which clattered heavily and began to tilt. Jesse, very near and very swift, reached out and steadied us both, one hand on the frame and the other on my shoulder.

He was a genie, a wizard, a boy who'd materialized from nothing but cigarette smoke and shadows, because he had *not* been there a second ago.

"All right, Lora?" He waited for my nod, then used both hands to straighten the painting. "What did you just say?"

"What?" My heart was still pounding. I'd flattened a palm over it, pressing back the fright.

"Just now. You said something in a foreign language."

"No, I didn't. Did I?" I dropped my hand. "Where did you come from?"

Jesse stepped back from the duke and his disturbing attire—properly aligned once more, still smiling down at us bloody cold—and faced me, too tall and real and solid to have simply appeared from thin air.

"You'll find this castle keeps many secrets, some ancient, some not." His fingers clasped mine, instant warmth. "This is one of the oldest ones. I'll show you."

He stepped back again, and again, pulling me with him all the way to the wall, only the wall wasn't there any longer. A gaping black space was where there should have been stone, where there *surely* had been stone when I'd first crept down this hallway.

One final step, and the darkness consumed him. His voice floated out to me.

"Don't be afraid."

"I'm not," I replied, irritated that he'd guessed the truth. I made myself follow without him having to pull. "Of course I'm not."

"Good. There's a landing here, feel it? Hold on while I . . ."

We had paused just inside the wall, standing almost chest-to-chest. He shifted against me, his arm reaching past my head, and without any noise at all the wall closed up again, sealing us inside— what? I didn't know. The innards of the castle, I supposed. It smelled like rats and dirt and rotting wood. It smelled like a crypt.

Jesse struck a match, held it to a lantern hung on a hook behind us. Yellow brightness bloomed.

We were in a tunnel. On a rickety wooden landing in a very narrow tunnel that plunged down and down into the depths beyond the light. There were stairs going down it, too, just as rickety, as clear an invitation to *this is a bad idea* as anything I'd ever seen.

Jesse grabbed the lantern, holding it up high. "The early defenders of this land built the fortress to withstand all manner of attacks. But they were men of short lives and brutal deaths, and they knew that nothing was ever foolproof. So the walls of Iverson are hollow. There had to be a way to get the castle folk out should the invaders get in. A secret way."

"*All* the walls?" I asked, shocked.

"No, not all. But many."

"Is that how you manage—"

"Yes." His arm lowered. The lantern burned between us, painting gray and gold along the contours of his face; he sent me a sideways look. "Not the walls of your tower, Lora. Rest easy. You're truly alone up there."

Yes. Until His Right Royal Lordship decides to show up again.

"Does Mrs. Westcliffe know?" I asked.

"Not that I've been able to tell. It's possible she knows about them but thinks they're sealed up or filled in. Some are. In all the years I've been here, I've never seen any footprints in the tunnels, besides my own. I don't think even Hastings knows about this. At least, not about all of it. He knows about the grotto, of course."

"The . . . ?"

"Come on. It's why I called you. You're going to like it."

He took my hand again, and the honey-sweet pleasure of his touch mingled with the thrill of fear that was skittering up and down my spine. The combination was nearly unbearable.

"You called me," I whispered.

"And you came," Jesse Holms answered, a green-eyed glance back at me, a half-smile that dissolved my bones. Then we were moving hand in hand down the rotting plank stairs.

I seethed with questions. I was ready to burst with them, and at the same time I was focused on putting one foot in front of the other, avoiding the gaps in the planks, trying not to examine too closely the rot in the wood or the thick pitch black that yawned beneath us. I could not smell an end to it. We might as well have been descending into the center of the earth.

It's Jesse. I'm safe. It's Jesse, so I'm safe.

I found myself watching either the lantern or the back of his head, both shining, both slipping deep into the dark heart of Iverson without falter, even when the air began to change and smell more of salt than stone. More of trapped waters than long-dead rodents.

Eventually I realized I could see more than just Jesse and his lantern. I could see the ceiling and walls and the outline of his body glowing an unlikely, pale slate. The stairs were revealed to look, if possible, even more rickety. Some of the planks had fallen away altogether.

"Mind yourself here," he said, and paused to help me over a particularly large gap.

I could have jumped it alone. But of course I never said so.

There was something both foreign and hair-raising about having a boy hold my hand, not only for pleasure but for protection. I had no memory of it ever happening before and could not imagine that, if it had, it could ever have been better than this: a firm grip and a callused palm, sweet honey thrills zinging from my fingers all the way up my arm.

Because this was not just any boy. And beyond his silhouette was that growing glow that lent him a sort of unearthly halo, as if he really were made of starlight.

"Cheers," Jesse said, and sent me another glance. "We're here."

Here was a cavern with glimmering seawater as most of its floor, wet limestone walls streaked with minerals and moisture, and rivulets of crystals twinkling in the uneasy light like fireflies. Manmade columns, eight of them, broke the waters, reaching from seafloor to ceiling. They looked colossal enough to support the weight of the whole island.

The slate-colored light was shining up from the water. A half-moon wedge of day blazed a brighter gray against the far wall, where the top of the sea met the top of the cavern entrance and air still got through.

The tunnel had ended in a wide, cut-stone embankment that fronted the salt water. Centuries of restless tide had lapped its edges smooth as glass.

As with the castle and it secrets, a long-dead someone had thought up the scale and bones of this space. Someone had discovered the grotto and constructed the rest, hauling in the rounded blocks for the columns, swimming down to the unknown bottom of the cavern to anchor the base of each. Someone had labored over every inch of the glassy embankment beneath my feet, using minds and hands and tools to ensure evenness, stability.

Many someones. Generations of someones, perhaps.

Except for where Jesse's palm met mine, I felt clammy with cold. The weight of all those spirits in the air seemed to press down on me, pushing into my skin.

"You'd moor your boat here." Jesse used the lantern to indicate the column closest by, exposing eerie, ring-shaped stains of rust marking a row down its side. "You'd wait for the tide to go nearly all the way out at night, just high enough so that you could still row away in the dark. By the time anyone in the castle noticed you, hopefully their ships would be beached, and you'd be far enough gone to find safe harbor. Or at the very least be beyond the range of cannons or crossbows."

"Jesse," I said, and he turned around.

I wanted to address what had happened last night, our kiss, my fainting, him carrying me back to the tower. There was a weight in my chest that felt like an apology, although I didn't know how to phrase it or even if I should try. There were too many layers of truth between this boy and me, obvious layers like, *I don't even know you,* and layers more subtle, ones that whispered, *I've known you forever.*

I let our arms stretch out into a bridge between us. The flowered cuff crooned its pretty song. And what I said was, "Am I dreaming this?"

He hesitated, then shook his head.

"Then"—I swallowed—"am I crazy? Have I gone truly crazy?"

"No, Lora."

"But how . . . *how* am I a dragon? How are *you* a starman?"

"I don't think of myself as a *starman,* exactly," he said soberly, though I sensed he wanted to smile. His hand released mine, the bridge broken; he moved to hang the lantern on a shiny new hook dug into the wall behind us. "I was born here, on earth. Not even far from here, in fact. Just over in Devon. My parents died young, when I was only five. Hastings is my great-uncle and he took me in, and I've lived here ever since. But I've always known what I am, as far back as I can remember. I've always been able to do the things I do. The stars have always spoken to me."

"And you . . . speak back to them?"

"Yes," he said simply.

"But not to people."

"No. Just to Hastings, and to you."

A shiver took me; I crossed my arms over my chest. "What do the stars say?"

"All manner of things. Amazing things. Secret things. Things great and small, things profound and insignificant. They told me that, throughout time, there've been only a scattering of people like me, folk of both flesh and star. That even the whisper of their magic in my blood could annihilate me if I didn't learn to control it. That I'd crisp to ash without control. Or, worse, crisp someone else." His smile broke through. "And they told me about you. That you were born and would come to me when the time was right."

"Did you summon me here?" The muted echo of my voice rebounded against the firefly walls: *here-here-here*. "To Iverson, I mean?"

. . . mean-mean-mean . . .

He didn't answer at first. He looked at his feet, then walked to the edge of the embankment and squatted down, raking his fingers through the bright water near the toes of his boots.

"We are such stuff as dreams are made on," he said softly to the water. "Both infinite and finite, human and not. I'm of comet and clay and the sparks of sun across the ocean waves." He sighed. "I know what it's like to doubt yourself, to comprehend that you're so unique you're forced to wonder about . . . everything. But, yes, I called you to Iverson."

It made dreadful sense. It actually made far more sense than anything anyone had told me so far. More sense than the notion that an orphan girl, a girl so mentally damaged she'd been institutionalized, would somehow find herself accepted into the finest finishing school in the kingdom just because there'd been an opening. . . .

I understood then that from the moment I'd heard Director Forrester first utter the words, I'd been invisibly balanced along a razor's edge, waiting for everyone else around me to snap to and realize what I did: The entire situation was preposterous.

"You did this?" I moved to Jesse's side, gazing down at the crown of his head. "All this, me and the school, and the bombs—"

"I only called you. The universe arranged the rest."

"And the *war*," I continued, abruptly queasy, "my God, the war. Are you saying that you and I are the reason for *that*?"

"I'm saying that the true nature of our world is for matters to arrange themselves along the simplest of paths. The war happened, and you came here because of it. Through it. We all slide along our destinies, Lora, and the war is how you came to slide to me." He stood and flicked the water from his hand. "I've been calling you since the day you were born. Every day. Every night. If I dared to praise any single consequence of this tear between nations, it would be that it brought you to me."

I was surprised to discover myself suddenly sitting on the stone floor, my tailbone aching. Luminous water sloshed before me, up and down and up, and I had to look away.

Then Jesse was there, his face close to mine.

"You don't eat enough," he said, frowning.

I covered my eyes with one hand and let out a laugh; I couldn't help it. "I agree."

"Your metabolism isn't ordinary, especially now. You burn energy at a much higher rate than regular people. You need to consume more."

"Perhaps you'd care to inform Mrs. Westcliffe," I suggested, still hiding my eyes. "If I attempt anything beyond two paper-thin slices of cake at tea, she looks as if she's planning to throttle me in my sleep."

"No," he said, decisive. "I'll do better than that. Hang on."

I drew up my knees and rested my head on my crossed arms, listening to the sounds of Jesse and the sea, both of them moving in small, mysterious ways beyond the red of my lids. When he returned, he was carrying manna in a woven reed basket: a round loaf of flour-dusted bread, a block of orange cheese, and a bottle of liquid, corked and greenish-dark.

He settled beside me and broke open the bread, handing me a chunk.

"Have you had wine before?"

"No," I said. "Maybe. I don't know."

"Try some now. Just a sip. You'll feel better."

He uncorked the bottle and handed it over. I smelled cherries and sugar and something like chocolate. Mindful of what had happened with the whiskey, I tipped the bottle to my lips and touched only the tip of my tongue to the liquid.

"Sorry there's no water. Next time I'll bring some."

"This is nice," I said. I took another swallow. It was red wine, not green. It tasted like nothing I'd ever had before.

"I thought you'd be hungry. I packed this last night, so the bread might be stale."

"No, it's delicious."

And it was. All of it. The cheese, as well, every last tangy speck. I ate like I was famished, like I hadn't put away a heap of kippers and bacon a few hours before.

I held out the last hunk of bread to Jesse. He refused it with a smile, so I ate that, too.

I suppose that would have sealed the deal, were he Fay. I'd eaten his food and drunk his wine, and if he offered I'd gladly have taken more.

Fay or fateful stars, same difference. I looked at him and thought, *Now I'm surely yours.*

But I didn't say it aloud.

"I thought this would be a good place," Jesse said. He had drawn up his knees and wrapped his arms loose around them, like I had, gazing out peacefully at the water. I could feel the heat of his side so close to mine, as if he radiated it. As if the golden light that lived under his skin was really a fire, banked now but steady. Eternal warmth.

"Good place for what?"

"For you to find yourself. Your true self."

I didn't respond.

"You're going to have to do it sometime, Lora. I can help you with it. Some of it, at least. It's going to happen whether you will it or not. Better to plan ahead now, don't you think?"

I stared down at the twill covering my knees. I stared hard at the tufts of wool that poked out here and there, the sturdy, diagonal weave of brown over brown.

"We can meet down here on weekends or after your classes. We might consider the woods, too, but there's always the danger there of someone passing by."

"Doesn't anyone else ever come here?"

"No. People say it's haunted."

I looked back up at him.

"By a single ghost," he explained, the corners of his lips lifted. "A very gentle one. I'm sure she won't mind sharing the space with us."

"I—I honestly can't tell if you're joking."

"Either way, does it matter? I told you you're safe with me, and I meant it. The grotto is perfect for us. It's secluded but still open enough to hide something . . . large."

"I don't understand. What is it you think I'm going to be able to do? I'm just a girl."

"To begin, you can stop thinking of yourself as *just* anything. I have a word for you, one I want you to keep in your heart." Jesse unlocked his arms and turned to face me fully, holding me in a gaze that resurrected that shiver of before.

"Drákon," he said.

And I knew it. I knew that word, even though I was positive I'd never, ever heard it fall from anyone else's lips.

Drákon.

If the beast inside me had still been raging, it would have sucked on the word like Jesse's sweet cherry wine. It would have gotten drunk on it.

"That's what I am," I said, as the truth of it rolled through me over and over, riding that cherry-wine crest. "That's what we're called. My—my kind."

"Yes."

"How did you know that? How do you know *any* of this?"

His hand lifted, a graceful palm cupped toward the ceiling, toward the universe we could not see beyond water and rock.

"Is there a word for you?" I asked.

I glimpsed a dimple in his cheek with his wry new smile, one I'd never noticed before. "Jesse."

"That's it?"

"Do you prefer *starman*?"

"No."

Jesse, star-bright. Jesse Holms. Jesse-of-the-stars.

I heard myself say, "Are you going to kiss me again?" and realized, horrified, that maybe I was the drunk one.

"Yes," he answered.

"Er . . . soon?"

"I hope so. But not right now." He climbed to his feet, reached out a hand and pulled me to mine, looking down at me ruefully. "Next time I'll definitely remember to bring the water."

. . .

God, he hated tea.

Armand Diego Lorimer Louis stared down at the steaming liquid in its cup, wan brown with little chewy bits of leaves mucking about near the bottom, and came to the conclusion that it was actually more than he could bear to lift the cup to his lips to drink.

There was lemon or cream to add to it, if he wished. Sparkling white sugar. All of it set out in silly little china containers painted round and round with podgy, smirking cherubs.

But nothing helped tea. It simply was what it was, which was boiling hot and flavorless.

Tea was the beverage, Mandy thought, of dreary, civilized people. People who would never lie without guilt, never steal without reason, never fornicate anywhere but in their own beds. With the curtains closed. In the dark.

He shouldn't have stayed. He should have gone home after leaving her room. Truth was, his hair was mussed and his cuffs were damp and she wasn't even present, and now here he was trapped beside Chloe yet again, suffocating in her noxious perfume. Pretending to listen to her natter on about a dress or a hat or her new gloves—it was always a dress, a hat, or new gloves; all right, and sometimes shoes—with his spoon gripped so tightly in his hand that his thumb and forefinger had gone white, and the tea bits whirling about in some awful, endless pattern, everything the same, every day the same, just as it always was. Just as it always was going to be.

He had a swift and utterly lucid vision of himself in this position in thirty-odd years. Loathsome tea, hot steam, silver spoon, and fifty-year-old Chloe seated opposite him talking about clothing, because to her it was categorically, absolutely, the most fascinating topic on the planet.

Besides, of course, herself.

For an unflinching instant, Armand wished with his whole heart that he were dead.

Then, at the very edge of his perception, something changed.

He glanced up.

She was passing by the doorway, walking with that fluid, nearly animal grace that no one else seemed to capture or even notice.

He was given four steps of her.

One: She moved from the hallway shadows into the light cast from the parlor. He saw her illuminated, drab colors gone bright; her skin alabaster, reflective; her hair tinted pink and gold and pink again.

Two: Her gaze met his, finding him past all the other people crowded inside the stuffy mirrored room, dying by inches and taking their tea.

Three: He was paralyzed. He couldn't move, couldn't smile, couldn't nod. He was pinned in the gray of her eyes, a prisoner to their piercing clarity.

For an unflinching instant, Armand felt his heart explode like a firework, and the future seemed unwritten.

Then four: Eleanore looked away and passed the doorway. He was stuck with tea and dresses once more.

Chapter 17

We drank, of course, at the orphanage.

We were crafty about it, or at least tried to be, and nearly universally tight-lipped regarding the specific whens and wheres and whos. Rules ensnared every aspect of our lives, Blisshaven's rules and our own, which were tacit and far more savage. From the time we were old enough to understand what gin was, we procured it and drank it. Anyone suspected of being a snitch tended to end up in the infirmary, usually missing teeth.

We had no money. We were given no allowance, not even a ha'penny for a peppermint stick or a cup of lemonade during our precious few outings into the city. So those who landed the gin were usually the quick-fingered older boys. The ones on the verge of something larger than themselves, with cracking voices and cunning gazes, who knew that the future rushing toward them was going to be even more desolate than their lives in the dorms. Who bonded into packs for dominance, who skulked about like hungry dogs let loose in the halls.

Who could slink away from our minders without getting caught. Who could distract a shopkeeper or pubmaster—and then run.

But even though they got their gin for free, they were still dogs. The gin wasn't free to any of the rest of us.

As I said, we had no money. So it won't astonish you to learn that although I'd never tasted fine wine before—or even mediocre wine or whiskey or champagne—I *had* tasted the raw, crude distillation of juniper berries in alcohol, quite a bit.

Jesse's kiss, staggering as it was, was not my first.

I had learned the same lessons as most of the other girls in Blisshaven. Bargain for limits on time and body parts. Don't let them use their tongues. Avoid Billy Patrick at all costs—grinning, vicious Billy Patrick—because no amount of gin he ever offered would be worth the bruises he left.

And never drink so much that you regretted your morning. The teachers were particularly short-tempered before noon. They weren't likely to go soft on anyone lethargic, even if you said you were feeling off.

I had measured out my sips, my kisses, savoring the one while pretending I was someone else for the other, and in all my years there, I never went to bed intoxicated.

It was disheartening to discover myself so quickly affected by Jesse's sweet red wine, but at least I knew the cure. I couldn't risk the Sunday tea—especially after I'd glimpsed Armand in there, his blue eyes like flames—so I retreated to my room and slept.

By breakfast the next morning, aside from a dull ache in my forehead and a fuzzy coating on my tongue, I was more or less hale again.

Drákon.

I whispered it to my mirror-self before dressing, watching her face, her eyes, round black pupils, purple-gray irises shrunk into gleaming rings.

"Drákon," I said aloud, and the girl in the mirror slowly smiled.

Even now I don't think any lingering consequences of the wine were responsible for what happened that Monday. I think it was just something that was bound to be: Jesse's all-knowing stars casting their own directions for the unruly path of my life.

. . .

"All right, then, ladies. Let's be off," commanded Professor Tilbury.

Tilbury was our history professor, potbellied and aged and with a voice that reached dangerously close to a squeak whenever he tried to raise it. He stood before us with his back to the large slate that had been fixed to the wall of our classroom. A single word, *Iverson,* had been chalked across the slate, with a long, uncharacteristic flourish of a tail completing the *n.*

We sat two by two in assigned rows, because the history classroom was crammed up short against the southern edge of the castle, which meant it was very narrow and unexpectedly lofty.

My chair was next to Lillian's in the far back. From our shared desk, Professor Tilbury looked like a white-bearded gnome against the slate.

He surveyed the lot of us; no one had moved. "To your feet, young ladies! Today is a most special day indeed. Today we will enjoy a walking tour of the history of our own fortress."

Beatrice and Stella, directly ahead of me, exchanged eye rolls.

"Sir," said Mittie from the very front, in her most piteous tone, "isn't it cold out for a walk? We haven't even our shawls."

It had dawned another overcast day, with a brisk spring wind blowing spray in fitful spurts across the channel, rattling the windowpanes. Still, pug-faced Mittie was far from any danger of freezing. She just liked to whine.

Professor Tilbury must have heard every whine before.

"The majority of our tour will be within the castle walls, Miss Bashier. If you didn't need your shawl for this chamber, you will not need it for the rest of them. However, if you truly feel a shawl is indispensable to your attire, you may fetch it now. The rest of us shall await you here. Naturally, any amount of time taken from the scheduled class period by your absence shall be made up by all of you at its conclusion."

The hour after history was luncheon. Even Mittie wasn't stupid enough to push matters that far.

I arose from my chair, glad to be doing something besides sitting and scratching down notes, anyway. One by one, the other girls did the same.

Confident that he had made his point, Professor Tilbury offered us what, for him, passed as a smile. He had blocky yellow teeth.

"Excellent. Let us begin at the beginning. Do any of you know what this room used to be?"

None of us did.

"Iverson's original keep was constructed by the conquering sons of Normandy. It was ruled by barons who commanded the wealth of the ports and all the fertile lands nearby." Someone tittered at the word *fertile*; Tilbury forged on. "Therefore, this fortress, even from its inception, was home to a powerful, prosperous lord and his family. It also would have been home to all his knights and servants and their families, as well. A castle this size might have had several hundred people living inside it, and that is before we even begin to consider the livestock."

"How primitive," sniffed Caroline.

"Primitive, mayhap, but necessary. So imagine you are that

powerful lord who controls this castle, if you will. Where do you go for your privacy? Where do you retreat with your family to escape the everlasting noises and smells and demands of the general populace?"

A word came to me, a word from the past. It bobbed up from the blank ocean of my memory, untethered.

"The solar," I said.

Professor Tilbury angled his head to find me standing in the back. "Yes, Miss Jones. Very good. The solar. Solar as in *solaris,* a place of the sun. Note our tall southerly windows, the near-constant light. Castles such as Iverson typically included a construct like this for the exclusive use of the ruling family, built above the ground floor so that the baron might observe the workings of his people below."

"It's terribly small for a family," doubted Stella, looking around.

"Correct, Miss Campbell. The solar of Iverson is no longer in its original configuration. It was partitioned off, probably sometime in the late seventeenth century. The remaining portion of it," he gestured toward the wall with the slate, "was converted into private quarters for the dukes and duchesses of Idylling."

We all pricked up our ears at that. The conjugal room of all those dukes, just beyond our slate? Only a layer of stones—and perhaps a secret tunnel—between us and a marital bed?

Malinda and Caroline jostled each other, snickering. Pale Lillian had blotches of pink spreading up her throat.

"If you please, sir," said Sophia sweetly, covering the snickers, "who stays there now?"

Likely Mrs. Westcliffe. She might not be a duchess or even a baroness, but there was no question about her rule.

Yet the professor surprised me.

"No one," he answered, curt. "No one has occupied those quarters in years. They are locked off."

"Why?" asked Mittie.

"It is the wish of the current duke. And that is all I know on the subject, so kindly don't request that we venture into them. We will not. However, there are many, many other fascinating facts about Iverson to explore. Come along."

He led us out of the room, talking all the while. I hung at the back of the crowd, as usual. I'd found I liked skulking behind the rest of the girls. It gave me the opportunity to disguise myself in their shadows. To the teachers I appeared proximate enough to be part of their group. The truth could be glimpsed only in the shifting, untouched space that stretched from the hems of their skirts to mine, never closing.

Good enough.

Everyone has a favorite something, and on that day I discovered that Professor Tilbury's was castles. The eight of us trailed behind him in our sluggish, uneven line, but he was so enraptured with his subject he never noticed our dragging feet; he practically danced a wee gnome dance ahead of us.

We learned about great halls and granaries, moats and bowers. A buttery was not, as might be assumed, a place where butter was produced. But the kitchen hearth might, as would be assumed, be large enough to roast a pair of oxen for the great lord's pleasure, should the need arise.

Oxen. We snaked only briefly through the kitchens, disrupting the hectic rhythm of the workers there, to their silent, tucked-chin displeasure. I saw Gladys arranging forks and white doilies on trays. Almeda was fussing over a cabinet of linens, snowy starched piles folded and stacked one atop another, towers of white.

A stink of blood and fried onions hung hot in the air. One entire counter was heaped with oozy plucked chickens; a sweaty brown-haired girl of about twelve was the plucker. Sticky bits of feathers dotted her apron and arms.

Everyone stopped what they were doing as we passed, dropping into half bows or curtsies, which my classmates regally ignored.

Only Gladys lifted her eyes to mine when I walked by. Her mouth hardened, taking on a scornful slant. I could tell exactly what she was thinking: *Just you wait, governess.*

It shamed me for some reason. I don't know why. My world was a hidden blossom of gold and Jesse and the promise of searing magic, but through no fault of her own, stick-skinny Gladys would likely only ever be what she was right this minute. A servant.

I dropped my gaze from hers. For the rest of the tour of the kitchens, I kept it fixed to the floor, stepping over errant feathers.

Frankly, even before Tilbury's outing I'd experienced rather enough of Iverson's unspoken motto of *We few versus the masses.* The jolt of coming from Blisshaven to this cool and sparkling place had been shock enough for me.

I heard sighs of relief from both sides of the Great Class Divide when our tour snaked out the kitchen doors again.

Upward we climbed. Flying buttresses. Lacy Gothic wings of marble arching over us, fantastical and airy enough for an angel's delight. I began to sense that peering at the minutia of Iverson was like peering at a slice of petrified tree. Every ring from the past had been crystallized in situ, held frozen in place for all time. Had there ever been any real changes, they were unseen, fissures invisible to my naked, untrained eye.

Anything new was simply rough bark on its way to transforming into stone.

It *would* petrify. Someday.

We ended our tour at the tip-top of the keep, emerging from a winding, enclosed set of stairs to the relative brightness of a section of the roof.

It was flat and scalloped with stones along the edge, designed for protection. For archers to run along and duck behind.

"Note the relatively small size of the merlons," Tilbury enthused over the gusting wind. "Imagine fitting oneself against this sole slab of limestone between taking shots, knowing that it is all that stands between you and a very messy death. There are pockmarks still discernible on Iverson's outer walls, even after all these centuries."

Mittie had hugged her arms around herself and was giving off fake shivers.

"I think it's perfectly dreadful," she complained to no one in particular. "We shouldn't have to see such things. We're ladies, not beastly knights or soldiers."

"Ladies of the castle were not immune from the fight," countered Tilbury, as the wind lashed his hair into wild white spikes. "Should the men fall, or should they have been on a quest elsewhere when the attack commenced, the womenfolk would defend the fortress."

"I should've *never*," gasped Mittie. "How very *ple*beian!"

Sophia snorted. "Then you'd have been slaughtered. Or worse. Isn't that so, Professor?"

"Indeed." Tilbury squinted at the pair of them, then at the rest of us. He blinked a few times, apparently just now grasping where the conversation was headed. "But let us reflect more on the bravery of such souls rather than the outcomes. It happens that, despite numerous attempts, Iverson was never completely overrun, not once. So the gentlewomen who dwelled here surely led lives of uncommon fulfillment. . . ."

I stopped listening. I walked away from the others to the edge nearest me and let my hand slide lightly along the border of a hiding-stone, feeling for pocks. The rock was cold and chipped, whether from invaders' arrows or time, I could not tell.

The channel opened before me in a wide, flat spread of navy chopped with froth and melting into forever. Even beneath the clouds, it was beautiful. More than beautiful.

It was . . . touchable. The high wind as well, now a tangible thing, thick as pudding. It filled my mouth and nose and ears, rushed into my senses. I leaned forward into it, testing its resistance.

I was certain, *certain*, I could raise my arms—a goddess of sea and sky, celebrating her reign—and allow the wind to lift me. And I'd be safe. I would not fall.

After all, I'd done it before, hadn't I? I'd forgotten about it—forgotten on purpose, let the grimy haze of my London life smear away the memory. Or perhaps it had been only a dream . . . but surely I'd stood like this before, tilted out over an abyss. If it *had* been a dream, it seemed so *real*.

I'd climbed out the window at Blisshaven. I could still feel the slick cold glass against my fingertips, hear the squeak of the frame as I'd hefted it open.

Smoggy air on my face. The empty dark. My body feeling lighter and lighter, lighter than air.

I had tipped into that emptiness below, and then—

"Eleanore."

I opened my eyes, just now realizing I'd closed them. Sophia had her hand on my sleeve.

"Watch it," she said, quiet. "You're about to make a hash of yourself."

I looked down. I had climbed atop the low barrier between two merlons and was balanced at the rim of the stone. The tips of my shoes poked out over a dizzying drop, black leather against faraway boulders and a viscous, surging sea.

No smog. No darkness. The violence of the surf below me was clear as crystal.

I came back to myself in a sickening rush. My stomach lurched. My knees buckled. My fingers clutched at the stones.

I moved my left foot, then my right, slinking down again to the safety of the roof. Sophia released my arm.

Bloody hell. I'd nearly done it, I'd nearly stepped clean over that edge—I'd *wanted* to—

"Tedious lecture," Sophia murmured while gazing at Tilbury, who was still rhapsodizing to his captive audience about the joys of medieval life. "But hardly worth ending it all, I would think."

"Hardly," I murmured in return, when I was convinced my voice would not break.

A frown creased her perfect brow; her eyes skimmed my frame. "You know, for a moment there, it almost looked like you were . . . smoldering."

That caught me short. "I beg your pardon?"

"Like you were smoking. Your hair—your neck and hair—blurring into smoke." Sophia shook her head once, hard. "Never mind."

"I—"

"It's all this wretched wind and salt, no doubt. I cannot wait to graduate from this pile of rocks, I swear."

She walked back to the cluster of the other girls. They parted and reabsorbed her into their midst without seeming even to notice.

. . .

It wasn't until we were leaving that I saw it. The lesson was concluded, and Mittie's shivering had finally started to look real. Tilbury opened the access door and there was a short, ladylike tussle to see who would get through first, but I waited. I wasn't sure how my knees felt about creeping down those corkscrew stairs just yet.

The clouds had thinned sheer overhead, transforming the sun into a hard silver disk. It lent a peculiar light to the limestone, blurring some crannies but heightening others, and when I gave a final glance back to the merlon I had first touched with my hand, I detected a faint tracing there that I hadn't noticed before.

It was a single word carved along the side, where it was not readily visible. The lettering was scripted, even graceful, although stone meant to withstand the ravages of a catapult must have been damned difficult to incise.

Just as I had perceived the flicker of thoughts behind Gladys's eyes, somehow, inexplicably, I understood that this word had been meant to serve as a final admonition, engraved as deep as desperation could manage into unyielding stone.

The word was: *Don't.*

. . .

What if, that moment in the grotto when I asked Jesse if I was crazy, he had answered *yes*?

What if all this persistent strangeness about me, all the dreams and songs and the wicked voice, was not the product of mysterious magic but merely my own mundane insanity?

No such things as dragons. No such things as boys made out of stars or girls going to smoke.

I would do anything to avoid being imprisoned again. I would absolutely lie or cheat or steal.

Perhaps I would even kill.

I would kill myself. I knew that. In a soundless and static corner of my soul, I knew that.

If it meant I'd go to hell—well, it happens that there are many levels of hell, and I'd already visited a few of them.

Jumping off a castle roof would be no worse a fate.

. . .

I waited until twilight before attempting to find him again.

Unlike the last time I'd ventured outdoors for Jesse, I did not run through this descending eve but walked most decorously from the main doors of the castle instead. Bundled in my shawl and uniform, I might have been partaking in any one of Mrs. Westcliffe's permitted after-supper al fresco activities, like:

Strolling to the edge of the rose garden to admire the sunset.

Strolling to the edge of the orchard to admire the sunset.

Strolling to the edge of the bridge to admire the sunset.

At England's foremost educational opportunity for young women, strolling to the brink of things was allowed. Leaving the green—plunging beyond brinks—was not.

As the sunset tonight consisted of a watery gray cloak of clouds, it was not especially worth admiring. I was the only student even pretending to want to slog along the grounds.

Still, I tucked my shawl closer to my chest and glanced around very carefully before easing into the woods. I even scanned the castle windows, searching for telltale faces, but the panes all shone empty. If anyone did see me go, they didn't care enough to raise a fuss.

Twilight is the best time for Fay trickery, or so I'd read. Not yet all dark, the last brief luminance of the sky fighting its inevitable death. Shadows that seemed to reach out and snatch at you; rustlings behind trees too near for comfort. Wisplights blinking off and on in the distance. Birds skipping from crown to crown of the blackened trees, calling *Farewell! Farewell!* in full-throated, mournful cries. . . .

Gooseflesh pricked my skin, and it had nothing to do with the cold. But I was not going to be afraid of these woods, not for any reason. These were the woods that led to Jesse, so I would not be afraid.

From far away, the false thunder of airships and bombs began, a short shuddering of the air that rippled through me, but feebly, like the echo of an echo.

I walked a little faster.

In the end, it didn't matter. By the time I found Jesse's cottage, twilight had faded into ordinary night, and Jesse wasn't there.

I knocked anyway, in case I was wrong. Maybe he was muting his music, like before.

The door swung open on silent hinges. No lock. No candles lit inside.

With my hand on the jamb, I took a half step forward into his home, breathing in the scent of him, subtle cinnamon overlaid now with pinewood and soap and coffee—and something else. Something that smelled very much like grass, sweetly pungent but fading rapidly.

My fingers found the bump of the cat's-eye knot. I traced three long circles around it before turning about and leaving.

My path back to the castle looped toward the stable. I looked askance at its plain stone sides in the distance, the light leaking through the planks of the doors to lay stripes across the dirt. It appeared dollhouse small next to Iverson's walls but in reality was likely large enough to keep horses for an entire manor.

No Jesse-music emanating from there, either, but the sweet grass smell of before billowed up and over me in waves.

Hay. Of course.

From across the yard I heard the slow, restless snufflings of very large penned animals, and the softer footsteps of someone who was likely more human-shaped.

The top level of the barn had windows of glass set back beneath the rafters, like those of a home. A figure moved behind one of them, thickset and hunched, a cap atop white hair. Mr. Hastings. He saw me and paused, then curled a hand at me from behind the glass.

Enter.

The wind puffed and the fringe of my shawl began a flutter; it seemed that as the air swept by me, the animal snufflings grew more agitated.

The gnarled hand beckoned again, more impatient.

For the second time that day, I thought, *Bloody hell.*

Chapter 18

What he wanted, Jesse knew he could not fully have.

The logical part of him, the serene and celestial part of him, accepted that. She was too young; she was untested. She didn't understand what was to come.

The enchantment threading through his every atom—tissue, bone, sinew—understood that and was strong enough and bright enough to make allowances for all those things.

But he was more than enchanted. He was a man, too. He was born of dirt, into a world of chaos and lust, and that was also his heritage. And the man in him didn't care about her tender young years or that she had no idea what she could do or what she would have to give up to do it.

The man in him just wanted. Purely wanted. *Burned* with want, exactly as he had from the moment he'd watched her walking toward him that night across the train station lot, manifest at last.

Behind tonight's mask of clouds, the stars whispered to him, cold and insistent:

she is yours and not. forever to be yours, forever to be not.

Right.

It was why he'd stayed to muck out the stalls after today's journey into town, even though he and Hastings had done it yesterday. Even though it was well past dusk and he'd declined the shared supper of bread and stew that Hastings had offered, and the thought of retreating home was just that. Retreating. He wasn't fit company for aught but the horses and the stable cats, who endured his ill humor well enough.

Going home meant darkness, and bed, and precious little to distract him from his own thoughts.

Placid Abigail flicked her tail at him when he ventured too near with the pitchfork. The tangerine tom, which had no name, hunched low on the crossbeam separating the stalls, following Jesse's every move with slitted orange eyes.

The Germans were bombing again tonight, miles up the coast. He wondered if she was hearing it, too, then pushed the thought aside, concentrating on the arc of the iron tines, the span of the ash handle against his palms. Hay mounded up, moved. Mounded, moved. Abigail's hooves like black crescent moons against the straw.

forever yours, forever not.

Pain began to gather between his shoulder blades, a welcome thing, knifing lower down the path of his spine. He was breathing harder, immersed in the earthy aroma of manure and alfalfa and the greasy bite of the smoke curling from the lanterns. He wished absently for a kerchief; drops of sweat began to sting his eyes.

He didn't need Abigail's sudden stiffening to know that she was there, nor the tom's swift desertion.

The stars announced, *here, here she is,* and he didn't even need them to know.

Jesse knew she was there because, very simply, his pain vanished. His irritation with himself and the world: vanished. And as he straightened and turned, all the star-brightness within him flared into that *want* again.

Abigail backed up hard, knocking into the stone wall. He set the pitchfork aside and placed both hands on her to soothe her, looking past her to the stable doors.

Lora stood uncertainly at the entrance, her arms and torso shrouded in a wrap, one foot cocked back behind her with her toes in the dirt, as if she meant to turn and bolt at the slightest sound.

So he didn't say anything. Only looked at her, helpless, yearning.

Zula, Abigail's foal, began to snort. She kicked at her stall door, once. Twice. Like a cue in a play, a pair of distant explosions echoed it.

"Those dreams I've had," Lora said, beneath the increasing clamor of horse and bombs and door. "The ones where I come to you at—at night. Were they truly dreams?"

her time is coming, her time, the sacrifice. tell her.

Jesse turned his face away so she couldn't see what lived within him. He gave Abigail a final rough pat, grabbed the pitchfork, and left and latched the stall.

"Come on," he said, walking past her, tossing the fork behind the trough outside. "You can't stay here. Come with me."

The stars approved, a swelling chorus of sound that he could not have blocked from his ears any more than he could his own heartbeat.

destiny along this path. delight both dark and bright.

A concept so cerebral as *destiny* wasn't what lit him to fire inside.

Delight, though. That was another matter entirely.

. . .

"I started to dissolve today. Into smoke or mist or something."

We were walking away from the castle and the stable and Hastings's view, enfolded nearly at once by the soft charcoal dark. I didn't see the need for subtlety.

"Did you?"

If Jesse was surprised or appalled, none of it was revealed in his tone. He didn't even glance at me, not that I could tell. His pace didn't falter.

"Yes," I said firmly. "Atop the roof of the castle. At the very edge. I was—I don't know how to describe it. I was almost in a trance of sorts. I had climbed out to the edge of the battlement, but I didn't even see it. In my mind, in my memory, I was back at the orphanage, back during this one night when I was much younger, and I . . ."

"You what?" he asked, still undisturbed.

"I jumped out the window there. From the top story. I *jumped.*" I heard the doubt in my own voice and hurried on. "And there was only the courtyard below me, not even a dirt one but one made of cobblestones. I'm *sure* it was real—but I never got in trouble for it. And I wasn't hurt. I don't even remember how I got back inside."

"How do you know you almost went to smoke today?"

"Sophia saw it, though she thought it was an illusion. She stopped me just before I—" I shuddered despite myself. "Before I jumped again."

"I see."

I bit my lip. "I think it was real. That time at the orphanage. So I need to know if it was also real with you."

We'd ended up next to a hedge pruned to resemble a loping hound. In a few weeks it would probably come into ferocious bud, but tonight it was skeletal, all bare branches and thorns.

Jesse was staring at me; I felt it, although I didn't raise my gaze above his chest.

My dreams of him had been so . . . intimate. The thought that they might have been more than dreams both excited and mortified me.

I reached out and touched the nose of the hound, pressing the pad of my thumb into a thorn. Behind us, Iverson loomed, a monolith dividing the wind and clouds.

Jesse shoved his hands into his pockets. "What do *you* think, Lora?"

A flash of irritation took me. "I think that I asked you first. And I'd appreciate a straightforward answer, if you please."

"Do you hear them? The bombs?"

"Yes, but—"

"Do you smell the burning?"

"What burning?"

"From the bombs," he said patiently. "From the fires they're starting in the towns."

I started to shake my head. My lips began to form the word *no*, but then I hesitated. I became aware that I *did* smell something, something faint and horrid. Acrid chemicals. Singed meat.

The *no* strangled in my throat.

He nodded grimly, reading my face. "It's not supposed to be like this, you coming into your gifts in stages. But, then again, you're exceptional in every way, Lora Jones, so perhaps the regular rules don't apply to you. I don't know. And I don't know if what happened to you at the orphanage was real, but from what I understand, when you transform fully—especially the first time—there is a price to pay."

"What do you mean? What price?"

"Pain," he confessed, on a hard exhale. "I'm sorry. There's always a sacrifice for every gift. It's . . . it's rather a rule of the universe, really. You were granted a great gift, so your sacrifice will be great, as well. That ensures the balance of all."

I recoiled from the hound, balling my hand into a fist against my stomach. "Well, what manner of pain? I mean, how much?"

"A *great* gift," he emphasized, low.

"Oh." I was abruptly short of breath. "Of course."

Stupid, stupid—how stupid that I hadn't thought of it before, that it would hurt. Obviously it would. And then I couldn't stop imagining it: my body bloating, mutating, into something hideous and snakelike. Something grotesque. My skin stretching shiny thin, my bones cracking and shifting and reknitting. My teeth sharpening, my tongue splitting. My hands and feet twisting into claws—

"Stop," Jesse said.

I stared up at him, almost panting with fear.

"Stop, beloved," he said more gently, and took up my clenched fist with both hands. "I've upset you, and I shouldn't have. I don't want you to dread yourself. I don't want you to dread what is to come. Like I said, you're exceptional, so there may be nothing to worry about at all. But whatever happens, whatever you face, I'll face it with you. Do you hear?"

"How can you say that? It nearly happened *on the roof* today. You can't know—"

"I *will* be with you. We're together now, and the universe knows I won't let you make your sacrifice alone. Dragon protects star. Star adores dragon. An age-old axiom. Simple as that."

I looked down at our hands, both of his curled over mine. I unclenched my fist. Blood from the thorn smeared my skin.

"The universe," I muttered. "The same universe that has produced the kaiser and bedbugs and Chloe Pemington. How reassuring."

With the same absolute concentration he might have shown for turning flowers into gold, Jesse Holms smoothed out my fingers between his, wiping away the blood. He turned my hand over and lifted it to his lips. His next words fell soft as velvet into the heart of my palm.

"Those nights, in the sweetest dark, we shared our dreams. That's your answer. I was stitched into yours, and you were stitched into mine, and *that* was real, I promise you." I felt his lips curve into a smile. The unbelievably sensual, ticklish scuff of his whiskers. "Very good dreams they were, too," he added.

It was no use trying to cling to mortification or fear. He was holding my hand. He was smiling at me past the cup of my fingers, and although I couldn't see it, the shape of it against my skin was beyond tantalizing, rough and masculine. I was a creature gone hot and cold and light-headed with pleasure. I wanted to snatch back my hand and I wanted him to go on touching me like this forever. I wanted to walk with him back to his cottage, to his bed, and to hell with the Germans and school and all the rest of the world.

But he looked up suddenly.

"They're searching for you," he said, releasing me at once, moving away.

They were. I heard my name being called by a variety of voices in a variety of tones, all of them still inside the castle, none of them sounding happy.

"Go on." With a few quick steps, Jesse was less than a shadow, retreating into the black wall of the woods. "Don't get into trouble. And, Lora?"

"Yes?"

There was hushed laughter in his voice. "Until we can see each other again, do us both a favor. Keep away from rooftops."

. . .

"This kind of behavior will not be tolerated, Miss Jones."

"I beg your pardon, ma'am."

"Students are absolutely *not* allowed outside after sundown without proper escort."

"I'm so terribly sorry."

"It was incredibly irresponsible of you. I had to summon half the staff to help search for you. From their suppers, I might add."

"I never meant to—I only nodded off in the gardens, I swear. I fell asleep."

"So you've said already. Twice. Are you ill, Miss Jones?"

"No, ma'am."

"A sound sleeper, is that it?"

"Yes, ma'am. I mean, I suppose so. I am sorry."

"I really must think you have no notion of the world in the least, Miss Jones. A child like you should know better than to trust the night. There are dangers beyond these walls—yes, even out here. It is my responsibility to ensure that every girl here remains *safe,* remains *healthy,* remains *untouched.* . . ."

"Yes, ma'am. Are . . . are you all right, ma'am?"

"I am perfectly well, Miss Jones. A touch of the catarrh, perhaps. Ahem. The duke is holding a celebration Saturday next to honor the birthday of his son. It is an Idylling tradition, and the tenth- and eleventh-year girls are invited every year. I am tempted—sorely tempted—to exclude you as punishment."

"Oh?"

"But as the duke has specifically requested your presence, and since this is, after all, your first offense, I shall not."

"Oh."

"Perhaps he wishes you to play again. We'll see."

"Oh."

"That will be all for now, Miss Jones. Tomorrow we will discuss a proper punishment for your transgression. You may retire to your room now, as it seems you are in such critical need of slumber."

"Thank you, ma'am. Good night."

"Good night."

. . .

I shall not wander the school grounds alone at night.
I shall not wander the school grounds alone at night.
I shall not wander the school grounds alone at night.
I shall not wander the school grounds alone at night.
I shall not wander the school grounds alone at night.
I shall not wander the school grounds alone at night.
I shall not wander the school grounds alone at night.
I shall not wander the school grounds alone at night.
x 100.

. . .

Days of rain. Days and days of rain, and nights, too.

It put the castle out of sorts. It forced everyone indoors all the time, not just the spun-sugar girls but the maids and menservants and teachers and everyone.

The only people I ever glimpsed mud-spattered from the weather were Hastings and Jesse, who drove the Iverson wagons on and off the island, because the food had to come from somewhere.

Should the rains never cease and the fish flee and the sea rise to flood the earth, we'd have nothing but soggy herbs from the kitchen garden to sustain us. It was a tad too easy to imagine my fellow students resorting to cannibalism—they definitely appeared the type—but it seemed to me a dire prospect. I had no doubt most of my classmates would taste like vinegar.

Naturally, preparation for the duke's party consumed them. Even the girls too young to attend gossiped and sighed over the notion of dancing in Armand's arms, and bickered over which of them would make the best sweetheart. Sophia and her band of merrymakers, who *were* attending, pretended they had much better things to do than worry about one single, provincial little party, even if it was being hosted by a duke. But it was all they talked about, anyway, outside class.

Outside class, I sat alone and dreamed of anything but the party.

Outside class, I sat and dreamed of the coming night.

At night, every night, I was no longer alone. Whatever time we could spare, whether it was hours or just minutes, Jesse and I met in the grotto, and we practiced my Becoming.

That was how I had begun to think of it privately. Becoming, capitalized. I still wasn't certain *what* I was Becoming. I tried to hold on to the image of a butterfly emerging from a cocoon. That seemed safe enough.

I'd never seen any picture of a dragon, however, that looked anything like a butterfly. Less wings; rather more teeth.

The small, sleepy hours of early Saturday morning found us seated, as we usually were, on the upper slope of the grotto's embankment. We had blankets and food and water—no wine—and the soft, antiqued light of Jesse's lantern bathing us in amber. I en-

deavored with my entire heart not to think of these stolen moments as anything romantic. Jesse was not courting me. He was not
wooing me, certainly not as I'd heard boys usually did, sending
girls posies or poems or buying them sweets or taking them to the
theater. He didn't attempt to kiss me even once.

We met like this because he was teaching me to Become. And
yet every night I sat there opposite him on the blankets and looked
at his attentive, handsome face and I thought, *This is our wooing.
This is our Becoming.*

I'd had no luck with going to smoke again. During school I tried
so hard to stay . . . as myself. But later on, down beneath the castle,
when I *did* try to dissolve, it simply didn't happen.

There were times when I felt ready to burst. My skin felt
shrunken, my heart hammered in my chest. I was *so* close. I willed
myself back to that moment at the brink of the roof; I willed the
fiend back inside me; I willed the voice to come to life . . .

. . . and, nothing.

The tide came in. The tide went out. Nights alone with Jesse in
this haunted, sparkling cave, and all I had to show for it were dark
smudges under my eyes and a constant chill I couldn't seem to
shake, even during daylight.

I didn't ever speak the words aloud, but it wasn't going to happen, I knew. And I couldn't blame it on the weather, or the stars, or
my uncertain age. Deep down, what prevented the Becoming was
purely me.

Because, deep down, I was afraid.

It was selfish and cowardly and low, I admit it. Certainly there
were people beyond my cloistered world who were suffering far
worse terrors than my own. The Tommies forced to live and die in
mud trenches, for example, or the townsfolk trapped beneath the

deadly zeppelins—I had *smelled* them burning; the most craven part of my soul thanked the heavens I could not hear the screams. But Jesse had said *pain*.

The pain of the war seemed far from me, but the promise of my own was as near as a sword dangling over my head.

And I was afraid. Sincerely.

"Let's try something new," he said now. We spoke in undertones, even though there was no real chance anyone above us would overhear. No matter how careful we were, however, the grotto took our words and sighed them back at us.

. . . new-new-new . . .

"Like what?" I asked.

"Anything else. Obviously, concentrating as you've been isn't helpful. So let's not think about the specifics of what we hope for. Smoke or anything like that."

I sat back on my hands. "Fine with me."

He had walked from the woods tonight, I could tell. The fresh, dark scent of the night still clung to him, and his boots were damp, with bits of grass and leaves flecking the leather.

Jesse reached down and peeled free a small, perfectly oval spring leaf from near his ankle, holding it up by its stem.

"I'll tell you a story instead," he said, gazing at the leaf.

"Tell me about the ghost. Who was she?"

"Ah, the ghost. Her name was Rose."

"Was she one of the builders?"

He twirled the leaf between his fingers, back and forth. "No."

"One of the students?" I shivered. "That's it, isn't it? She was a student."

"It's not my story to tell you. I'm sorry. It belongs to someone else."

"Don't you know?"

"I do know. But I have in mind a different tale entirely."

Without warning, his hand glowed bright. The little leaf was engulfed in a globe of brilliance; the cavern flamed to life, all the sparkles on the walls transformed into countless flashing suns. I lifted an arm to cover my eyes—then the light was gone.

When I looked at him again, Jesse was looking back at me, his jaw set and his face masked with shadows. The leaf was exactly as before but now, of course, solid gold. He offered it to me, unsmiling.

"Once upon an age—"

"Can you do that with anything?" I cut in.

"No." Since I hadn't taken the leaf, he placed it on the blanket between us. "Only living things. Nothing inanimate."

"That's why it's flowers," I said, realizing. "You transform flowers and plants, like the brooch and my cuff. But could you do it to—"

"Yes. But I won't. Life is precious, Lora. All life is precious, even roses. Even frogs, or snails, or the lowest of crawling things. I have no desire to be the arbiter of life or death over others, despite this gift of alchemy. Perhaps because of it. Transmuting the living into gold destroys it, even as it preserves its physical shape."

My mind raced. "What about a tree? Could you transmute a tree?"

"Yes."

I sat up straighter. "You could be *rich*. You could be richer than the king, if you liked. My God, Jesse. You could have a whole forest of gold! You could have *anything*."

. . . *anything-anything-anything* . . .

"*Rich* is a matter of perspective. I think my life is rich enough.

And I have already"—he gave me a significant look—"nearly all that I want."

"But you could *also* have a mansion. And servants of your own. A cook! And motorcars and chauffeurs and a telephone and—"

"I'm a country lad, Lora. I'm happy like this."

I shook my head, exasperated. *I* was a city girl and had lived poor for as long as I could remember. Lived poor and hated it. It never would have occurred to me—or to anyone else from St. Giles, I'd wager—that someone with the means to escape the grind of poverty would simply choose not to do so.

A forest of gold. In my mind's eye, it was glimmering and endless, a shimmery warm paradise. Like a scrap of proof of what could be, the oval leaf gleamed next to my thigh, shiny as a newly minted coin.

I picked it up. Nothing warm there: It had taken on the chill of the grotto already, cold against my fingers. Even its tiny treble song felt cold.

And then all the exasperation in me began to fade. I looked down at the leaf. I felt its firm chill and recalled its green spring softness from moments before. Its life.

A thought scratched at me, elusive. Jesse had shown me something and it had slipped by me; I had missed a message tucked between words and actions. I had missed a lesson. What was it?

I said, very slow, "Alchemy is surely a great gift, one of the greatest. What sacrifice do you make for it?"

For a long minute, he was quiet. Finally he said, "I'll strike you a deal, dragon-girl. You listen to my story now, and I'll tell you of the sacrifice later."

"Later? When?"

"When you truly need to know."

"I think I bloody need to know right now."

"I'll tell you later, I promise. But now—we've only an hour or so before the maids are up. So, please." He leaned forward, pressed his lips swift and cool against mine, and, even though I didn't mean to, I stiffened, surprised. "Just listen. And relax."

I nodded and Jesse drew away, almost smiling. I lay back on the blanket and closed my eyes, clutching the leaf. Between the sting of pleasure that lingered on my mouth and the tinkling leaf song in my hand, I felt anything but relaxed.

Once more, his low, measured voice filled the cavern.

"Once upon an age, there were no humans on the earth, only Elementals, beings of pure form and intent, very powerful. We would call them spirits today, I suppose, or gods, except there were no people around to worship them. Yet the humans did come eventually, and the Elementals discovered they could not compete against pragmatic mankind. One by one they ceased to exist, until finally there was but one left. A goddess."

"What did she look like?" I wondered aloud, not opening my eyes.

"She was too compelling to look at directly. Bright like the sun, bright and terrible. Only one other being could look upon her, and that was Death. And so . . . they became lovers."

He said the word like a caress, like velvet again, and my face began to heat.

"Together they forged great and hellish things," Jesse murmured. "Lightning and waterfalls that churned into clouds off the tip of the world. Chasms so winding deep that daylight never traced their endings. They dreamed through golden days and silvered nights. All the other creatures envied or adored them, because Death and the Elemental were destruction and creation joined as One. In the natural order of things, they should not have been stronger joined. And yet they were."

He shifted, coming closer to me. A hand settled lightly atop my chest, directly over my heart. At our feet the seawater splashed a little, as if disturbed by something rolling over in the dark, distant deep.

"Centuries passed, and mankind began to devour the earth, even the wildest places. They had tools to invent and wars to fight and grubby, short lives. Nothing about them dwelled in the magic of the ancient spirits. So although Death, the Great Hunter, prospered as he sieved through their villages, the Elemental, strong as she once was, thinned into a web of gossamer. Human lives simply tore her apart."

His hand was so warm. Warmer than I, warmer than the air, and still just barely touching me. The light behind my lids never lifted, so I knew he wasn't glowing, but it felt as if he held a tame coal to my skin. It felt like something painless and ablaze, drawing my heart upward into it.

"The time had come for them to divide. Like all the rest of her kind, the goddess would cease to exist; she had no other course. So Death and the Elemental severed their joined hearts. For a few generations more, she drifted alone through the last of the sacred places, deserts and fjords, lands so savage no human had yet desecrated them."

Jesse's voice dropped to a whisper. Without moving his hand, he bent down, his breath in my ear. "And Death, who had tasted her brightness, who would never cease to crave it—who knew her better than all the collected souls of all mankind's weeping dead—became her Hunter."

I was hot and strange. I was light and lighter, and curiously my breath came so slow.

"Until at last, one starry night beneath the desert moon, she surrendered to him. She allowed him to come to her, to make love to her. To unravel her . . ."

. . .

It was happening. He sat next to her and bore witness to her change, her pulse slowing, her skin blanching, the fans of her lashes stark against the contours of her face. He kept his palm there against her chest, up and down with her respiration, and watched the smoke begin to curl around his fingers.

"And by his hand, in the bliss of her unraveling, she touched the stars. . . ."

Lora's breath hitched. Her heart skipped—then stopped.

If I could take this from you, Jesse thought fiercely. *If I could take this one moment away from you and keep the agony for myself—*

Her eyes opened, went instantly to his. Panic lit her gaze.

Then she was gone.

His fingers sank to the floor through her empty blouse, and the blue dragon smoke that was all of Eleanore Jones rose into strands above him.

Chapter 19

It did not hurt.

It took me a while to comprehend that. I think mostly what I felt in those first few seconds, beyond astonishment, was an extreme sense of loss: loss of gravity, loss of orientation, loss of Jesse's touch. Yet, by some means, I could still see. I could hear. I was still myself, with my own thoughts but none of my own body.

I was lighter than the air. I was diaphanous, bobbing and floating and unable to control it, and the dripping-wet stalactites poked down around me, and Jesse was a boy on his feet below me, his face tipped up, gilded hair and eyes glinting like emeralds.

He mouthed my name. It came to me distant and smothered, but, weirdly, it didn't seem to matter. The boy down there didn't matter nearly as much as these fascinating rock formations that combed through me now with their solid teeth, because I knew that they were only the lid on a ceiling, and beyond the ceiling was freedom.

And, oh, how I yearned for it. I twined and spiraled and searched for a way out, and the waiting stars sang hallelujahs to me and pulled and pulled—*yes, this way*—

"Lora. Lora!"

I bubbled against the ceiling. The smoky fragments of me stretched longer and longer; I realized I could become less than smoke. I could flatten myself, sheer as a sheet of molecules, a shimmering hint of next-to-nothing. Even thinner.

And it felt . . . *good.*

That was when I knew that, if I wanted, I could just keep thinning. Let myself unravel. Final freedom. No weight, no pain, no worries. Not ever again.

"Come back to me, Eleanore. Listen to me. You have to come back now."

The boy spoke sternly, and I paused. A fire burned within him. How peculiar that I could see it now, in this form, when he could do me no harm. It burned inside him without even a flicker, just this strong, steady light that illuminated him in flame and gold, every cell. Every beautiful bit.

"Dragon," snapped the boy. "I command you to come back."

I wanted to laugh at that. Command. Indeed.

But . . . he'd done something to me. I couldn't maintain my lovely thin stretch. I was changing, thickening, even as I fought it. I was pouring back down to the floor of the cavern in a darker mass, coils of smoke that tightened into the shape of the girl I'd once been, a girl with feet and tucked legs and a body hunched over them, her head hanging and her long hair sweeping the stone.

My fingers curled against damp rock. I sucked in air.

Then Jesse was crouched beside me, an arm tight around my back, his head bent over mine. He might have been breathing harder than I was.

"You—" I gulped some more air. "You can *command* me?"

"I didn't want to have to."

"That is completely unfair!"

"Aye."

He pulled me to my feet and embraced me fully, something he'd never done before. I allowed myself to sink into the heat of his body for a minute, then lifted my head from his chest, blinking. The cavern seemed more sparkly. Everything looked sparklier and brighter. Colder. On the ground a few feet away lay a familiar pile of clothing in a very familiar layout, and I was wearing none of it.

Perhaps he noticed, too. Perhaps he just read the subtle signals of my body, the sudden rigidity of my spine, because he stepped back and began to shrug out of his peacoat.

"Here." He draped it over me. "How are you? How do you feel?"

"Naked," I grumbled. "You can *command* me?"

His hands tightened upon my shoulders. "Eleanore." When my eyes lifted to his, Jesse broke into a grin. And right then I glimpsed again the ineffably divine fire that burned within this child of the stars; it was there, right there behind the summer beauty of his gaze. All the brightness around me, all the sparkles, the heat and cold and the rising joy that welled through me so sharply it almost hurt: all reflections of him.

"You did it," he said. "You went to smoke."

I touched a hand to his cheek, awed. "Crikey. I did."

. . .

Smoke, of course, is not quite a dragon. I reminded myself of that as I lay in my bed that morning, waiting for Gladys's knock. The sun was rising and the sky flushed a vigorous pink, but I knew there'd be no sleep for me for some while.

I had *lost* my human body, even if it had been for only a few short minutes. I had Become something less than corporeal. I had defied all logic and all proper sanity, *and* I'd had a witness.

I wasn't mad. But I wasn't quite a dragon yet, either. I felt itchy and odd. Like the twilight, I was now a thing between worlds, and I felt . . . incomplete.

Before we'd left the grotto, Jesse said that maybe the pain of my transformation wasn't supposed to be with smoke. That maybe it was going to be when I shifted into a more monstrous shape.

He hadn't actually said *monstrous*. I thought it fairly implied.

I squirmed against my sheets, imagining wing bones digging into my back. I held up my hands and spread my fingers before my face. I squinted at them, turning them this way and that in the rosy light, then bent my fingers into claws.

For a second—no more than that—I could have sworn there was an impression of scales along my wrists, ridged and perfect. Then I looked closer, and all I saw were wrists.

A shadow zipped by the window, too swift to follow. Then another, and another. I got up, stuck my head beyond the sill.

The flock of gannets shot like bullets past my tower, flying hard and fast away from me toward the sea, into the rising pink sun.

I heard the hiss of the air sluiced from their wings. I smelled the fish-feather muck of their scent.

The itching inside me crept nearer to the surface of my skin.

. . .

To the tenth- and eleventh-year girls' open dismay, the duke's party was considered a scholastic function. Therefore, we would all wear our formal Iverson uniforms, which looked nearly exactly like our everyday uniforms but for a frothing of lace along the shirtwaists and skirts of satin damask instead of broadcloth.

I wanted to inquire what scholastic function, precisely, attending a birthday party fulfilled but knew better than that. Mrs. Westcliffe had made it clear that I was expected to attend, so whatever punishment she might devise, it wouldn't include getting to stay behind.

I shall not ask intelligent questions.
x 1,000.

We all waited in the parlor for the duke's automobiles—how many did he have, anyway?—to show up and ferry us in excellent style to the celebration. Mrs. Westcliffe and Miss Swanston were to be our dutiful shepherds, and they waited with us, standing in the middle of the room with crossed arms and jewelry spangling their persons. Even Miss Swanston, it seemed, had the means for a pearl choker. A gaggle of younger girls clustered about the doorway, shoving at one another for the best spot from which to eye us with envy.

I sat in my horsehair chair, gazing at my knees, thinking about smoke and sacrifices and how Mrs. Westcliffe's garnet earbobs thrummed to a beat that resembled a Sousa march, which seemed exquisitely appropriate.

I'd never before worn anything made of satin. I was fairly certain I'd never even touched it.

The skirt was aubergine and textured with poppies. The poppies felt nubby against my palms; the rest of the material was smooth smooth smooth. Beneath my outward elegance, my plain cotton chemise and corset chafed at my skin, and it seemed like something of a cheat.

I'd heard of nobs with satin sheets on their beds. I'd heard of street girls who saved up for months for satin petticoats. And now one entire half of me was wrapped in this thick, slippery cloth, and all I could think was, *How could anyone sleep in this?*

"Good gad, it's absolutely *sweltering* in here," groused Malinda, but softly, because we weren't allowed to say *gad*. I'd noticed that when she was particularly peevish, her voice took on a singsong edge. "Must we have *all* the lamps burning?"

"The better to see ourselves by, my dear," murmured Sophia, scrutinizing her face in one of the mirrors. Her earbobs were of diamonds. She looked stunning, and she knew it.

Lillian was fanning herself with one hand. "I feel as if I might melt. How is my hair? Is it positively limp? It is, isn't it? It is. I can tell."

Caroline shouldered up next to Sophia in the mirror, pouting. "At least your complexion holds up. I'm red as a beet."

"I'm going to look positively wilted for the party. I am."

"I *do* wish they'd bother to *get* here already. Do you think the duke *knows* how *tardy* his servants are? They *are* in his employ. Should someone *inform* him?"

"They're here," I said, and stood.

"Oh, *really*," snarled Malinda. "Now you have the hearing of a *dog,* is that it, Eleanore?"

"How fitting," chimed in Chloe from nearby, I suppose because she couldn't resist.

The duke, as it happened, had at least five automobiles, because that was how many showed up to carry us off the isle. I rode to Tranquility with Mrs. Westcliffe again, Miss Swanston on my other side, and took comfort in the thought of all the other girls crammed into the other autos, sincerely hoping that the wind blew them to rags.

In defiance of the war and the airships and any sort of two-candles-a-month rule, Tranquility was lit to blazes when we pulled up. It appeared that every window in every room shone with light, and it turned out that the party wasn't even to be held indoors.

We followed the butler through a ballroom to the formal gardens in back, and even the headmistress couldn't contain her gasp of wonder.

Beneath the rising moon, the grounds opened up in a spread of rolling grasses and marble stairways and gazebos and trees, finely garbed people swirling through it all like flower petals loosed to the wind. Torches burned along the farther paths, bright dots of orange against the blackening sky; Chinese lanterns glowing red and green and turquoise swayed more placidly from the trees. A string orchestra played a waltz from a corner of the courtyard just below us. No one danced to it; the rest of the courtyard was taken up by elaborately dressed tables of food and champagne.

This was a far more momentous event than a tea party, clearly.

"Well," said Mrs. Westcliffe at last, remembering to close her mouth.

"Quite so," agreed Miss Swanston, with a sideways, smiling look at me. "Miss Jones. Would you care to lead the way?"

I descended the steps from the ballroom to the courtyard with satin clenched in both hands, making my way to the duke's receiving line, stationed right by the first champagne table. Armand stood beside him, both of them in black tails and pomade so sleekly perfect they looked cut from a fashion journal.

Without making eye contact, I curtsied, mumbled my greeting, then moved quickly aside to allow Mrs. Westcliffe room to fawn.

"Your Grace."

"Irene. Welcome. Miss Swanston. And, er—you, as well, Miss Eleanore. I trust the journey here wasn't too taxing?"

"Not in the least. You are, as always, the most gracious host. . . ."

Because I'd moved, Armand was now directly in front of me. Our eyes locked. He did not speak. I did not speak.

". . . you have certainly outdone yourself this year! What a truly handsome transformation to the gardens, truly inspired . . ."

I sighed, giving in first. "Happy birthday. I don't have a gift."

His brows drew together. "Excuse me?"

"I said, I didn't bring a gift. Sorry."

He stared down at me. "Why would you—wait. Did you think . . . all this was for me?"

"Isn't it?"

And he started to laugh. Really laugh, genuinely laugh; it snared his father's attention and that of Mrs. Westcliffe. Miss Swanston, angling behind me, placed a gloved hand on my elbow.

"How heartwarming to see young people getting along so well! Miss Jones, we mustn't keep His Grace and Lord Armand. There are far too many guests eager to speak with them."

"Have a grand time," Armand managed, still chortling, as we moved off.

Mrs. Westcliffe found a lost flock of her little lambs milling about; apparently the other motorcars from Iverson had arrived. With a word to Miss Swanston, she left to tend to them.

Miss Swanston remained with me. By unspoken accord, we headed to the nearest table of food.

A maid bobbed at us and handed us plates. As the waltz shifted into a polonaise, we only stood there, taking it all in. Oysters on platters of chipped ice, haunches of beef waiting to be carved, fat lobster tails, strawberries, glazed duck, roasted artichokes, sturgeon in lemon sauce, salads, brandied fruits. Breads and breads and breads, a thousand kinds of cheeses and grapes—it was without question the most food I'd ever seen assembled in one place.

As if the war did not exist. As if rationing did not exist; as if hungry children stuck in foundling homes did not exist.

I might have remained as I was for hours, stunned and starving, but Miss Swanston took the tongs for the strawberries, which were nearest, and placed a few on my plate.

"How are things, Eleanore?"

I woke up fast. In my experience, when adults asked this question, it never led anywhere pleasant.

"Very fine, ma'am."

"Good. I'm pleased to hear it." She moved on to the roast beef, nodding to the footman behind the table for a slice. "I imagine it's been something of a transition for you. Coming all the way out here from the city, I mean."

"Yes," I agreed, straight-faced.

"But, I must say, I think you've adapted nicely. You seem a resilient girl."

"Thank you, ma'am."

"You're quiet but smart. Modest, I suspect. Watchful." She sent me that sideways look again. "Watchful is good. Learning by observation is a most useful skill, especially for someone in your position."

I had nothing to say to that, so only took up the cheese tongs.

"I lived in London for a few years after my own schooling. Islington. Do you know it?"

"No."

"No, perhaps not." She smiled, but it seemed wistful. "London is a colossal place, after all. A splendid, stinking jewel of humanity. I read that somewhere, and I don't believe I've ever come across a description more apt."

We had reached the end of the table, and my plate was full. I looked around for a space to sit, but the duke's truly inspired décor apparently didn't include tables and chairs. We strolled toward the only vacant spot left on the patio, leaning together against the marble railing. One of the Chinese lanterns hung directly above us; it colored us and all the food candy-red.

"Why did you leave, ma'am?"

"Ah." Miss Swanston was rolling a cube of cheddar around on her plate with her fork. "Well, my parents died one winter, both of them. And the house had to be sold."

"I'm sorry."

"Yes. I am, as well." She abandoned the cheddar. "As I said before, Eleanore, I know you're smart. I also have a reasonably clear understanding of how very . . . difficult your life has been up until now. Please don't look so distressed. Mrs. Westcliffe shared your records with me under circumstances of strictest confidentiality. Your past is your own, and, as far as I'm concerned, no one's business but your own."

The roll I'd just bitten into had gone dry as sand in my mouth.

"Yet I find I cannot help but offer you some unsolicited advice. Stay focused on your studies. Iverson will open doors for you that you might never have conceived. Your future could be as happy as your past was not. Don't allow yourself to waste that chance. Don't succumb to any . . . distractions."

I could only imagine my expression. Miss Swanston lowered her candy-red lashes and glanced back at Armand.

"Oh," I said, swallowing. "No. Definitely not."

"Forgive me. He seems quite taken with you."

The bite of roll lodged in my throat; I coughed. "He isn't, I assure you."

"Eleanore, it grieves me to correct you, but he is staring at you even now. He hasn't been able to tear his eyes from you since we arrived."

I couldn't tell her the truth. I couldn't say anything like, *Armand doesn't count. Armand's not even in the game. I'm in love with a boy made of stars, and we're going to live together ever after on gold and smoke and moonlight, and* that's *my happy future, no matter what any of you think.*

I scowled down at my plate. "He's simply . . ."

"Yes?" she prompted, very mild.

I searched for the right word. "I don't know what he is," I admitted finally, frustrated. "Bored, I suppose."

"Yes," she said again, just as mild. "I'm glad you've realized it, too."

"But I'm not dense. He's nobility. I know—I know what I am. I know what to avoid."

"Good," Miss Swanston said once more, and gave me her wistful smile.

. . .

Eventually, I ate my fill. Eventually, Miss Swanston became convinced that I wasn't about to go fling myself at Lord Armand and left me at the railing, saying that no doubt the headmistress would be missing her.

Twenty wily girls roaming free in the night and three unguarded tables of French champagne. I suspected Mrs. Westcliffe *was* rather outmatched.

The receiving line had dissolved, and the duke and his son were nowhere in view. Adults of all sizes and shapes stood elbow-to-elbow around me, admiring the gardens and one another. Chloe and her group were making their way through the food tables; Sophia and hers loitered at the foot of the stairs below me. So I left my plate with a maid and slipped back inside Tranquility.

I'd return for the champagne later.

It was easier to breathe away from the crowded courtyard. As I entered the ballroom, the music from the orchestra dimmed from strident to agreeable, and the peculiar aroma of banquet mixed with ladies' perfume gradually faded in my wake. But the ballroom was as empty as the gardens were full; obviously the guests were supposed to remain out there. The only other people in the chamber besides me were a pair of footmen stationed by the main doors, perhaps to ensure no one got inside.

The best way to publicly succeed at anything forbidden is to seem as if you know what you're doing, even if you don't. Especially if you don't. Don't stop, don't hesitate, and don't look back. I glided past the footmen into the main hallway with my chin up and my expression bored, an air I'd seen nearly every girl at the school assume whenever someone of a lower station was near.

Of course you must let me pass; clearly I'm a lady; I belong in satin and mansions and I know where I'm going and I definitely, definitely, won't be filching the silverware.

Like the ballroom, the hallway seemed deserted. It stretched long and mysterious in either direction, far darker than the rest of the house; all the electric lights had been set to low. When I passed directly beneath one of their dangling glass domes, a humming drone swarmed through my head so nastily that, after that, I sidled around them.

A runner of blue and mottled olive, rich and plush, absorbed my steps. Paintings, huge and framed in filigreed wood. Discarded scaffolding, bare frames of lumber and metal holding up nothing but air. Splintery pinewood crates, most unopened but a few showing their stuffings of straw and what might have been antique firearms.

And—voices behind me. Adult voices, male, subdued, discussing something about Americans and naval blockades.

I had my hand at once on the knob of the nearest door. By the time the duke and his companion passed by, I was well hidden in the shadows of what looked to be a study—a very masculine study, with panels of mahogany and massive leather furniture and a portrait above the fireplace of Himself with a family, so it was pure blind luck that they didn't follow me in.

But they walked on down the hallway.

I released the breath I'd been holding, suddenly fatigued, the itch inside me beginning another crawl along my nerves. I wandered over to one of the chairs and tested it for softness. It was far more comfortable than it appeared, a reading chair, clearly, with a newspaper neatly ironed and folded atop the stand by its arm.

A London paper. Yesterday's date.

HUN DIRIGIBLES FLYING FARTHER INLAND, warned the headline. I touched my fingers to it, spinning it about to scan the rest.

Germany's cowardly use of naval airships upon the civilian population is expanding. Bloated and slow, the zeppelins cruise far above any altitude ground artillery may reach, and often even above the firing altitude of our valiant boys in the sky.

The Minister of War has recommended that all eastern and southern coastal towns implement immediately our own very ef-fective nighttime blackout rules. . . .

Well. Perchance His Grace hadn't read this particular article yet.

I sat back in the chair and crossed my feet at the ankles. Then I glanced up at the portrait.

Definitely the duke in his younger days, and a fair-haired, gray-eyed woman who must have been his duchess. They were both gazing straight at me—at the artist who had painted them—Reginald with a trace of a confident smile, but the woman with a delicate, pensive sort of gravity, as if she felt that smiling wouldn't be appropriate. He was standing, but she was seated on what looked to be a garden bench, her hands resting on the shoulders of not one boy but two: the first a toddler with an unmistakable blue stare; the second an older child, probably around five, and fair like his mother.

She didn't really resemble me the least bit. I couldn't imagine what the duke had been going on about.

I studied it through half-lidded eyes, picking out the details, how roses bloomed pink and cream in the foreground. How the clouds above their heads looked stormy, and the wedge of sea in the far back was more of a suggestion of color and shape than anything literal.

Toddler Armand held something in his hand. A key, it looked like . . .

I'd stay for just a moment. I'd close my eyes for only one minute. Then I'd return to the party.

. . .

He found her in the study. He hadn't even known he'd been searching for her until he opened the door and there she was, relaxed in one of the chairs, her head tipped back and her hands in her lap, very much asleep.

The bracket clock on Reginald's desk ticked away the seconds, *six, seven, eight,* as Armand remained at the doorway, taking her in. Then he stole inside his father's sanctum, closing the door carefully behind him. Making as little noise as possible, he settled into the chair closest to Eleanore's.

What was it about her, he wondered, that made her so impossible to ignore? Little orphan girl, proud skinny waif, with secrets and music inside her that filled him with a crazed combination of exhilaration and fear. Like morphine pumping through him, but sharper than that. Not muddy. She'd made it as clear as could be that she didn't even like him, but still Mandy found himself thinking of her and fantasizing about her so often it was stupid. *He* was stupid.

Yet here he was yet again. Because *she* was here and, for whatever the hell reason, he couldn't stop wanting to be near her.

Her eyes opened. She registered his presence without an ounce of surprise.

"It's not your birthday, is it?" she said, straightening. "It's his."

Neither of them glanced up at the portrait. Certainly Mandy didn't need to look at it; he'd memorized it years ago.

"Aubrey Emerson Hugo, the Most Honourable Marquess of Sherborne. He's a glorious twenty-one years old today, wherever he is."

"No one told me you had a brother."

"Didn't they?" he said lightly. "I'm flabbergasted. It seems to me I can hardly go anywhere without people singing his praises."

"Is he dead?" she asked, with that open candor no one else ever offered him.

"I hope not," Mandy replied. "Because I don't want to be a sodding duke."

She nodded at that, unoffended. Another rare quality. Nothing he seemed to say or do ever amazed her.

"He's a pilot," he heard himself explaining. "Royal Flying Corps. Somehow even Reginald's bluster couldn't keep him from enlisting, although God knows Reggie tried. He bribed everyone he could think of to keep his golden boy here at home, but in the end, Aubrey just left. Just got up and went. And since he was of age, there was nothing Reggie could do about it."

"You're almost of age," Eleanore said quietly, leaning forward with her elbows on her knees.

"Yes." He smiled at her and wondered how it looked, if it was as bitter and twisted as he felt inside. "But Reginald learned his lesson, you see. He learned that when bluster and money don't work, class does. Associations do. Family links. Insinuations. I went to the recruiting station at Eton with Laurence. I did everything he did, exactly the same. And now Laurence is part of the University and Public Schools Brigade, and I'm stuck here. I was told, officially, that as I'm still months short of the legal age, I should try again later. And then I was told, unofficially, not to bother."

She held him in that frank, luminous gaze. "Why?"

"Oh, because I'm touched. Just like my mother."

He stood up. He walked to his father's desk, then to the window. The rage in him felt like a clenched fist in his chest.

"Such is the power of words, waif." He fixed his focus beyond the panes, beyond the splash of light that was his father's party to the very blackest part of the night. "Such is the power of having the ears of mighty men. Lost your heir to the cause? Don't lose the spare. Whisper to all the right people about how your second son *isn't* right. That his mother's blood flows too freely in his veins. No one's going to give a regiment to a madman."

He heard her moving. He heard the rustle of her clothing as she stood, the footsteps that took her up to the fireplace and the portrait above it. He turned about to see her.

"She died of consumption. That's what we say. I've repeated it so often now that I half-believe it myself. Consumption. As if anyone dies of that any longer."

Eleanore kept her silence, but her eyes went back to his.

"She leapt from the roof of the castle," Mandy said. "She killed herself, and Reggie moved us here. Not one mad parent but two. Bodes well for me, don't you think?"

God, there, at last: He'd reached her. Her face drained of color, and she swayed and braced a hand against the mantelpiece for support. It wasn't much, but he'd *done* it, he'd penetrated that stone-cold façade, he'd broken through to some deeper heart of her, he knew it. It was as gratifying as a fresh rush of morphine, and now the words spilled free and he couldn't stop them if he tried.

"She heard voices, she said. Odd songs no one else could hear. Told my father there was something inside her, another person or something, and it kept telling her to jump. She'd tried it twice before, but Reggie had managed to stop her, so this time she waited until dark. Her body wasn't found until the next afternoon, when finally they thought to search the grotto." The bitter smile stretched across his face again. "So. At least I know I won't lose my cunning in the end."

"Armand," Eleanore said, making his name a terrible sound, a sound so lovely and sweet and awful it pierced him to the core.

He sealed his lips together. He stood in place without moving, glaring at her, unwilling to surrender more of himself to any part of her.

"Armand," she repeated, and lowered her arm. "Do you hear songs?"

"No," he answered instantly, because he *was* cunning and he always knew the right thing to say, but this time it didn't work. His glancing blow to her heart had opened her to him, or him to her, and he realized right then that not only had he broken her enough to see into her, but that she could see into him.

And she didn't believe him.

Lies, rumors, masks; he was composed of little else. She saw it now.

He did the only thing he could. Mandy walked away, out of the study, back into the celebration of his blessed brother's life.

He did not seek out Eleanore again.

Chapter 20

Third letter from Rue, dated November 17, 1809

Darling girl,

Time has stolen too much from me. Time has ensured we shall never again meet face-to-face. But there are a few things more I must share with you before I Travel On.

The first is a Word.

How strange it seems to me now, but there was an era when even penning this Word would summon grievous punishment from our tribal Council. We dared not write it, we dared not speak it. We lived it only in whispers. In public locations it seemed best not even to think it, lest some Sighted human steal it from our very minds.

But the Council is gone now, all those hoary old men finally Turned to dust. I confess I find no small satisfaction in surviving them. Little difference their laws ever made to me. I was always too bold for their liking. And so I tell my friend who is my eyes and useful hands in these hard, blind years to inscribe the following letters on this page: Drákon.

That is who we are. That is what we are. And your blood, my child, ensures that no matter how many of us are gone now, done in by humans or our own foolish devices, we are not quite extinct.

Not damned quite.

I've hidden you well. I hid your entire line from the Council and the tribe, and of all my many notorious accomplishments—I am not so modest as to deny they are many—the secret of your life and that of your progenitors is my greatest.

They never guessed where Kit and I went, or why. They never thought beyond Europe, certainly not so far as a land of warlords and rice fields and misted mountains.

A land where dragons are worshipped instead of butchered. A place where our boy, your great-grandfather, could show his true face to the sun and fly free.

Those dead old Councilmen, those iron-fisted bastards who strangled us nigh to death with their Rules. How I wish I could gloat in their faces.

You are my final vengeance upon them, and my final grace. You hold all my hopes now, as well as my heart.

Fly well,
—Rue

Chapter 21

How did the rest of the evening play out? I've no idea. I exited the study after Armand in a daze, in a heart-thumping confusion of shock and incredulity. Even though I'd followed him nearly right away, I didn't see him anywhere, not in the hallway, not in the ballroom or the gardens after that.

I do remember some of it. I remember the duke on a graveled path with torchlight in his hair, watching me, surrounded by his fellows. I remember Miss Swanston speaking gaily to a man with silver spectacles, her head tipped to the side and him bouncing nervously on the balls of his feet. Sophia and Mittie beneath a tree, sharing glasses of stolen champagne. The colored lights gleaming, the orchestra always playing. An immense tiered cake had been placed on a central table, iced white and yellow and trimmed with garlands of marzipan. The cloying scent of it nearly turned my stomach.

At some point the cake was cut. Toasts were made. I was there for that, standing by myself beyond the bulk of the crowd.

Armand never returned to the party. And all the rest of the night, all the way back to Iverson, one thought kept rattling through my head, obsessive, persistent, offering no solutions and absolutely no peace:

Could it be possible . . . ?

I fell asleep that night in my tower without an answer.

Tomorrow I would find Jesse. Jesse would tell me the truth.

. . .

He looked down at the key in his hand and thought of all the reasons why he shouldn't be where he was, about to do what he was about to do. It was Sunday; he was technically just a visitor to Iverson, no longer a resident; he didn't want to run into Eleanore or Chloe or Westcliffe or any of them; he didn't know how believable his lies would be right now should anyone discover him.

He used to be so good at lying. At guile. At deflection. It occurred to Armand in that unlit, desolate hallway, holding that key, that he hadn't felt like *himself* in a long while. If he truly considered it, he seemed more a circus-mirror likeness of who he used to be, all wavy and wrong, stretched in impossible directions. Even thinking about it too much made him dizzy, perhaps because so much of who he was now was zigzag reflection, not truth.

So he didn't leave. His hand moved, fit the dull iron key into the dull iron lock. He was honestly astonished when, after an initial moment of stiff resistance, the tumblers turned. Unless the students had learned how to pick locks, it had to be more than a decade since anyone had tried this.

The door to his parents' bedchamber cracked open—not much, because the door was heavy, ancient planked wood scrolled with wrought iron, most of it rusted, but enough so that a stale puff of air hit him in the face.

Mandy fought a sneeze. He swiped at his nose, pushed harder at the door, and managed to open it enough to squeeze through.

It was dismal enough, all right. Easy to believe this place had been kept in shadows for nearly all his life. The floral curtains pulled across all the windows looked riddled with rot and moths. Pinpricks of daylight shone through the sagging flowers, tiny spears of sun illuminating motes.

The curtains, the bed coverings, the upholstery on the chairs and settees: all of it decayed, forsaken. He stood in a medieval suite disguised in old chintz and kingwood, and it was just as depressing as he'd expected it to be.

He'd been born in this chamber, right there in that bed. He'd had a crib in the corner, where a grimy dressing table now stood, and then a cot. Only months after he was old enough to join Aubrey in the nursery, Rose had taken her final step from the battlement, and Reginald had abandoned the castle.

They'd lived in London after that, all three of them broken and so . . . dreadfully quiet about it. All three of them just waiting for Tranquility to be completed, because somehow, *somehow,* that was going to help.

"Soon," Reginald would tell his sons, when they begged to return to the sea. Mandy remembered Aubrey crying silently at night, and how the Thames smelled like sewage instead of salt, and how Reginald always promised them the same thing in the same hearty tone: "We shall live there again soon."

Soon had proven to be a word to last nearly twelve years. *Soon* meant a succession of nannies, then tutors, in their Grosvenor Square mansion. *Soon* meant a thumping city rhythm hammering a new tempo into his life that proved so loud and busy that, in time, young Armand barely recalled the blue salty sea. Or the castle. Or his mum.

And when the day at last came that they moved back to Wessex, all three of them again, that glorious, hope-filled day . . .

How he'd wished at least one of the workers had had the consideration to knock over a lantern and burn goddamned Tranquility to the ground.

But no one had. Perhaps they'd not dared. The duke's mad vision come to life was a fearsome beast, after all.

Armand dropped his hands to his sides and closed his eyes. He breathed in the musty scent that surrounded him now—still holding the bright bite of salt beneath it—and pushed back thoughts of anything but this room. This place. His mother's realm.

Reginald hadn't changed a thing since the night of her death. He hadn't even bothered with dustcovers.

The soles of Mandy's wingtips pressed grit into carpet and stone. Dust gathered along the hem of his trousers and covered his fingers as he opened the drawer of the dressing table.

Rose had kept a diary. It was one of the few vivid memories of her he'd retained. It had been of lavender leather with the pages gilded along the edges. As a child the gilding had obsessed him; she'd let him fan the corners with his fingers over and over, trying to rub off the gold.

It wasn't in the dressing table. Or the writing desk. Or the armoire, the washstand, or the dresser. He found it, incredibly enough, beneath the mattress of the bed.

The *mattress*. Was Reginald truly that obtuse, that he'd never think to search there? Or had she kept it there as a joke, knowing it was the most obvious place to look?

Mandy glanced around, located a chair, and perched at its edge. He ran a thumb along the diary's same frayed, familiar corner. Habit.

Then he opened it and began to flip through the pages.

His mother's voice found him at once.

13 Aug., 1896: Archery Tournament. Second spot. A brisk east wind, else I should have got First.

6 Dec., 1896: So happy! Cannot sleep. Another boy, I am certain of it.

8 June, 1898: Ladies Garden Tour. Ladies Garden Tea. (Make certain Cook knows about the scones!) Ribbon Presentation at Noon. All done by three. Armand viciously fussy. Nanny says colic.

12 June, 1898: A foggy, dreary day.

25 Nov., 1898: Dear Reg says to smile more. A cheery face! That will help.

14 Feb., 1899: Leg of lamb, mint sauce. Peas. Buttered noodles. Speak to Hastings about more candles for the great room.

22 March, 1899: No sleep again. Songs songs songs. I think this latest from the diamond collar he just bought me. It seems like it it seems like it it seems so. I will not speak of how much I loathe the thing.

1 Aug., 1899: She haunts me. I am convinced the answers are there in her letters. Why can't I find them? Why couldn't she clearly say? I've been so foolish, dismissing her all these years.

3 Oct., 1900: It will not settle. It will not lessen. No peace, no no no not at all.

30 Dec., 1900: Is this what I am to suffer for the rest of my days,
    this ceaseless Voice? She never mentions such a symptom,
    only the music and the pain. What is this affliction? So
    much of my family line remains indistinct. Her words are all
    I have. Tainted blood. Have I cursed my boys, as well? How
    willingly I would offer my days for theirs.
15 March, 1901: The sky is so open. I might fly straight into it.
    no wings but I might i might.
17 March, 1901: I tried. Dear Reg. Found me.
9 May, 1901: Second try. REGINALD.

Mandy slapped the book shut. There were no more entries after that.

She haunts me.

Who was *she*?

In the dead silence of his dead mother's room, the motes danced. He sat there in the closed-up tomb of it with the channel seething beyond him, feeling his heart beat. Feeling his lungs, his hands, his feet. The pastel-skinned book between his fingers.

Hearing . . . songs . . .

The dressing table, said the sly thing inside. *Secret space. Look again.*

He dropped the diary. He went to the table, pulled out the drawer once more. Pins, pearls, an Asian-looking fan, a silver-backed comb and brush.

He went to his knees. He reached his hand in as deep as he could and knocked against the end panel.

Hollow.

Armand made a fist and shattered it.

Amid the shards of wood, his fingers found paper. He pulled out a slender stack of folded sheets, yellowed with age, tied with a peach-colored ribbon that was improbably still crisp.

The ribbon fell into a loop on the floor, only a little smeared with blood. He selected one of the sheets at random, opened it, and began to read.

> *I've hidden you well. I hid your entire line from the Council and the tribe, and of all my many notorious accomplishments— I am not so modest as to deny they are many—the secret of your life and that of your progenitors is my greatest. . . .*

. . .

Jesse was going to be off the isle for most of the afternoon. He'd told me yesterday that he and Hastings would be traveling inland to run errands for Mrs. Westcliffe. But from the instant I awoke, the itching consumed me. I discovered I'd scratched my arms and thighs raw in my sleep, great red furrows dug into my flesh.

On top of that, I felt jangled. Fidgety. Colors that had been ordinary yesterday now burned brash. The morning sky hurt my eyes. The giggly, hectic rustling of five-score girls getting ready for breakfast downstairs grated in my ears as if they had all invaded the tower and swarmed into my room.

Armand had been correct: There were spiders along the ceiling. Their webs shone garish, opalescent. They picked their way from strand to strand, loud as elephants.

Somehow I endured breakfast and chapel, eating, not thinking, not listening. As I walked back to the castle with a hand shielding my eyes from the sunlight that glared along the grass, I considered how cool the air in the grotto would feel on my skin. How very soothing its dimness would be. How just overall damned perfect it sounded, with or without Jesse.

I'd go without him. There was no reason not to, actually. If nothing else, I could sit there in the dark and eat the handful of almonds I'd stolen from the sideboard this morning. He could find me when he came back.

It was still odd to think about the dual nature of his life. The sorcery that ran through his blood, all that wisdom and song . . . and his public face, the mute, simple boy who worked at the school because his uncle did, who dwelled alone in silence in the uncultured woods.

I supposed his life was no less odd or dual than my own. Both of us understood the safety of a public face. I didn't want to imagine what might happen should either of our secrets come out.

Another tie to bind us. Another silken bond. If I spun enough of them, we'd be woven together forever, a single tapestry of Eleanore and Jesse.

But for Armand, now the loose thread in my little dream. What to make of him?

"Why, Eleanore, where on earth are you off to in such a rush?"

Sophia. She'd caught me right inside the main doors.

"Oh . . . the library."

"Oh," she echoed, nonchalant. "As it happens, so am I. Shall we?"

I was stuck then. She fell into step beside me, and together we strolled in exactly the opposite direction of where I needed to go.

I tugged my sleeves lower over my wrists to hide the scratches.

"Did you try the fizz last night?" Sophia inquired, not looking at me.

"The champagne? No."

"I must say, it wasn't swill."

We broke through a cluster of prattling sixth-years heading the other way, parting them like sharks moving through minnows.

"I didn't know we were allowed to have any," I said.

"Mercy! If you feel the need to ask permission for every little adventure, what a tedious life you're going to lead."

"True," I agreed, matching her drawl. "The absolutely last thing I would want is to lead a tedious life."

"Well, naturally. I mean, for a girl like you, life has likely had its little excitements already. You've come from some hovel near Cheapside, I presume. Some dreadfully squalid place. And now you're here. You should have tried the champagne is all I'm saying. You would have quite enjoyed it."

"Perhaps Lord Armand will smuggle some in for tea," I snapped. To my surprise, Sophia turned and regarded me with sparkling eyes.

"Wouldn't *that* be marvelous? I wager he would, if *you* asked him."

I laughed, uncomfortable. "Not likely."

"You'll never know until you try. It'd be such the coup."

We'd reached the library. I walked purposefully up to the nearest set of shelves, hoping to shake her from my heels, and pretended to study the titles.

The Ladies of Leicester's Guide to Successful Housekeeping, 1906.

Charts of the Principal Cities of the World, Including Railroad and Telegraph Lines.

One Hundred Uses for Pigs.

Sophia had lingered at my side, very much unshaken. She leaned her back against the shelves and twirled a strand of flaxen hair around one finger. "You are, after all, Armand's inamorata of the moment."

I gave up on the titles. "I'm his what?"

"Inamorata. It means *lover.*"

"I know what it means."

She took in my face and slanted a smile. "Dear me. Have I offended you?"

"Only by your ignorance. I'm not his lover. I'm not—anyone's anything."

"But you could be, if you wished it. If you looked at him the way he looks at you . . ."

"You're imagining things."

"I'm not. Everyone's noticed."

"What does it matter to you?" I flashed.

Sophia's smile faded; she gazed at me thoughtfully. "It matters to Chloe. Isn't that enough?"

I glanced around the room. Lillian and Stella were watching us from a table by a window, worry etched along their mouths. Mittie and Caroline stood taut nearby. What was their queen bee doing talking to the worker drone?

I smiled back at Sophia, pleased to etch their worry a shade deeper.

"You're right. It's enough."

"I like you, Eleanore," she said, straightening. "Believe me, I'm just as astounded by that as you are." She took a couple of steps toward the others, then paused, sending me a pale-blue look from over her shoulder. "But my head is *not* tiny."

. . .

I laid back against the smooth clamminess of the embankment. Water purled near my feet, the sound a balm against my skin. Without the light of a lantern—I hadn't chanced carrying one—the entire cavern glowed with its unearthly cool light, as if the moon had sunk to the bottom of the sea and now shone upward at me, silvery and serene.

Better. Much better here. Even the press of stone against the back of my head and shoulder blades didn't bother me. It felt like relief.

I *could* try to become smoke again, I realized. I didn't need Jesse for that. Did I?

As soon as I thought it, the itching returned, ten times worse than before.

"All right," I said aloud.

. . . *right-right-right* . . .

"Smoke," I whispered, staring hard at the stalactite directly above me. "Smoke."

Graceful and thin. Weightless. Less than air, less than . . .

It happened.

And once again it happened without pain and before I could fully even take it in. One second the stalactite loomed over me; the next I was sliding sideways toward it, rising in curls. No more itch, no more gravity. No more Eleanore, just the outline of my clothing below me, still laid out on the stone.

I wanted to laugh. I wanted to dance! I could see myself, how I'd become like vapor. I could control—mostly control—all the tendrils of me. My density.

I heard that celestial song beckoning again from beyond the roof of the cavern, the summoning of the stars, and I ached to reach them. I coiled and tumbled, wrapped around the fangs of rocks, and searched for a fissure to slip through. I was going to *fly* so, so far away—

The hidden door inside the grotto creaked open. The boy who stepped through it wasn't Jesse but Armand Louis.

I churned in place for a moment in confusion, concealed in the toothy pattern of the ceiling.

Armand, not Jesse. Armand, who'd spoken to me once about the grotto, who was likely the only other person alive who knew the secrets of the castle as well as Jesse did.

He saw my garments straightaway, crossed to them, and bent down, lifting my blouse in his hands. I wouldn't suppose him to think they belonged to anyone but me. He'd seen me wearing them at least twice before, and the mud brown of Blisshaven was distinctive.

The golden flowers of my cuff gleamed up at me like a smile.

"Eleanore?" he called, looking around. But the grotto was echoing and empty. There wasn't exactly anywhere to hide.

"Eleanore!"

He was searching the water now, so close to the end of the embankment, his shoes were getting wet.

I'm not here, I thought, frantic. *Don't look up; go get help, just go, just leave, so I can come down and get my things.*

He was stripping off his coat and then his waistcoat. He was yanking at the laces of his shoes.

Yes! That could work! I could assume my human body again while he was underwater, snatch up my clothes and boots, and dash for the tunnel—

Yet it was only my second time transforming to smoke, and it appeared there were aspects of it I hadn't precisely mastered. As Armand pulled off his first shoe, I began to thicken.

I could not prevent it. I could not slow it. And I didn't even make it down to the ground before I was a girl again. I dropped from the ceiling with my arms and legs flailing, a surprised yelp wrung from my throat, and hit the water hard.

It seems almost unnecessary to mention that I was never taught how to swim.

Chapter 22

I knew to hold my breath but not to close my eyes. It turned out that saltwater stings.

I was a fish without fins, sunk into the deep. I was engulfed in silver glow and bubbles and treacherous, looming chunks of pillars and craggy island stone. I was flailing still, unable to manage anything else, my body smacking against one of those huge ancient columns, scraping off muck.

Then there was a frothing of more bubbles, and a new shape was beside me. Armand, fleet as an arrow, grabbing me by the hair and then the shoulders. I clung to him and tried to breathe too soon when we broke the surface together, so I ended up inhaling mostly water.

He got me to the embankment, I'll say that for him.

My fingers fumbled along the slick stone but couldn't find a hold. Armand's hands had become a painful pressure against my rib cage, but no matter how hard he pushed at me, I couldn't do it. We were both flailing now.

Then, a miracle. Jesse was there, hauling me up to my feet, twirling us both about so that he stood between Armand and me.

I held on to him because my legs felt weak. I dropped my head to his shoulder because I was still heaving for air. I was naked and made of rubber and my hair was a long wet river draped along Jesse's arm, and I wasn't about to try to move anywhere else.

You can envision how it looked.

"Don't," Armand spat, pulling himself up atop the embankment with no apparent effort. I raised my head to see him better. He was pushing his hair out of his eyes and glaring at Jesse, his face white with rage. "Don't you touch her!"

He was at us at once. At Jesse, I mean. He was shoving himself between us, trying to pull me away.

"No," I rasped, holding on tight. "Let go, Armand! Let go!"

Jesse hadn't released me, nor had he defended himself. He simply lifted a hand to Armand, grabbed him by the sleeve, and said a single word.

"Stop."

And Armand did. He stood there dripping and panting, his gaze raking us both. Then he jerked his arm free.

"So this is how it is. *This* is what you're about, Eleanore? This is what you like?"

"Don't be smutty! It's not what you think."

"Actually, it is," said Jesse.

Armand took a surging step toward us again. "Bugger you, Holms, and—what? What the *hell*? You can *speak*?"

I looked up at Jesse, who glanced down at me and offered a grave hint of a smile.

"What have you done?" I whispered.

"Right." Armand was still furious. "What the bloody hell *have* you done, you lying bastard?"

"Not what you suppose, mate. Not yet, anyway."

That was the barb that hit its mark. Jesse said it and instantly something in Armand shifted. It was real and utterly unmistakable: He was standing right there next to us, so close I could feel his exhalation on my neck, and that connection that had always existed between the two of us frosted into deathly ice.

"Get your hands off her," he said, very quiet, very composed. "Or I swear I'll kill you."

Jesse met his eyes, then gave a nod. "You're not going to kill me, Lord Armand. But I'm going to give Lora my coat now, so take a breath, and take a step back."

"And close your eyes," I added around clenched teeth, because I'd started to shiver.

He glowered at us a moment longer, then turned his back. Rigid shoulders, ramrod spine, legs apart, spoiling for a fight. If his eyes were closed, I couldn't tell, but I took advantage of the moment, anyway, as fast as I could.

"I think you should just keep this," Jesse said to me, again with that smile. He brought the lapels of the peacoat together over my chest. "You can grow into it."

Armand turned back around. When he spoke again, it was still in that ghastly, deathly voice. "What's happened to your legs?"

I glanced down. The coat reached to the middle of my thighs; the scratches I'd made last night gleamed a vivid red against the bluish-pale rest of me.

"Did he do that to you?"

"No," I said. "I did it. I was asleep."

"Fuck," said Armand, very clearly, and walked back to his own pile of clothing and shoes. "Get on with whatever you want. I'm leaving."

"Wait." I trailed after him. "You can't tell anyone about this."

"Can't I?"

"Armand. Mandy. You can't tell."

He slung his coat over a shoulder and smiled at me, but it was a dire smile, as deathly as his voice.

"How charming," he said, "to hear you say my nickname at last."

"Please."

From behind us, Jesse sighed. "It's no use. It's time to enlighten him."

"Oh, are we going for enlightenment now?" Armand's eyes narrowed; he pushed again at the chestnut hair plastered against his forehead. "Excellent. Here's some for you both. I'll have you sacked, Holms, and I might have you expelled, Jones, but I've not quite made up my mind about that yet. After *he's* gone you might be more in a mood for a toss with me, since it's clear you're that sort of girl. All it's going to take is one quick discussion with my father to end your liaison forever, as no doubt you both know."

I walked forward. My hand lifted. Before I had realized it happened, I'd struck him, a ladylike slap that would have gotten me mostly jeers back at the orphanage, but I was angry enough to put some force behind it. His head whipped to the side.

Time stopped. None of us moved.

A slow, spiky throbbing began to flood my palm.

Just as slowly, Armand brought his face back to mine. There was my handprint upon him, red on white, just like the scratches along my body.

"You have no idea what you're set to destroy," I bit out. "You're not thinking. You're acting like a child."

"Actually," murmured Jesse, wry, "he's acting like a *drákon.*"

We both shifted to stare at him.

"What?" Armand said, a stifled sound.

"What?" I said, much louder.

"Show him, Lora." Jesse placed a hand on my shoulder. "Show him what you can do."

I shook my head. Of course I wouldn't. Of course not. Going to smoke was one of the very best secrets that lived between *us*. I wasn't going to add Armand to that.

"Lora. It's important."

"He won't tell on us. I'm sure he won't—"

"Dragons do not exist," Armand interrupted, still so white.

"You've got to show him." Jesse held my eyes, sober and determined, love and light behind his gaze. "He must see to know."

"But—"

"He said *dragon,* and I said *drákon.* Didn't you hear it? In his bones and in his heart, he already grasps the truth. His mind needs to see."

Armand clenched his fists. He looked from me to Jesse, back to me, and the fear that enveloped him now was strong as stink. "You're barking mad. Both of you. I won't listen to this."

"Oh," I said, hushed. "Oh."

Because in that moment, that heavy and wild moment there in the cool moon grotto, with the sea and the rocks and the sparkling walls, I understood what Jesse was telling me but what he had not actually said. I took in Armand's sharp, unhappy face and saw my handprint again, saw myself.

And everything clicked. Everything sorted out into big, obvious truths. I understood the connection I'd always felt with this reckless son of a duke. I understood his stifling fear. Without me even speaking to him of it, Jesse was confirming that all I'd suspected of Armand and his mother last night was, in fact, real.

. . . the true nature of our world is for matters to arrange themselves along the simplest of paths. . . .

What could be simpler than grouping us all together?

"You don't have to be afraid," I said, looking past Jesse to Armand. I tried to smile at him, but my lips felt numb and I don't know how successful I was; he glared back at me like a cornered animal, desperate to bolt.

Jesse's fingers tightened on my shoulder, a silent message of reassurance.

"I'm sorry I hit you," I said, and meant it, right before I went to smoke.

Jesse, I noticed, caught the peacoat before it reached the ground.

. . .

We met that night in Jesse's cottage. Armand had wanted us all to go to Tranquility, but Jesse pointed out, correctly, that it was far less risky for Armand and me to steal away to the cottage than it would be for Jesse and me to steal into the manor house.

"You've got a staff of—what?—thirty? Thirty-five these days?" Jesse asked. "Lora can't be found alone with either of us at Tranquility. Her forced departure from the school would be an inconvenience to all of us. But the only person who cleans my home is me."

I thought personally that if I was able to evaporate quickly enough, it wouldn't matter who caught me where or what they said. It might even prove amusing.

Oy, guv'nor, she was there and then she turned into bloomin' smoke, I swears it! Only three pints of ale tonight at supper, guv, I swears!

But I didn't want to sneak all the way out to Tranquility, so I said nothing.

Armand and I sat across from each other at Jesse's table. A stack of letters and a diary had been placed in the middle between us. The diary was mostly jaunty and newer, but the letters were very old, combed with very old, spidery writing. Combined, they'd spelled out a message that was nothing short of electrifying.

When I'd finished reading the last page, my fingers were trembling.

Jesse, of course, had noticed. He'd said we could discuss everything after eating and was now moving about in the tidy little kitchen, slicing bread, finding jam. Stoking the coals in the oven into brightness for a kettle and tea. He'd muted his music again and so these small, comforting sounds were the only noises to be heard; thankfully, tonight had a brilliant moon, so the Germans weren't bombing. Even the crickets were quiet.

It jarred me to see Armand in Jesse's setting. His dark hair, his intense blue eyes. His posh tailored shirt and high starched collar and clean fingernails. He seemed to just *gleam* more than either of us. Perhaps that's what being born into a fortune could do. Polish you up to a shine, light up the world, no matter where you wandered. I expected this was as informal as he ever got, but compared to schoolmiss me and hired-hand Jesse Holms, he was done to the nines.

Even in the half-light of the candles, Lord Armand looked ill-suited to this rustic place, a foreigner discovering himself in a foreign land.

The kettle began to steam. The berry-ripe scent of the jam caught in the vapor, wafted over to me in long, draping coils.

Do you even know how to do that? I wondered, watching Armand from beneath my lashes. *Have you ever even had to boil your own water for tea?*

I should try to be kinder. He'd had more than a shock today, I knew, and it wasn't as if I didn't understand how it felt. But a mean little part of me still smarted over being derided as *that sort of girl*. If he was uneasy, that part of me was glad.

The brittle cold ice that had frosted inside him, that had connected us in the grotto, had melted. In its place was . . . I wasn't sure what. Something new. Something that felt like swords and power. Gleaming, like him.

"What is it?" he muttered, his eyes moving to me. "Why are you staring?"

"I'm not," I replied. But I felt the blood rise in my cheeks.

Jesse thwacked a plate piled with bread between us, followed by half a brick of butter and a crock of raspberry jam. A knife—the long skinny kind that looked like it should be used for poking things, for digging insects out from tree bark—stuck up from the middle of the red goo.

Armand regarded it all without moving. I reached for the bread.

"How can you eat? After everything, how can you be hungry?"

"I'm always hungry." I used the knife to smear butter across the bread, and then jam. It was brown bread, sour to the jam's sweet, but I didn't care. It tasted superb.

Jesse served the tea, then took the chair beside me. As soon as I was done with the bread, he laced his fingers through mine and brought our joined hands to rest atop the table, in plain sight. Happiness began its tingling spread up my arm.

It wasn't subtle, but it was clear. Armand leaned back from the light, staring disdainfully at a fixed point beyond us both.

"How long have you known about him?" I asked Jesse, using my free hand to gesture toward his guest.

"Forever. Nearly as long as I did about you."

"God, Jesse. Why didn't you say anything?"

"He was a shadow of you." Jesse shrugged. "His background is diluted, his dragon blood less strong. Even with you in his proximity, I wasn't certain any of his *drákon* traits would emerge. He hasn't anywhere near your potential."

"Pardon me," Armand said, freezingly polite, "but he is still right here with you in this room."

"Do you mean . . . I did it?" I asked. "I made him figure it out? What he is?"

Jesse gave me an assessing look. "Like is drawn to like. We're all three of us thick with magic now, even if it's different kinds. It's inevitable that we'll feed off one another. The only way to prevent that would be to separate. And even then it might not be enough. Too much has already begun."

"I don't want to separate from you," I said.

"No." Jesse lifted our hands and gave mine a kiss. "Don't worry about that."

Armand practically rolled his eyes. "If you two are quite done, might we talk some sense tonight? It's late, I'm tired, and your ruddy chair, Holms, is about as comfortable as sitting on a tack. I want to . . ."

But his voice only faded into silence. He closed his eyes and raised a hand to his face and squeezed the bridge of his nose. I noted again those shining nails. The elegance of his bones beneath his flawless skin.

Skin that was marble-pale, I realized. Just like mine.

"Yes?" I said, more gently than I'd intended.

"Excuse me. I'm finding this all a bit . . . impossible to process. I'm beginning to believe that this is the most profoundly unpleasant dream I've ever been caught in."

"Allow me to assure you that you're awake, Lord Armand," I retorted, all gentleness gone. "To wit: You hear music no one else does. Distinctive music from gemstones and all sorts of metals. That day I played the piano at Tranquility, I was playing your father's ruby song, one you must have heard exactly as I did. Exactly as your mother would have. You also have, perhaps, something like a voice inside you. Something specific and base, stronger than instinct, hopeless to ignore. Animals distrust you. You might even dream of smoke or flying."

He dropped his arm. "You got that from the diary."

"No, I got that from my own life. And damned lucky you are to have been brought into this world as a pampered little prince instead of spending your childhood being like this and still having to fend for yourself, as I did."

"Right. Lucky me." Armand looked at Jesse, his eyes glittering. "And what are you? Another dragon? A gargoyle, perchance, or a werecat?"

"Jesse is a star."

The hand went up to conceal his face again. "Of course he is. The. Most. Unpleasant. Dream. Ever."

I separated my hand from Jesse's, angling for more bread. "I think you're going to have to show him."

"Aye."

A single blue eye blinked open between Armand's fingers. "Show me what?"

. . .

He must have known this moment was near, because only this morning he'd gotten up in time to venture out to the back meadow, where lush knots of foxtail and buttercups nodded through the grasses. By the light of dawn he'd picked a dewed bouquet—he'd thought for Lora—and brought it back to the cottage.

It rested now in his mother's green glass vase on the sill of his bedroom window, all the dew dried, fragrance sowing wild and heady into the blankets and pillows of his bed.

Too much to hope, it seemed, that he could have shown it to his dragon-girl in there.

Jesse beheaded one of the buttercups, brought it to the table where the two of them waited, Lora with her hair down and her gaze steady on his, still chewing her slice of bread. A smudge of jam traced an endearing curve along the bottom of her lip.

And Armand, leashed but so coiled inside, looking absolutely as if he'd rather be anywhere else in the world right now than here with the two of them.

You and me both, mate, Jesse thought.

He uncurled his fingers to reveal the buttercup in his palm. Armand's gaze flicked to the flower, but that was all. Lora, who knew what was imminent, wiped at the jam, closed her eyes, and turned her face away.

He would never, ever let her down. Jesse steeled himself, opened his soul to the fire, and let the agony come.

. . .

"A star," Eleanore said once more, after the light had faded and Mandy had gotten his vision back.

He'd shoved away from the table without being aware of it; his chair now laid on its side by his feet. Holms no longer had that brilliant, horrifying glow that had blinded Armand, that had seemed to boil his blood to a peak and send his mind into a fierce frantic babble: *It can't be, it can't, it cannot be.*

"Dragon protects star," Eleanore announced coolly from her place across the table, her half-eaten bread pinched between two fingers. "Star adores dragon. And now you can't betray us."

. . .

Like a dazzling reminder of the impossible made possible, the golden buttercup shone upon the table, lucent metal against the duller wood. Armand couldn't seem to stop staring at it, even as we talked about the letters. Even though he'd held it in his hands and turned it over and over, searching for the hoax that wasn't there.

The metal buttercup sang a metal song now, and it was clear both of us heard it. A very pretty song, too, jingling soft as fairy bells beneath our conversation.

I'd definitely remember to slip it into my pocket before I left. Armand probably had mountains of gold stashed away somewhere inside his mansion, anyway.

"I knew it was your mother's side," Jesse was saying, perusing one of the letters, "but I didn't know how far back it went. These are over a hundred years old. That's, say, four or five generations. Possibly even six. And for each generation, they could have passed through either the matriarchal line or the paternal. It's astonishing your mother had them at all."

"But who was the author?" I asked. "Who was Rue?"

"No idea." Armand ran a hand through his hair. "Reginald hasn't been too keen to talk about my mum or her family. I do know she was the only child of a baron and that her parents, my grandparents, died right before the marriage. He mentioned once that their estate was sold off, taxes or something. And it seems that Rue was a member of the nobility, whoever she was. It's signed *M. of L.* in each. That's how titles were disguised from the public in the news back then, the dailies and such. So maybe she was still wary enough of this 'tribe' to hide her true name."

"And that of your ancestor." I tapped my finger to one of the sheets. "Or someone was, since she dictated it. That might be why there are no other proper names besides *Kit,* and no envelopes."

"*M* could only stand for *Marchioness*. Surely not too difficult to track down. We've a copy of Standish's Peerage of the Empire back at Tranquility. I think it traces lines back past the fifteenth century."

"Unless your Rue wasn't *of* the empire," Jesse pointed out.

"Or she fabricated it," I added. "That's what I would have done, if I'd truly wanted your line kept hidden."

Armand dropped his head into his hands and made a sound like a groan. "If I wasn't barmy already, I'm going to be."

From somewhere in Jesse's bedroom, a clock gave a single chime.

"It's half past three," he said abruptly, standing. "You need to get home, both of you. Louis, I'd like to keep the letters here, if you don't mind. I want to go over them again."

I came to my feet. "And ask the stars about them?"

Jesse nodded. Armand only shook his head, gloomy. There were bruises under his eyes that hadn't been there yesterday.

"Ask the—fine. Splendid. Keep them if you like. Burn them. Turn them to gold or silver or lead. In the morning I'll wake up and none of this will have happened."

"No, lordling," I said to him. "You're never going to wake like that again, and you're never going to be able to forget."

"Bugger you, waif."

"And you."

He walked past both of us without another glance or another word, opened the door, and disappeared into the night.

I went to Jesse and wrapped my arms around him. After only a second's hesitation, his arms lifted to embrace me, too.

"I don't want to go," I whispered.

I felt his chest expand beneath my cheek. "This is going to be much more difficult than I anticipated."

"Which part?"

"All of it." He brought a hand to my hair, his fingers weaving through. "Things are about to change rapidly now, Lora. He'll come back to us stronger and stronger. He's going to crave you more and more, and not having you will eat him raw."

I frowned up at him. "What do you mean?"

Jesse tucked a strand behind my ear, his eyes emerald dark, his lashes tipped with candlelight. "It will be in his nature. He'll feel compelled to claim you, and he won't stop trying to do that. Ever. When that happens—"

"That is not bloody going to happen."

"When that happens," he said again resolutely, "I want you to remember two things. One: I've loved you since before he even knew you lived. Two: Spare a little pity for him. This isn't entirely his fault. He was born into his role, just as you and I were. But, Lora-of-the-moon—only a *little* pity, all right?"

"My pity may reach as deep and wide as the ocean," I answered. "But my heart is already claimed."

To prove it, I clutched his shirt and lifted myself to my toes and brought my lips to his.

Sweeter than raspberry jam, warmer than candle flame, softer than bread.

People often spoke with religious rapture of milk and honey, but if I had nothing but Jesse to consume for the rest of my days, I'd die a heathen beast, content.

Chapter 23

Monday dragged on. The lack of sleep I'd been accumulating over the past week or so was creeping up on me. I fell asleep in my chair during Vachon's lesson in the ballroom, listening to Caroline struggle to add some *brio* to her Rossini.

She wasn't succeeding. With Vachon tapping his wand hard into his palm, she repeated the same passage again and again, and the world went fuzzy and my head dipped down to my chest.

I awoke to my classmates' giggles and monsieur's wand whacking me upon the shoulder.

At least he hadn't hit me across the knuckles. I fancy it was that he didn't want to risk bruising them; the duke might ask for an encore any day.

I staggered through the rest of my classes. I took notes; I conjugated verbs. I sketched pomegranates and limes in fat, crumbly strokes of charcoal on Bristol board and earned a word of praise from Miss Swanston, who seemed to think my simple lines were the product of modernist inspiration, instead of *I just want this done*.

I listened for Jesse's music, which came to me finally during supper, floating up from beyond the windows of the dining hall.

He would be standing out there in the dark, I knew. Standing in the moonlit gardens, looking up at the glass.

We had no better reliable means of communication. Paper notes could be intercepted; I might get caught at any time whenever I tried to sneak to the grotto or out to the green. But if Jesse was near enough for me to hear him, I could understand him. Intricate music, dulcet music, his silent symphony moved from *brio* to lullaby with such effortless beauty, Vachon would weep. And every bit of Jesse's song was meant for me, a one-way message only I could receive.

Tonight it said, *Rest, love. Sleep.*

That seemed a fantastic suggestion. But I decided to drop by the library before I made my way up to my tower.

The truth was, despite what I'd told Sophia yesterday, it was the one place I tended to constantly avoid.

Imagine a man crawling through a desert, dying of thirst. He needs water; his parched dreams are of water; only water is going to save him.

And then at last help comes. A bloke walks up to him and says, "Sorry, chap, no water for you. But here's a lovely glass of powdered sugar. You can have as much as you like!"

Books had always been my lifeline. Even at Moor Gate, they'd offered me books to keep me biddable, and I'd plunged into worlds I'd never guessed existed. Fiction or fact, it hardly mattered; books transported me beyond my own mental borders. Maybe they even helped preserve my sanity. What there was of it.

Iverson girls were not exactly encouraged to dream beyond their borders. There'd be no tales of amazing submarines or folklore of the Fay found here. Mrs. Westcliffe didn't even subscribe to a newspaper.

However, if I wanted to read about needlework or making cheese, I had my pick.

I don't think I was the only one unimpressed with the selection. After supper, the library always filled with students, most of them from my class and Chloe's, but all they did was sit around and play games and chat about things like fashion and boys until curfew—until I would have been blue in the face with boredom. Usually a teacher or Westcliffe sat with them, I suppose to ensure no spontaneous moment of meaningful conversation erupted.

It was yet another part of life at the school in which I would be considered an interloper, and on any other night I'd walk past the library entrance without a second thought.

But . . .

Armand had mentioned that he had a book of peerage at Tranquility. All these blue-blooded girls mucking about: I thought it a good chance Iverson might, as well.

Perhaps I could riddle out the mystery of Rue and Kit. Perhaps I could find them before Armand did.

Perhaps . . . I could find my own family somewhere in there.

It was a notion I'd not allowed myself to surrender to until now, but it had been boiling inside me for hours, bubbling up against the thin wall of my resistance. It was feverish and stubborn and full of absolutely stupid hope, so of course I'd tried to ignore it.

Armand was a dragon. I was a dragon. Armand's genealogy could be traced. My genealogy . . .

We might be related, even distantly. I didn't have any familial feelings toward him, really, but for the first time ever in my memory, I had a place to start.

The library itself was just as anyone might picture a library in a castle would be, jammed with tables and overstuffed chairs, long and very tall, with shelves and shelves of books that reached so high—at least two stories—that there were sturdy wooden ladders affixed to hooks on every wall. The ladders were on rollers, and the hooks attached to brass rails, so in theory one could slide from one end of the room to the other without having to descend.

In practice, though, we were forced to climb down again if we had to move over even one shelf. It was tedious and likely yet another reason why there wasn't a great deal of reading done in this place.

Somewhere up there, shelved away, might be the answers I sought. There might even be some forbidden Poe or Wilde or Stoker hiding amid the many uses for pigs, crouched back in the shadows and hoping for the light.

No one paid me any mind as I made my way to the catalogue bank. I flipped through the handwritten cards of authors and titles; the only way to find something here was to know at least one of those things. The shelf number for the book would be inked in beside it, but each shelf contained about fifty books, so you had to hang there on the ladder and read every spine of every one until you came across yours.

Let it be said that nothing was ever accomplished in haste at Iverson.

I didn't know either the author or the name of the tome I wanted. I couldn't even remember the title Armand had mentioned last night. I tried looking under *Peerage,* but the only book listed there was *Peerage of Royal India,* circa 1835, which I doubted would help.

Yet there I was ten minutes later, perched high on the ladder of the eastern wall, perusing shelf number 229, which probably no one had gone near in decades, the dust was so deep. I found India's peerage right away; the spine featured ornate lettering stamped in real gold foil and what looked like a sapphire affixed near the top, but it was only paste.

All the rest of the titles seemed geared toward specific family lines, especially ancient Saxon kings.

Not useful.

Below me, the tables were all rimmed with girls. And there was Mrs. Westcliffe in a chair cozied up to the fireplace, a trio of eighth-years at her feet. She had a book in her lap and was reciting what sounded like a sonnet to them. I was near enough to catch a few lines and realize I'd read it. It was one about love and a noble knight whose sacrifice for his pure maiden grants him a place of honor amid the constellations forever and ever.

Right.

I was getting filthy up here. I'd have to be careful not to touch my shirtwaist before washing my hands or I'd catch hell from Gladys about the marks.

A small commotion began at the door. Almeda hurried in, trailed by two other maids and a man in a khaki riding uniform, who had taken off his black-brimmed hat and was holding it under one arm. The chevron markings of an officer were stitched onto his sleeves.

All the girls at all the tables fell silent. I doubted anyone recognized the man, but we all recognized what he meant.

Mrs. Westcliffe found her feet. She handed the book of sonnets to one of the eighth-years and went to meet the man. They conferred for a moment, his head to her ear, and then she stepped back again and gave a terse nod. Her gaze searched the room.

"Miss Bashier," she said.

Everyone looked around. Mittie sat, unmoving, at a table beneath a stained-glass window. A lion with a mane flaming outward like the corona of the sun pranced behind her, locked in the glass.

Sophia was sitting next to Mittie, and she finally gave her a small bump with her elbow, so Mittie got up. Sophia stood, as well, but only Mittie walked around the table and crossed the rug to the newcomer and the headmistress.

"Come with me, my dear," said Mrs. Westcliffe, and put her arm about Mittie's shoulders and drew her from the room.

The man offered a bow to the rest of us, then followed. Almeda followed him, the other maids followed her, and then there were only students left, staring at one another with round, round eyes.

· · ·

Mittie's father had worked for the office of the prime minister. He wasn't even a soldier. But he'd been in Paris, consulting with a general there, when a bomb from an airship blew him and his hotel to pieces.

· · ·

Two more days passed, and Jesse still hadn't let me know it was time to meet.

Unsurprisingly, I hadn't heard a peep from Armand, either. When a boy tells you to bugger off, it usually means he's done with you. For a while, at least.

I leaned out my window on my third night alone and studied the stars. With some effort, I'd been able to pry open my thousand-diamond window far enough so that if I pressed my body to the wall and let the stone take my weight, I could fit my head and shoulders through to the open air.

A night of patchy clouds and moon. A night with a tinge of

purple but not that full, amazing saturation of color it sometimes had. The clouds were mauve lined with platinum, drifting against the tinsel stars.

The sea sloshed against the island bridge, regular as a heartbeat. It was oddly comforting to think that it would always do that, always be like that, no matter who won the war.

But it was the stars that fascinated me. I heard them singing now. Rather, I'd always heard them singing, but since Jesse, since I'd Turned to smoke, I heard them singing *to me*. Before it had always seemed as if they were just another chorus in countless strange choruses troubling my life. Now I heard the words.

dragon-girl, come, come, last of the chosen, beloved of our beloved, come up.

All three times I'd Turned to smoke in the grotto, I wanted to reach the stars so badly it obsessed me. I wasn't sure what would have happened had I escaped the cavern. Would I have gone up and up? Would I have ever returned to earth, even for Jesse?

I couldn't say. As I looked at them now, they winked and twinkled back at me like a fiery scattering of my most bosom friends.

There was only one way to find out.

I Turned to smoke, sifting up and out through the window.

They pulled at me right away, drew me in threads from the castle. I blew out over the liquid silver of the channel, marveling at the shrinking world, at a pod of seals darting beneath the surface of the waves. At the nests of gulls dotting the mainland cliffs beyond the island, eyes that stared and beaks that clattered.

Higher. The separation of land and sea below me was a jigsaw line of rough forest and fields edging rougher water.

yes, yes, you're free like us! come up!

There were winds up here, brutal ones. I felt myself begin to tear in their currents and tried to duck down beneath them again, but they were too strong.

up!

This was bad. I was having difficulty holding myself together. Within minutes I'd been swept so far out to sea, I couldn't even see the coast any longer. Everything was indigo and silver and dark, and the stars in their almost-purple heaven.

up!

I strained to obey. Attempting to slide beneath the river of wind only thinned me more; I gathered my strength and forced myself upward, becoming more like a blade than a sheet of vapor, and when I ripped free of the current I found myself in blessed calm, tumbling about until I was able to right myself and go calm, as well.

hello, sang the stars, their hallelujah chorus of lights twinkling now every color of the rainbow.

Hello! I would have sung back, a hallelujah of my own, had I a voice.

. . .

I Turned back to a girl inside Jesse's cottage. He was in the bedroom; it was all very dark. I Turned by the pair of chairs near the back window, because there was a blanket slung over one of them and I used it as a wrap.

I stood there, feeling like I needed to catch my breath, although I wasn't even winded.

I was wearing flesh again. I was firm inside a body, feet flat on the floor. I made a fist and pressed my nails into my palm. When I released them, red crescent moons marked my new skin.

Jesse emerged from the bedroom carrying a candle spilling wax into a holder, closing the door behind him. He didn't look sleepy, like I'd woken him up. He looked tired, though. There were lines bracketing his mouth. His hair hung long and limp.

"I've been out," I said.

"I know."

"I listened to your friends. The stars."

"I know."

"I want you to finish the story now, Jesse. I want to know what happened to the Elemental after Death came to her in the desert. What was their ending?"

He walked to the chair that'd had the blanket and folded himself into it slowly, one limb at a time, as if he had to consider how it would happen. He was wearing a regular shirt and trousers and even shoes. Surely I hadn't actually woken him?

"Where did I stop?" he asked absently.

"When she—the unraveling."

"Oh, yes. Death had come and done his work. But in her dying moments, even as she unraveled, the goddess reached up and dragged what stars she could from the sky down to earth and sent them into the seeds of men. So that a few humans, a very few, would be born with fragments of her power and theirs. It was a gift of gold and death."

"Death? That's a gift?"

He gazed up at me.

"Wait a minute," I said. "Do you mean to say—are you telling me that your powers are linked to your death? Is *that* your sacrifice?"

"Power begets power. It requires it, too."

"For God's sake." I stomped over and threw myself at his feet, just like one of the eighth-years with Mrs. Westcliffe. "Would you please stop talking like that? Would you please tell me in plain words what I want to know?"

Jesse leaned forward and touched the fingers of one hand to my bare upper arm.

"Everyone dies, Lora. I don't mind knowing how my own death is going to come about."

"That's—that's—" I groped for the right words and could only come up with ones I'd blurted to him before. "That's completely unfair!"

"Aye," he said, softly.

"You've got to stop, then! Stop making gold. Stop doing anything like that that brings you nearer to dying."

Despite the lines of exhaustion, his lips smiled. "Breathing? Existing? Being who I am?"

I buried my face against his knees, then wrapped my arms around his legs to pin him in place. I realized then that the blanket I wore was one of the fleece ones that had been in the carriage on the very first night we'd met. It was his, not the school's. All along it had been his, and he must have put it in there for me.

Because, even then, Jesse Holms had known what I needed.

His fingers began a glide up my arm, across my shoulder. Down my back. He drew figure eights upon me, five-pointed stars, our initials entwined.

"When will it happen?" I asked, to his knees.

"Well, not tomorrow, in any case. Or the next day, or the next. I've years in me yet, dragon-girl. Don't fret."

We stayed like that, he in the chair, me on the floor, with his hand tracing those clever, soothing patterns along my skin, until the sky began to pale and the morning larks began to stir in the woods and break into their own versions of heavenly songs.

Chapter 24

"The Duke of Idylling has invited you to go yachting with him and his son."

"Yachting?" I knew I was gaping at Mrs. Westcliffe, but I couldn't help it. The last thing I'd expected was for Armand to try to reach me by way of his father. I wasn't even entirely certain what yachting was.

I guessed my expression made that clear. "Yes, Miss Jones," said the headmistress testily. "Yachting. It means to go out to sea on a yacht. For pleasure."

It was a bright and balmy Friday afternoon, and I was trapped in her office. Blue sky, blue as cornflowers, shone through the tall windows around us. One of them had been opened; bridal lace surged and fell with a lazy breeze, and everything smelled of cut grass.

All the other students were off enjoying the hours of freedom that stretched from now until Monday morning, but I had been summoned here and directed to one of those fat, sinking wing chairs to contend with a person whose mood seemed far more suited for a wintry day than this one.

"How kind of him," I said. It seemed a benign enough response.

"The trip is scheduled for Sunday. I suppose, just this once, you may be excused from chapel."

I sat in silence, trying to make sense of it. Was this good? Was this bad? Was this how I wanted next to encounter Armand, trapped on a boat with him?

Mrs. Westcliffe talked on. "I am unclear on the precise number of guests attending. A few of the better sort of locals might be present, along with any visitors currently staying at the manor house. Everything will be perfectly proper. I am confident you will have a most delightful time."

"Yes."

"But," she added—a hard, expelled sound; perking up, I thought, *Ah, here's the rub*—"none of the other students are included in this invitation. Only you."

I pursed my lips. I looked innocent.

Westcliffe pressed her palms together atop her desk, forming them into a steeple. "Miss Jones."

"Yes, ma'am."

"I understand that you have been without proper social or maternal guidance for most of your life. It's possible you do not understand all the potential consequences of this situation."

"Indeed," I said, waiting for her to simply go ahead and forbid it.

"It is considered an honor to be . . . plucked from the crowd, so to speak. There are fine families in the district who have lived here for generations, none of whom have been so favored with the duke's attention. Yet I wonder if it's not truly His Grace himself behind this invitation, but his son."

"Perhaps there's a piano aboard."

Her nostrils flared. "Don't be pert. This is not a matter of jest,

Eleanore. If you go on that yacht, your every move will be scruti-
nized. Your every word will be dissected. Your manners must be ir-
reproachable, and they must be so at all times, even if you believe
you are alone. Do you understand me?"

Do not steal anything. Do not belch or scratch your arse.

"Yes, ma'am."

"Should Lord Armand choose to favor you with *his* attention,
you will react politely, graciously, but always with an aloof, dignified demeanor. It could be that he believes you to be . . . less than
what you are. You will show him the error of that thought."

"Yes, ma'am."

He'd already seen me naked. I supposed everything from there
would be a step toward *dignified.*

"Do you still have the bangle he presented to you?"

The *cuff,* I wanted to correct her. As if I was going to lose it.

"I do."

"Wear it. Let him see that you value it, but take my strong advice on this, Eleanore. Do not accept another such gift from him.
One is permissible. Two becomes a suggestion."

"Oh."

"Do we understand each other?"

"Yes, ma'am. We do."

A smatter of laughter and applause reached us from beyond the
open window. Some of the girls had set up a game of lawn pins, and
the sudden *crack!* of a ball hitting its mark echoed through the room.

"One last thing," said Westcliffe.

"Yes?"

"Wear your uniform. It won't hurt to remind everyone of where
you belong."

I puzzled over that for the rest of the bright day.

· · ·

That night, Jesse said to me, "You should go."

We were in the grotto, the remains of our midnight meal scattered around us. I was sleepy and full and in his arms, and I'd never known that wet stone and a couple of blankets could be so comfortable.

I'd gone to smoke five times more since my trip to the stars, but no dragon.

I'd tried, though. For Jesse, I'd tried. Smoke was all I'd been able to accomplish.

"Armand needs to see you. He's had all this time to think things through. He'll have questions. He'd rather go to you with them than to me."

"I hardly have answers."

"Then guess."

I huffed a laugh. "Are you serious?"

"I am. Either you guess or I do."

That brought me upright. "You mean, you've only been guessing at what you've been telling me?"

He gave a grin, folding his arms behind his head. "Not entirely. Sheathe your claws, love. The stars tell me most of it. I hypothesize the rest."

"You *guess.*"

"Very well. If that's the word you want."

"That was *your* word!"

"Come back down," he invited silkily, opening up the blanket again. "It's cold without you."

I didn't, not right away. I fixed him with what I hoped was a steely look, but Jesse was right. Without the shared warmth of our bodies, the grotto rippled with cold after nightfall.

"What *is* a yacht?" I asked, burrowing back against him, yawning. "Is it like a fishing boat? Like a steamer?"

I was a child of the city, remember. The only boats I knew were the punts and masted ships that went up and down the brown waters of the Thames.

"It's a symbol for the sort of men who've never had to fish to eat, and who would board a steamer only if it were one of style. You were born on a boat, you know."

Every muscle in my body went rigid. "What?"

"Not a boat," he corrected himself. "A steamship. A big one."

"Jesse—"

"Aye, I got that from the stars. But that's all they'll say of it. Believe me."

I lay there, my mind spinning, trying to make sense of this gift I'd been so casually given. Trying to seize hold of its enormity.

I knew something about my past now. I *knew*.

A steamship! I'd only ever seen adverts for them in the papers. They were huge, sharp-edged iron monsters topped with funnels big enough to swallow whole homes, far too massive to dock anywhere near London. They had names like *Mauretania, Lusitania, Olympic*.

So I hadn't spent my entire life in the city, as I'd thought. Once I'd known the ocean and at least a port town.

"Water dragon," Jesse whispered. "If you don't accept the duke's invitation, people will talk."

"I don't care about that."

"I know you don't. But it's not merely you who will be affected by this."

"Really? You like Armand so much?" I heard the skepticism in my voice.

His chest expanded on a long inhalation, lifting the upper half of me with it, since I had draped myself over him. "Star adores dragon. Although I wouldn't say I adore him precisely, or even like him. It's more that . . . now that you've come, now that his powers are awakening, I'm connected to him. Like brothers, almost. And we don't get to choose our families."

"If you say so."

"We're in a bubble here, Lora. The island, the school, even the countryside. We're all encased in a beautiful bubble, and the war seems far beyond our ken. But it's not. Anything might happen. It won't hurt to have Armand on your side, no matter what comes."

"On *our* side, you mean," I said sharply.

"Yes. That's what I meant."

I chewed on my lip. "I wish . . ."

He waited, no sense of urgency in his body or his breathing, only his customary, contemplative peace.

I tipped my face to see him. "I wish all this was over," I said. "I wish there was no war and that I wasn't in school. I wish I didn't have to do what everyone else says and that we could just . . . *be*. Together. The two of us."

. . . *us-us-us* . . .

I don't know if he heard the question beneath my tone, if it was as blazingly obvious as I feared it was, or too smothered to detect. But Jesse lowered his lashes and met my eyes; he looked much more like himself now than he had a few nights ago. Clear gaze, golden glow. Summer storms behind the green.

"We've all the time in the world," he said, and bent his head for a kiss, one of those sweet drowning ones that filled me with nectar and honey.

I hoped it wasn't a guess, but I didn't have the nerve to find out. I wanted too badly to believe him.

. . .

I walked into my room the next afternoon following tea and realized at once that it had been violated.

Not that you could tell by looking. It *looked* just as it should: bed made, furniture dusted, floor swept, pitcher of clean water. Everything looked right.

But it wasn't.

I stood poised at the doorway, my eyes reflexively searching for what they couldn't see. Sight didn't help; my other senses did.

The air feathered a chill across my skin.

It tasted of chemical perfume, of jasmine and sugar.

And the music of my tower had changed. Gruffer, coarser, a cry of warning rising from the golden buttercup and oval leaf tucked in the armoire, taken up now by my cuff—but the circlet of roses was silent. In its place wavered a thin new song, one I'd heard only once before.

I crossed to the bureau and opened the drawer where I had stored the circlet, stuffed behind my stockings . . .

. . . and pulled out instead Mrs. Westcliffe's green sapphire ring.

"Well, sod you, too, Chloe," I muttered, and clamped my fingers hard around it.

I raised my chin, closed my eyes, and listened. She couldn't have been here that long ago. I'd been gone only an hour, and her syrupy scent still polluted everything. She'd taken my brooch . . . where?

Downstairs. Its song came to me high and faint.

Not the wing housing my fellow students. Not the teachers' wing, either, which was a relief. And she hadn't taken it outside the castle. Not yet, anyway.

I stalked the corridors with the sapphire ring still in my fist, slicing my way through the listless Saturday clusters of students and maids.

Winding up, finally, in front of Mrs. Westcliffe's closed office door. My brooch sang from behind it.

Not good.

A pair of fifth-years by the turn in the hall spotted me and paused, curious. I bent down and began to work at the heel of my boot, as if it had come loose. They moved on, and I was alone.

I stood and tapped lightly at the door.

"Mrs. Westcliffe?"

No response. The door eased open.

"Ma'am?"

I took a step past the threshold.

"I just came by to ask if . . . you . . . knew . . ."

The office was empty. I tossed a quick glance back at the hallway, then tiptoed all the way in.

". . . that you could use some bleeding locks in this school," I finished.

Chloe's perfume began a fresh assault upon my nose. I wrinkled it in distaste as I hurried toward the desk.

As I'd suspected, one of the drawers had been left conspicuously agape. There were papers and glass weights and a broken jeweler's box inside, everything a mess. And there, right beneath it on the rug, was my brooch. The pin to secure it had been bent practically in two.

Amateur. Anyone wanting to wear it would have noticed if the pin was that damaged. She'd have been smarter to warp it just enough so it no longer met the hook.

Chloe Pemington was in sore need of a lesson in being smart.

I stuck the brooch in my pocket and straightened the contents of the drawer as best I could. I shoved the ring back into its box— there was nothing I could do about the broken hinge—and was closing it all up again when I heard an unmistakable castanet-clip of footsteps echoing down the hall.

I jumped up, looking wildly about for a place to hide: nothing. The curtains were useless, the bookcases too shallow, the secrétaire too exposed. If I went to smoke, I'd leave my clothes behind—and the brooch—and my cuff—

". . . excused absence, of course," Mrs. Westcliffe was saying. "I assume you will remain in contact with Miss Bashier during this time?"

"Yes, ma'am."

Sophia. Westcliffe and Sophia, right outside the door.

"Good. Good." The door began to swing wide. "And may I rely upon you to convey our continued condolences to her and her family?"

I leapt behind the door. I flattened myself against the wall as the wooden panel bumped to a stop against the toes of my boots.

"You may, Headmistress."

Westcliffe hadn't noticed the bump. She entered the chamber, leaving Sophia to linger at the doorway. With just the long, vertical gap of the door and jamb between us, we stood only inches apart.

"I wired for flowers, naturally, but one does wish to offer a more *personal* touch in such times. Miss Bashier has been with us for many years. And she has, I believe, a younger sister nearly of school age . . ."

"I'm certain the Bashiers appreciate your sympathy, ma'am." Sophia's voice had that unctuous pitch; she shifted on her feet, clearly ready to be cut loose.

"Yes." The headmistress had reached her desk and taken her seat. All she had to do was dismiss Sophia, who'd close the door and there I'd be.

"Very well. Good afternoon, Lady Sophia."

"Good—"

Perhaps I moved. Probably I did. With the door practically to my nose, I'd been holding my breath, and what likely happened then is that I released it. Regardless, what happened *next* is that Sophia turned her head a fraction toward the gap. Toward me.

And she saw me. One pale-blue eye grew wide, then narrowed. I glared back at her.

"I say!"

Westcliffe spoke up. "I beg your pardon?"

"Ma'am—did you see it?" Sophia dashed into the room, leaving the door untouched. "There, at the sill?"

I peeked past the door's edge. Sophia was pointing to the window behind the desk. Westcliffe rose to her feet, turning her back to me.

"What?"

"There—just there! It was a little bird pecking to come in!"

Westcliffe's shoulders relaxed. "Is that all?"

I angled around the door. Sophia prattled on.

"Oh, but birds can become such a serious nuisance. I'm sure it was a mudlark, and they're especially devious. One never knows what trouble they'll get into next."

"Mudlark? I don't believe I'm familiar with . . ."

I was away! I took a few running steps from the office door before stopping, waiting for the inevitable. I stuck my hand in my pocket and ran my thumb over the golden roses, stroking a fresh song from their ridges.

Sure enough, Sophia caught up to me within seconds, her eyebrows risen nearly to her hairline.

My voice came out like ground glass. "Where is Chloe?"

"The front parlor, maybe. Or her room. Someplace with mirrors."

I spun on my heel and headed toward the parlor, because it was closest. And that's where I found her, laughing, and seated and surrounded by her toadies, a box of chocolates on the floor being shared between them.

I walked up, and every one of them but Chloe glanced up at me—then began to snigger.

"My, my," Chloe murmured, studying the chocolate she held. "I do believe this one's gone off. It stinks like a cesspit." Her eyes lifted. "Oh, wait. It's only the guttersnipe."

"Or perhaps it's your perfume," I said cordially. "You always smell like a whore."

"It's *French,*" retorted Runny-Nose, before Chloe could speak.

"Then she smells like a *French* whore."

"Aren't *you* the eloquent young miss." Chloe's gaze cut to Sophia, standing close behind me. "Slumming, little sister? I can't confess I'm surprised."

"I'm merely here for the show," Sophia said breezily. "Something tells me it's going to be good."

I took the brooch from my pocket and let it slide down my index finger, giving it a playful twirl. "A fine try. But, alas, no winner's prize for you, Chloe. I'm sure you've been waiting here for Westcliffe to raise the alarm about her missing ring, ready with some well-rehearsed story about how you saw me sneaking into her office and sneaking out again, and oh, look, isn't that Eleanore's brooch there on the floor? But I've news for you, dearie. You're sloppy. You're stupid. And the next time you go into my room and steal from *me,* I'll make certain you regret it for the rest of your days."

"How dare you threaten me, you little tart!"

"I'm not threatening. You have no idea how easy it would be to, say, pour glue on your hair while you sleep. Cut up all your pretty dresses into ribbons."

Chloe dropped her half-eaten chocolate back into its box, turning to her toadies. "You heard her! You all heard her! When Westcliffe finds out about this—"

"*I* didn't hear a thing," piped up Sophia. "In fact, I do believe that Eleanore and I aren't even here right now. We're both off in my room, diligently studying." She sauntered to my side, smiling. "And I'll swear to that, *sister.* Without hesitation. I have no misgivings about calling you *all* liars right to Westcliffe's face."

"What fun," I said softly, into the hush. "Shall we give it a go? What d'you say, girls? Up for a bit of blood sport?"

Chloe pushed to her feet, kicking the chocolates out of her way. All the toadies cringed.

"*You,*" she sneered, her gaze scouring me. "*You* with your ridiculous clothing and that preposterous bracelet, acting as if you actually belong here! Really, Eleanore, I wonder that you've learned *nothing* of real use yet. Allow me to explain matters to you. You may have duped Sophia into vouching for you, but *your* word means nothing. You're no one. No matter what you do here or who you may somehow manage to impress, you'll always be no one. How perfectly sad that you're allowed to pretend otherwise."

"I'm the one he wants," I said evenly. "No one's pretending that."

I didn't have to say who.

She stared at me, silent, her color high. I saw with interest that real tears began to well in her eyes.

"That's right." I gave the barest smile. "Me, not you. Think about that tomorrow, when I'm with him on the yacht. Think about how he watches me. How he listens to me. Another stunt like this"—I held up the circlet—"and you'll be shocked at what I'm able to convince him about *you*."

"As if you could," she scoffed, but there was apprehension behind those tears.

"Try me."

I brought my foot down on one of the chocolates, grinding it into a deep, greasy smear along the rug.

"Cheerio," I said to them all, and turned around and left.

. . .

It happened that a yacht was a big, sleek boat, although to call it just a boat would be akin to calling a peacock strutting around in full plumage just a bird. It was made of wood, it floated, like the ordinary punts I knew. But all similarity ended there. The duke's yacht was three levels of hand-rubbed teak and glass and brass so polished I couldn't look at it directly. Beneath the open sun it looked trimmed in fire, too dangerous to go near.

Yet there *were* people going near: menservants in snowy-white jackets, plus the duke's other guests, a stylish crowd in cool linens and crisp straw hats poking about with walking sticks and parasols. They passed the other vessels moored at the village docks—the smelly rust-streaked trawlers, the battered rowboats, a handful of sailboats—as if they did not exist.

Armand and the duke stood by the plank that angled up to the yacht and watched as the motorcar they'd sent for me pulled in close. The chauffeur came around and opened my door and I scooted out, slammed at once by the wind.

I was beginning to realize that the wind was a constant here. In London we had days—weeks—of heavy, choking smog that ate up the streets and sky, trapped in place by all the buildings. But this part of the country was so wide and clean and open, the people so glossy and well fed.

Jesse was right. It was a land in a bubble.

I clapped a hand to my own straw hat, my same plain one from the donation bin. The brim flapped up and backward along an old fold, a line in the weave that was already cracked.

It was Armand who greeted me, stepping forward while his father only fidgeted in place.

"How good to see you, Miss Jones."

That debonair tone, the friendly press of his hand upon mine. It was such a contrast to our final moments in the cottage that I couldn't help but smirk.

"Thank you for having me," I replied, loudly enough for the duke to hear.

"But I haven't," said Armand under his breath. "So far."

I tugged back my hand. "Ever the gentleman, aren't you?"

"I try. Come aboard, waif. Come and experience a gentleman's world."

First I curtsied to the duke. He wore no hat, so his hair blew stringy and long and the sun lit the jaundice yellow beneath his skin to a sickly sheen. He gave me a nod, his gaze twitching only briefly to mine.

"Have you been out to sea before?" Armand asked me in his public voice, escorting me up the plank.

"Once. But I don't remember it."

"I think you'll like it. Most people seem to find it relaxing, but I've always thought it was more invigorating than not. Once we get going, I'll take you to my favorite spot at the bow. With enough wind in your ears, it feels rather like you're flying."

We exchanged glances.

"Or so I've always imagined," he said guilelessly.

Inside the boat—the yacht—twenty or so of the linen people had gathered in what resembled a formal salon, drinking and talking in clipped, nasal accents. The white-jackets meandered through them, bearing trays of tea and champagne and something darker, like sherry. The air was laden with gossip and jewel songs.

Armand snared a flute from the nearest tray. "Champagne?"

"Water," I said, which earned me an arched brow.

"Really?"

I shrugged a shoulder. The champagne sparkled palest amber in its glass, scented enticingly of grapes and yeast. But I remembered how it went with Armand and the whiskey. I wanted to keep my wits.

"Well, then. I'm sure we've a pitcher around here somewhere."

He murmured a few words to the waiter with the tray, who bowed and vanished into the crowd.

We were clearly the youngest people aboard. There didn't seem to be anyone else even near our age, and there was no question that we were being noticed. Eyes ogled. Hands were raised to mouths to hide the whispers. A few of the older men looked me up and down with a bold combination of interest and speculation, but most of the stares were merely curious.

The duke's son and the pauper girl. I suppose as a couple we were the most interesting thing in view.

I took the champagne glass from Armand and finished what he hadn't. As Sophia had said, it wasn't swill.

So much for my manners.

"Why am I here?" I asked curtly, handing back the empty flute.

"Because I invited you."

I dropped my voice. "Did you find out anything about Rue?"

"Is that why you came?"

"No, I came because I simply can't get enough of people looking down their noses at me. The girls at school are getting frightfully lax about it."

"Are they? How remiss of them. We're taught from the cradle how to look down our noses, you know, we rich sons of bitches. Perhaps Westcliffe's curriculum is a tad too liberal these days."

"Why, yes, my lord," I said very audibly, "I *would* enjoy seeing the rest of the boat."

"The yacht."

"That, yes."

He grabbed two more flutes of champagne and my arm, and we edged our way out of the salon to the wraparound deck.

To my surprise, the yacht was moving. It was very smooth and very quick; the dock had already receded to the size of a pencil, all the other boats dwindling to the size of toys. A cloud bank had mushroomed up beyond the hills and waterfront homes of the mainland, dove gray near the top, a darker pewter below.

"See those?" Armand gestured to the clouds, sloshing some of the champagne out into the channel.

I nodded.

"And see all the boats still docked? Even the fishing boats?"

I nodded again, uneasy.

"I believe it might rain," he said.

I had to keep a hand on my hat; all my pins were giving. "Why are we still heading out?"

"Oh, because it's such ripping good fun." He took a long gulp of champagne. "Being trapped at sea during a gale because Reggie wants to. What could be better?"

"Armand—"

"Don't worry. If we sink, we'll swim back together to shore. We'll use your bewitching chapeau as a float."

The nose of the yacht dipped hard, then rose. The wind began a low howl around us.

"I'm not blotto," he said, in response to my expression. He turned to the railing and chucked the empty flute to the waves. "Not yet, in any case."

I went to stand beside him. The flute had sunk beneath the surface already, on its way to an eternity of sand and tide.

"That's good. Because I can't swim."

"Why did you go swimming in the grotto, then," he asked too pleasantly, "if you can't swim?"

"I wasn't swimming there. I was smoke, at the ceiling, when you came in. Falling into the water was an accident."

"You're welcome," Armand said.

I refused to ask for what. We both knew.

The clouds built. The yacht nudged farther into the sweep of blue.

"Jesse thought you might have questions," I said at last.

His smile came sardonic. "Jesse."

"He thought you might like asking me better than him."

"Why does he call you Lora?"

I hadn't expected that, and angled a glance up at him. He was facing the distance still, his profile sharp, his jaw set. The color of his irises exactly matched the far waters.

"It's just my name."

"Not the way I heard it."

I pulled at some loose hair that had blown into my lashes, nettled. "Is that really what you want to know?"

"No, not really. I want to know if you've slept with him."

Oh, if I could be any girl but me. A thousand responses flitted through me, a thousand different things to say, ways to behave. And from the thousand, all I could capture was:

"Why?"

He faced me. He said nothing.

I found, to my dismay, that I could not hold that burning look. I ducked my head and began to remove my hatpins, and when I finally spoke, I made certain my words remained beneath the wind.

"Did you locate Rue?"

"There was no marchioness named Rue listed anywhere in the history of the peerage," he said tonelessly. "There was no name that even sounded like that."

Without my hat on, the world seemed abruptly much brighter, and much louder, too. I took hold of one of the brass-fire rails as the yacht gave another dip.

"Have you ever wondered," Armand said, "if anything around

you is really real? What if it's all made up? What if all this is just my mind playing tricks? Dragons and smoke and bloody gold stars. What if you're an illusion, Eleanore? Wishful thinking?"

I couldn't help my laugh. "Do you truly suppose you'd wish for me?"

His lips tightened. He shook his head, squinting out, and I knew I'd said the wrong thing. His knuckles had gone white on the railing.

"I want to show you something." Still clutching my hat and pins, I pushed back the cuff of my sleeve, lifted my arm before him so that my wrist showed. "Do you see that? That scar?"

Armand tossed the other champagne glass overboard—it whistled end over end before making its splash—then used both hands to bring my arm closer. "No . . . wait. Yes." He looked up. "What's it from?"

I said, very steady, "That's what happens when you tell other people about the foolish things that live in your head. When you begin to wonder aloud about illusions and reality to those around you, when you have none of the power and they have it all. You become dangerous to them. You're a threat, even if you're only a child. We hear the songs. They don't. But they're right and we're wrong, and when they strap you into the electrical-shock machine, they use these leather restraints, see, and they strap you in hard because they know that when the lightning shoots through your body, you're going to buck and scream. So they gag you, a special gag so you don't bite off your tongue. And you jolt against the board, and the leather binding your wrists and ankles cuts into you until it's actually red with blood. *Red* red, always stiff. And that is why, Armand, you should shut the hell up about the nature of illusions. Forever."

His face had gone, if possible, even paler than before. There was none of the horror I'd expected to see; I'd been trying to provoke it, because horror was more tolerable than compassion. But, once again, Armand did the unexpected. He bent his head and pressed his lips to the inside of my wrist, right up against the scar and my hammering pulse.

My fingers opened. The pins clattered to the deck and my hat floated free. Out to sea.

"I hope the Germans get them," I said. "I hope they blow that place to hell along with everyone in it."

"I hope it, too," he said.

. . .

The rains did catch up with us, but not before a group of the linen gentlemen had a chance to cast their lines off the back of the yacht. That was about all they did with them, too. They stood in the shade with their drinks and laughed and told jokes while three of the servants sweated and baited the hooks and minded the nets and everything else, calling, "Here, sir, if you please," should any of the strings hitch.

Then the gentleman in question would come up, grab the pole, and reel in his fish. Easy as pie—for them, at least.

The sky began to lower upon us. The clouds simmered black and grim. From a place that seemed not all that remote, lightning flashed and the thunder that accompanied it rolled in a deafening *boom!* across the waves.

The yacht started turning about. Everyone was packing it in, but then one of the lines snapped hard, lifting up from its dragging angle.

"Sir! Sir!" summoned the servant, and a man bustled up to take over the rod.

He couldn't spin the reel against it, whatever it was. Even with the manservant struggling to help, it wasn't working. In the white wake of the boat, the creature fought ferociously for its life, thrashing and twisting, trying to break free.

It took three men and a brace to reel it in. Two men to net it. There were cries of excitement and hands thumping backs in congratulations, and all the cheery fellows shouting, "A shark! A shark, by gad!" as it spasmed on the deck and gradually bled to death in the confusion of netting. Before it was completely lifeless, they hoisted it up by its tail on a hook and let it hang upside down while they all postured by it, still grinning.

I stood far back from the commotion; Armand had become swallowed in the crowd. I don't know how, I don't even know if it was true, but I felt that shark's dying gaze, its cold flat eye fixed on me.

I couldn't look away from it, all the blood and silver skin. An unspeakable thought had entered my mind and it would not leave.

This is what they do to monsters. This is what they'd do to me.

Chapter 25

Try thinking about something else after witnessing that.

I couldn't.

We'd landed back at the wharf in the pouring rain. I'd been driven back to Iverson in the pouring rain. I'd dragged myself out of the motorcar, along the driveway, wrenched open the castle doors, all through the pouring rain, and all I could see the entire time was the gasping death of that fish.

I'd bet that someone was eating it by now. I'd bet they sautéed it in chunks. Chopped off its fins, stewed its head. Tossed its guts to the cats. Hacked free its jaws to mount on a wall, good for drunken reminiscences for years to come.

I buried my face in my pillow. A scream was building within me, but instead of freeing it I dug my fingers into the sheets and pushed it lower and lower into my chest, until it came out as a rasping moan.

Why did you think there aren't any dragons around anymore? whispered a voice inside me—not the old voice, the familiar fiend, but one of plain ordinary common sense. *What did you think happened to them? That they all died off of old age?*

I hadn't thought of it. I hadn't considered it once, to be honest.

But the history of Europe had always included dragons. And knights. And lances. And lots and lots of stabbings through hearts.

I remembered what Rue had written about a *drákon* council and their rules about secrecy. Despite her obvious disdain for them, perhaps those rules had worked somewhere. Perhaps somewhere what was left of her tribe still existed, huddled and human-looking, like me.

But in a bottomless-pit-fearful part of me, I knew it wasn't true.

Don't worry about it. You're not really even a dragon, are you? All you are is a girl who's sometimes smoke. No one's going to stab that.

I sat up. I dragged the pillow to my lap and bit my lip and stared hard into the darkness of my room. I hadn't lit my lamp or candles.

Rain pelted the diamond window.

Just a girl. Just smoke.

It pelted my hands, then my arms as I opened the hinge.

Just an orphan. Just a guttersnipe. A nobody.

"No," I said out loud. "I'm a dragon."

For the second time ever, I Turned in the tower and flowed out the window, but I wasn't headed for the stars or even Jesse's cottage. I was going to the far woods, the ones that ended at the cliffs overlooking the sea, where no one lived, and no one worked, and no one would be.

Raindrops shot through me, but they didn't hurt. I might well have been part of the mist that curled up from the ferns and grass, that reached wraithlike arms up through the boughs. I skimmed lower and lower until I *was* the same, except that the mist was wet and I was not. Smoke is always dry.

I didn't really choose a place to Turn back. I was simply going until I wasn't any longer, vapor until I wasn't, and then I was standing in a small clearing. I was skin now. Definitely getting wet.

I looked up, blinking at the sting of the shower. I took in the clouds and the black crowns of trees encircling me, so much taller than I was. Branches shivered; water plopped to peat. Drenched bark gave off the scent of pungent wet wood. Mud and grass squelched soft between my toes.

I stretched my arms above my head. I tipped back my face to the elements and opened my mouth to drink in the storm.

Now, I thought, washed clean and cold. *I'm ready now.*

Since it was true, it happened.

Smoke came first, but only for a wink of a second, too quick for me to register anything like disappointment. Then smoke transformed into solid shape, and it was not my human one.

I was still standing in the clearing in the grass-threaded mud. Yet I was on four legs, not two. I blinked again at the rain beginning to bead upon my lashes, which had gone thick and were faintly shining. Looking around the clearing, I could tell that I stood higher up than before. Much higher. My neck was slender and long and I could bend it nearly all the way about to take in my body: also slender, also shining.

I was a dragon of gold, as if Jesse had touched me and transmuted me but not taken my life. I was sinuous and covered in lustrous golden scales, all the way almost to the tip of my tail, until they faded into purple.

I had a mane, too, mapping a line down my back. It looked like a ruff of silk or cut velvet. I folded my neck around almost double so that I could rub my chin on it. Silken, yes, but also jagged. Combing my chin through it sent quivers of pleasure down my spine.

Then I saw my wings. They were folded against my back, metallic. Without knowing how I did it, I opened them, using muscles I didn't even have as a person. The ache of moving them for the first time felt delicious; I did it again to fully bask in it.

I had *wings*.

I don't know how to describe what I felt then. I was amazed and afraid and boiling feral inside. I slashed my tail through the rain and realized that it was barbed when it hit an oak tree and I got stuck.

No problem. I pulled it out and danced around, delighted at the fresh, gaping hole in the trunk.

My new body came with a weapon. That pleased me.

I recalled my worry about my tongue splitting—which seemed beyond funny now; I mean, my tongue was the least visible part of me—and flicked it out to see if that had happened, but I couldn't tell. I could taste the air, though. I could taste everything in it, minerals and salt and fat, fresh rain. Houses miles out. Horses and sheep, dogs and cows and foxes. People.

It was then that I realized that Rue had been wrong about this Turn, too. There was no suffering. There was only wonder.

If I was a monster, then by the stars, I was a glorious one. Jesse had told me once that I was a beast better than any other, and now I knew it to be true. If the shark-hunters or lance-bearers came for me, I'd chew them to chum. Maybe I'd do it, anyway.

I slitted my eyes at the clouds. Just looking at them made me hungry in a way I'd never felt before. Ravenous, but not for food.

For flight.

I crouched down, got ready to spring, and beat my wings.

I made it as far as the treetops before losing control and crashing back to the ground, taking out another oak and a grove of ferns.

I tried it again.

Again.

All right. Flying was turning out to be stickier than the Turn, but that was fine, too, because I had the rest of my life to practice.

I settled into the mud and examined my talons. Shiny gold, sharp as razors, and I could dig them as deep as I wanted into the flesh of the earth.

I smiled, or tried to. I laughed, but no sound came out.

I flipped around and rolled in the mess of the clearing, ripping out what was left of the grass, getting filthy, feeling as gleeful as I'd ever been. When I decided to stop, I was panting, sated somehow, so I stretched out my neck and rested my chin in the mire and let my eyelids sink not-quite closed.

Only then did they emerge. Two boys, their faces sketched ashen in the dark, both of them in slickers. They approached me from opposite sides of the clearing with oddly identical gaits: halting, cautious, moving sort of crablike sideways with a palm held out in front of them—as if to ward off my temper, which to my mind was a very good thing.

The blond one reached me first. He touched me carefully on the neck. His hand felt like cool fire.

I opened my eyes all the way again, studying him.

Then the brown-haired one, still mimicking the other. Another hand on me, higher up, though, and his palm felt like pure heat.

"Lora." Jesse smiled. "Lora-of-the-moon."

"Good God," whispered Armand.

And with that, I Turned back into the schoolgirl they both knew, only one standing nude in the mud.

. . .

I thought I'd at least have the filth of my roll left covering me, but apparently when I Turned, I went stark clean.

Jesse got his slicker off first. The sleeves flopped past my hands and the hood obscured half my face.

"How did you know?" I asked, pushing back the hood.

Jesse only smiled again.

Armand said, "You—you called me."

He sounded bewildered. Even wearing his raincoat, he looked like he'd gone for a swim in a sea of debris. I brushed a soggy clump of leaves from his shoulder.

"No, I didn't."

"I heard you. I heard you clear as anything."

"Yes," agreed Jesse, as the rain flattened his hair and turned his shirt translucent. "I heard you, too."

"I didn't call either of you," I insisted. "I don't know what you mean."

Armand scowled. "I was in bed, and I heard you say my name. Like you were right there in the room with me. And then I . . ."

"What?"

"He was pulled," Jesse finished when Armand didn't. "Just as I was. Pulled out here by instinct to this place to be with you. To witness what you had become."

What I had become. I was a *what* now. I pressed both my hands over my heart, feeling its reassuring beat. Humanlike.

Jesse touched his lips to my cheek. "I told you I would be with you when it happened," he said softly. "Well done."

"Yes," said Armand, hollow. "Congratulations."

I went to my knees. I didn't want to, and as soon as I started to buckle, they each had me by an arm, but I still went down. Slowly, irrevocably, into the squishy suck of mud that didn't seem nearly as wonderful now as it had a few minutes past.

"Did you eat?" Jesse asked, just as Armand said, "Are you going to faint?"

"No, and no." I pulled until both my arms were released, then lay back on the ground. Rain on my face, pooling in the corners of my eyes. If there were a few hot tears mingled in there, the pair of shadows leaning over me wouldn't be able to tell.

"Jesse," I said. "Are there any more dragons left on the planet besides me?"

"There's bloody *me*," Armand interjected. But he knew that wasn't what I meant and shot a look at Jesse, as well, expectant.

Jesse came down into a squat at my side. "I don't know. I'm sorry. Sorry to both of you. But I honestly don't. If there are . . . I don't feel them. Not like I did you."

I swiped at my eyes and asked the question I'd never allowed past my lips before. "What about my parents?"

"No," he answered, a single word with oceans of meaning.

No. Of course not. Because if they'd been alive, they would have found me by now, wouldn't they? If Jesse could summon me, if Armand could awaken to his powers through me, then certainly the two beings who had given me life would have figured out how to claim me before now. They would not have left me in Blisshaven, abandoned me to Moor Gate, on purpose.

The logical side of me realized I wasn't truly alone. But, oh, right then in the storm and the sludge, logic was useless. Lodged in my heart was a splinter, one that I knew was the death of my parents. The death of my hope for them. So *alone* wasn't even the best word for how I felt.

Left behind. That was more like it.

My gaze landed on Armand. Like Jesse, he had given up standing to squat beside me. His hood had fallen away. His face dripped with rain.

"Remember that shark?" My lips barely moved. "From the boat?"

I didn't have to explain what I meant. He looked down and away. Nodded.

"Don't do this in front of anyone. Ever," I said to him. "Don't let them see."

"For God's sake, Eleanore, I seriously doubt that's going to be an issue. I have no clue how you did . . . that. I don't know how you spoke to me in my room at Tranquility. I don't know how you go to smoke, or flash your eyes like that—"

"Flash my eyes?"

"When you're angry sometimes," Jesse jumped in. "Or emotional, if you'll forgive the word. Your eyes luminesce. It's very beautiful."

"I just hear the songs," Armand said quietly, silvery black raindrops spattering his head and back and shoulders. "And I feel things. That's all."

"That's how it begins," I countered. I struggled to get upright again, and once again both of them helped. We stood linked in a row awhile longer, none of us speaking, until Armand dropped my hand and turned away.

"I've got to get the motorcar back before anyone notices. Bribery only goes so far, and I've already used up this quarter's allowance."

Before either Jesse or I could say anything, he gave a hard shake of his shoulders, like a dog trying to dry its coat, pulled up his hood, and walked back into the blind of the trees.

"He's good at that," I said.

"Lonely." Jesse raised his brows at my look. "I can't help it. I feel him now, too."

I didn't know why *Armand* would feel lonely. At least he had his father, and a brother. And a real home. And probably uncles and aunts and cousins, not to mention all of high society eager to befriend him.

Except for the ones who thought him mad, I supposed. The ones his father had turned against him.

"You should go, too." Jesse ran a hand down my arm; his palm came away covered with mud. "You'll sleep well tonight, dragon-girl."

As soon as he said it, I knew it'd be true, because the exhaustion hit me, drained what heat was left from my muscles, and sent me swaying again. But I held my ground.

"What about you?"

"I'll sleep," he said, coming close, shining with water. He was really, really drenched.

"No. I meant, what about if I sleep with you?"

It was already a night of firsts for me. Why not add another one to the pile? Actually, two: This was the first moment I'd acknowledged to myself that Jesse had been gradually putting a distance between us. Not physically, but in every other way, and I knew I wasn't imagining it. He'd mentored me, he'd fed me, he'd encouraged me and shone the only true light upon my soul that anyone ever had. I belonged to him. Dark wine, dark longings. I'd been his since the moment his fingers had brushed mine that amethyst night by the carriage. Since I'd eaten the orange. Since I'd followed him into the grotto and listened, enraptured, to the legends he'd spun around us both.

But I'd never spent the whole night at his house. I'd never done more than dream of us in his bed together.

He gazed at me, his expression veiled, though there might have been pain in the shadows behind his eyes. His mouth opened on a reply, but before he could say what I knew he was going to—*no, not tonight,* which could all too easily become *not ever*—I added quickly, "For an hour or so. That's all. Then I'll go back."

The veil lifted; he changed course without warning. "Yes. All right."

I was a very skilled liar. You had to be if you hoped to live by your wits. It was no wonder he couldn't tell.

Or maybe he could, and had decided not to care.

. . .

That was how I discovered a sweeter darkness than even the one from our stitched-together dreams. I drowsed in his arms in his bed with my head cradled to his bare shoulder, one leg thrown over him. I couldn't sleep and I couldn't stop smiling, so I was glad that with the curtains closed it was pitch-black and he couldn't see.

I let his body seep new warmth into mine. I listened to the sleepy, delicate songs of gold that lilted through his cottage, that lilted through him and me together, binding us in a net of notes, and thought, *Now you are mine, as well.*

. . .

"You seem different today, Eleanore."

"Do I?"

"Yes."

Sophia had caught up with me as I walked to French class. With her books hugged to her chest, she matched her pace to mine and gave me a leisurely perusal.

"Rather less glum than before. Rather more . . . content, I'd say. Glowing. Oh! Was it the yacht trip? Having Mandy all to yourself for a change? *Do* tell me all about it."

I shook my head. "Don't be absurd."

"Did he kiss you finally? Is that it?"

"No, Sophia."

"*Zut alors!* He did! He did, didn't he? You're blushing."

"I am not. I'm warm. That's all."

"It's an icehouse in this part of the castle. You're not warm."

We slowed to a stop. Students joggled by us, a few of them tossing us dirty looks for blocking the narrow hallway.

"I don't blush over kissing boys," I said to her, holding her eyes.

Her lips curled. "Well. That's worthy of note. Bold little Eleanore. What *is* bringing out that wholesome glow, I wonder?"

"We're going to be late," I said, but before I could push on, Beatrice rushed up to us both.

"Did you hear?" she gasped. She had a hand pressed to her side as if she'd actually been running.

"No, what?" Sophia was curious but was acting as if she mostly wasn't. Beatrice in general annoyed her; Beatrice being dramatic annoyed her even more. Interesting how I could tell that about her now.

Beatrice threw a pent-up glance at me. Whatever it was, she was dying to spill it but didn't want me to hear, too, in case it brought me further into their forbidden circle.

"What?" snapped Sophia again, aggravated.

Beatrice decided her news outweighed my insignificance.

"The Marquess of Sherborne is dead!"

I frowned. Why was that title familiar?

All of Sophia's cool pretense vanished. Her mouth made an *O* and her books slid down to her stomach. "Where did you hear such a thing?"

"Westcliffe was discussing it with some of the professors in her office with the door open, and I was passing by. The duke received the telegram this morning, and it's all the talk of the village. His aeroplane was shot down by the Huns!"

The Marquess of Sherborne. Of course. Aubrey, Armand's older brother.

Chapter 26

So it became that my third visit to Tranquility was not for a party but a wake.

Fittingly, the sky was overcast with storm clouds again, although the wind wasn't perfumed with impending rain. It was a tepid, muggy day, made muggier by the fact that I was dressed entirely in black, which seemed to repel the breeze but soak up the moisture.

We all wore black, we Iverson girls. It had taken Almeda and the castle staff nearly four days to dye all the formal uniforms.

I reeked of dye. Tranquility reeked of grief.

The manor house would be open to the public all week. Tradition dictated that the locals would come by to pay their respects in stages: fishermen, farmers, merchants. Today was our day, and a line of ebony-clad girls marched up the grand curving driveway—pinkish grit from the crushed shells speckling our shoes—without anyone speaking a word.

Mrs. Westcliffe led the way, carrying an offering of white lilies. Lady Chloe was just behind her, carrying nothing but her fine looks, which seemed even more heightened in black. I had tried to hang behind at the end of the line, but all the youngest girls were there, and the three teachers at the very back gestured for me to get ahead and move to the front with my own class.

That's how we entered the mansion. That's how we greeted Armand, because the duke wasn't even there. I heard people whispering from the corners of the black-and-white parlor that he was upstairs, locked in his quarters.

By the time I reached Armand, the strain was clear on his face. Most of the girls had just curtsied and gabbled a few words. Chloe, on the other hand, had thrown her arms around him and held her lips to his cheek, a few seconds too long for anyone to mistake it as a mere token between friends.

My turn. I gave no kisses. No embrace. I held out my right hand and he accepted it, his gaze drifting down, unanchored, to stare blankly at where we connected. His fingers were cold, barely curved around mine.

"Remember the shark," I said, the first thing that came into my mind.

Armand looked up again. A little of the focus returned to his eyes.

Be strong, I was telling him. *You are more than this moment,* I was trying to say.

He understood me, I think. His fingers regained their life, clasping mine hard.

Tonight, I mouthed to him, another something that just popped into my head.

He nodded, I moved away, and the girl behind me took my place.

Eventually, the duke did come down to make his greetings, and if it had been quiet in the room before, now you could hear a mouse squeak.

The best word to describe Armand's father was *ghoulish*. His suit hung off him—he'd lost even more weight since the day on the yacht—and his face reminded me of the jack-o'-lanterns we used to carve on All Hallows' Eve, all sunken red eyes and bony outline and uneven teeth. The Iverson girls shrank back from him en masse; his starving, jittery desolation looked actually contagious. Only Mrs. Westcliffe approached in her assured clip across the marble tiles. She'd already passed the lilies to a footman, so she was able to take up both of his hands and keep them in hers as she murmured something to him none of the rest of us could make out.

None of the rest of the people, I mean. Maybe I had dragon hearing since my transformation, because I heard her as if she had spoken just to me.

"Reginald," Mrs. Westcliffe had said. That was all.

And there was so much anguish behind that one word that I knew not to mistake it as a mere token between friends.

. . .

That night, I waited in the tower for the dark to reach its full bloom. My plan at first was to go to Jesse and then Armand, but Jesse himself had quashed that.

I hadn't seen much of him since our night together. Only a few occasions around the grounds, working with Hastings, driving the carriage or cart. Once a fleet, illicit caress of my cheek in the bamboo grove of the conservatory before class. His music to me since then—including tonight—had all been the same reassuring tune.

All's well, beloved. Catching up on sleep. We'll see each other soon.

I had decided to let him have his way, since he'd been gracious enough to let me have mine.

The sounds of the castle settling in for the night seemed both repetitive and heartening. How quickly I'd become accustomed to this place, I realized. I was even rather fond of it. My tower, the old-fashioned teachers and lessons, even the other girls, snooty and insolent and so untouched by grimy reality.

The bountiful food.

On an evening such as this, with the moon smiling and the stars sparking to life in milky, silvery bands, I almost wished I could stay here forever. Which seemed a very upside-down thought, because as much as I appreciated my life in the castle, it was a place that had been constructed with only one purpose in mind: to hide from death.

But there was no true hiding from death. It would hover and wait. It didn't even need a war to claim lives, although I'm sure the war helped. Death had taken Jesse's parents and mine, Mittie's father, and Armand's brother. Too many inmates from Moor Gate to count—if anyone but me had even been counting.

Everyone who'd built this fortress was dead. Everyone who'd set the stone and mixed the mortar and thought about the trajectory of arrows and swords with each new layer in place: dead. Everyone they'd ever loved, too. You could make all the secret tunnels in the world, cross your fingers for all the low tides to steal away, but Death was the Great Hunter, and he would still end up finding you.

"But not now," I whispered to the stars. "Not here, not tonight."

Almeda arrived for her final evening check. I bid her good night and got a nod in response, accompanied by a stern "Get into bed, then, miss. Dreams don't dream themselves."

Another half hour, just to be certain. And then, right as I was about to do it, lift into smoke, I heard a tiny scratching at my door.

I whirled about. It wouldn't be Jesse. He was back in his cottage; I could feel him there.

A voice spoke, the barest slight sound beyond the wood. "Eleanore."

I let out a *siss* through my teeth and yanked open the door.

"Sophia. What are you doing here?"

She stood alone on the landing in a robe of some voluminous, floaty material. Probably silk, like the dress she'd lent me. It billowed around her in white tucks and folds, turning her into a very pale ghost.

"May I come in?"

I couldn't think of a suitable reason to refuse her, and, anyway, it was likely the most civil thing she'd ever said to me. I backed up, lifting a hand in permission, and she floated into my room.

"Oh. This is . . . pleasant," she said, looking around at the plain stone walls.

"Yes, it is."

"I'm sorry I've not come before."

"We're not at Sunday tea, Sophia, and there's no one else listening. What do you want?"

She wandered to the bed, which took only a few steps. Her hair fell in a long bright braid down her back.

"I didn't want to ask in front of the other girls, but I wondered if you would deliver a message to Armand for me."

For a bizarre moment, I thought she knew what I'd been about to do, and how—but then she turned around and kept talking.

"I know you'll see him before I will. Maybe you'll slip out, or he'll find a way to come to you. Please don't bother to deny it. I can see the truth on your face. I've seen it on his ever since you came. I don't care about that, I swear. Mandy and I . . . We used to be friends. In childhood. In London. Only friends, I promise. He was such a sad little brat when we were first introduced, it was all I could do to endure him. But he's not *really* a brat. I'm sure *you* know. Deep down, he's quite funny and kind. And when I saw him today at Tranquility, in that horrid parlor, I just . . . I lost my words, I suppose. I lost what I'd meant to say to him. That I was sorry. I didn't know Aubrey as I did Mandy, but he was always nice to us. Not teasing the way some big brothers are, but good-natured. He was so clearly the duke's favorite; I know that must have been hard for them both sometimes. But Mandy loved him. So I wanted to say how sorry I was, that I remember Aubrey and I'll miss him, as well. But I didn't."

She seemed to run out of air. Even in the voluminous robe, she looked smaller and more vulnerable than she ever had, though that might have been only a deception of the shadows.

"All right," I said gently, and escorted her back to the door. "I'll tell him."

Tender creatures, these aristocrats. Who would have guessed?

. . .

I knew no other chambers at Tranquility but the ones I'd been in before. The parlor, the ballroom, the study. I figured Armand's bedroom would be on the second floor, possibly the third. But it turned out it was on the fourth, a lone secluded chamber, the last before the wing ended in breezes and open space.

A rough wall of plywood had been put up to block the sudden conclusion of the house. A tarpaulin had been nailed over that; it looked streaked with moisture, probably from all the recent storms.

I smoked around the gaps between the plywood and Tranquility's wall and found myself in one of those richly paneled hallways,
with embossed strips of copper going green decorating the tops of
both walls.

I hung in the air, obviously out of place. Had anyone emerged
from the stairway at the other end of the corridor, they'd think
there was a fire.

But no one came up. There was only one heartbeat on this level
of the manor house, and it emanated from the one room with a
closed door.

I thought about smoking through the keyhole or under the gap
at the bottom, but it seemed, well, rude to show up like that. This
was his home, not mine, and even though he'd had no qualms
about barging into my bedroom uninvited, I was not him.

So I Turned back to a girl in the hall, raised my fist, and knocked.

I heard him stirring. The knob began to turn. I grabbed it and
held the door in place before he could open it more than a crack.

"Do you have a blanket or something?"

The knob released. He padded away, came back with a quilt that
he thrust through the gap in the doorway. I wrapped myself up and
went in.

Electric lights, not even gas. No soot, no flickering. I'd never get
used to them.

Colored-glass chandeliers lit the room in pools of artificial
glow. Newspaper pages scattered the floor beneath the windows, as
if he'd been reading there for days and no one had bothered to
come and pick them up. There was a rumpled bed with stiffly
draped curtains, a few rugs, a desk holding empty wineglasses, and
a fireplace—no fire—with a mantel of polished red stone. None of
the furniture matched. It seemed as if they were pieces culled from

other sections of the mansion, lumped together for convenience and nothing else.

Even so, it was a remarkably spare space, considering its size. The students' suites at Iverson had more frippery than this.

Armand was staring at me, his hand still on the knob.

"I told you I'd come," I said. Then, when he didn't move: "You should close the door."

He did. I wandered forward into the chamber, the quilt dragging behind me in an angled, weighted train.

I looked up, stepped out from beneath the buzz of a chandelier, and turned around to find him again. He hadn't yet moved.

"I've a message for you from Lady Sophia."

His face remained empty.

"She apologizes for not expressing her condolences properly to you today. She said to tell you that she's sorry. That she liked your brother and she'll miss him."

"Sophia knew you were coming here? Tonight?"

"No. She thinks we're lovers. She thought we'd steal away somehow to see each other soon."

That seemed to wake him some. He took a step toward me, despair roughening his tone.

"Is that why you came?"

"No, my lord." But since I didn't have any answer beyond that, I went to his bed and sat upon its edge. I hooked my heels in place against the black-walnut frame and laced my fingers together in my lap. Then I waited.

It took him about two minutes to come over. He climbed up beside me, not touching, and sat with his shoulders slumped. He smelled of sandalwood aftershave and wine.

"I guess you'll have to be a sodding duke now," I tried—clumsy, tasteless, and he only winced.

"Sorry." I covered his hand with mine. "That was dumb."

"No, you're right. I'd be lying if I said I hadn't been stewing about it. Me and Reggie both. I think it's safe to say that this isn't remotely what either of us wanted."

"I'm sure you'll do swimmingly."

"Bugger that," he said, tired. "And bugger Aubrey, too. I wish I could say that to his face, even if he did go down a hero in a dog-fight. Tell him what an ass he is for dying. For leaving me here like this."

"I know."

His hand twisted around until it covered mine.

"Isn't it peculiar, Eleanore," he said, not making it a question. "I know that you know." He sighed. "They couldn't even scrape together enough of his body to return it to us. They had to identify the plane by its numbers. What they could see of the numbers. All the rest of it—all of *him*—burned up."

I'd never suffered another's bereavement before. I'd gone through the steps of my own, of course, but only in private moments, tears in pillows or hidden in the falling rain. This was something very new and different to me: Armand's unfiltered grief, so bare and so deep.

So naturally my instinct was to deflect it.

"How is your father?"

Armand squeezed his eyes closed. "You saw him. Looks splendid, doesn't he? The butler can't uncork the bottles of claret fast enough."

I glanced over at the wineglasses on the desk but said only,

"Maybe what he needs is you nearby. You know, just being around him more. That might help."

"He can't even look me in the face. Didn't you catch that? It's like if he looks at me, he sees only his dead son, not his live one. It fills him with hate."

"I'm sure it's not—"

"He's getting in guns," Armand said. "Crates and crates of guns. He's always been a collector. He and some of his blokes, they even formed a hunting club. But this is something different. This is . . . more. Today it was machine guns."

I tipped my head. "What's that?"

"They're quite modern." He scratched at his shoulder through his shirt and straightened some. "They use bullets on a belt that's fed into a drum. It's thoroughly—" He noticed my face. "They fire a lot of bullets very, very quickly. Quicker than anything else."

I looked up and around the bedroom, the mismatched furniture, the weirdly firm light. "Why? What could you hunt with those? What could they have to do with anything?"

"I don't know," he replied. "That's what's so unnerving."

I rubbed a hand to my forehead, feeling an ache beginning to build behind my skull. "Armand."

His eyes went to mine.

I had to say this carefully; I had no wish to add to his despair, but I couldn't let it go. "Do you think . . . do you suppose it's possible that your father might . . . mean to do you any harm?"

But I'd actually made him smile. A real one, too, even if it came acerbic and thin. "With a pair of Vickers? Not unless he means to mount them in the hallway and spray me with bullets when I'm not paying attention. Seems like rather a spot of work for him. Surely even an unwelcome heir is better than none."

I returned his smile as I pulled away my hand. "I think we need to teach you how to Turn to smoke, just in case. It's a handy thing to be able to vanish in a hurry."

His smile widened, but there was no humor left to it. "Handy." He fell back against the blankets of the bed, his eyes gone shiny and hard. "If I could vanish into smoke, Eleanore, I'd leave this place and never return. That's a promise."

"Just like Rue," I said softly.

"Yes. Why not? Just like Rue."

· · ·

"I'm spending until dawn with you," I said firmly. "Don't bother to argue."

"God forbid," said Jesse, solemn.

I pushed past him into the cottage. He'd been waiting up for me, I could tell. There was a book spread facedown upon the table, a pair of lamps lit beside it.

"I thought you said you were resting tonight."

"Aye. I was. But then it occurred to me that the bed wasn't nearly so comfortable without you. So I got up and hoped."

I crossed my arms over my chest and dug my toes into the soft nap of the rug. The cottage had been built within a protective circle of birches; even during the heat of day, it was never very warm.

"You hoped for me?" I asked, uncertain.

Jesse came close, put his arms around me, and buried his face in my hair. "As always. As ever."

"And I came," I whispered, closing my eyes, breathing him. The ache behind my forehead began to unbind.

"And you came," he agreed.

And he summoned the magic that was all his own, beyond stars and starfire. A magic of mortal lips and hands, of bristly new whiskers scraping my chin, of melting kisses that made the whiskers unimportant.

Our bodies entwined, our hearts. Our lives.

I think that was the night a very quiet, very powerful part of me began to comprehend how it was going to be. I think the part of *me* that was magic, that had broken away from the practical earth to slip along Jesse's celestial family of stars, to allow them to bind me in their spell . . .

That part of me knew.

. . .

A lethargy had taken the castle and all the girls in it. Very few of the students had known Aubrey, but we all knew of his family and his station, and that was enough to wash the color from the cheeks of entire classes. We were given black satin ribbons to tie as armbands along our sleeves. All the mirrors had been covered in strips of black crêpe, and a wreath of dried black roses hung on the head-mistress's door like the single baleful eye of a rook. I wondered if we'd gone through the entire county's worth of dye.

The professors spoke in weighty voices no matter the topic. Lightheartedness was not permitted. Laughter was not permitted. Even our meals had gotten more salty, perhaps from the cooks' tears falling into the stew.

I had not known the dead son of the duke. But I knew that if it were me—when it became me—I wanted none of this to infect the lives of those I'd be leaving behind.

No salt and endless black. No dragging footsteps of sorrow. I found myself hoping that when I died, the people who loved me would celebrate what I'd had instead of weep for what I would not.

The liveliest people at Iverson weren't its residents. The duke had decided to store some of Tranquility's spare fixtures and furnishings here in the empty chambers; apparently he'd finally noticed that half his mansion was rotting unprotected beneath rain and sun. For the past few days a stream of village men had delivered crate after crate on their backs, like picnic ants carrying sugar cubes. A line into the castle. A line out. At least they smiled as they were leaving.

I was making my way to the tower stairs after supper, walking slowly because rushing was sure to earn me a scold. At the end of the main hall, Mrs. Westcliffe stood with one of the younger maids, their arms filled with unlit lamps.

"Here, of course," she was saying. "And at every window along the wall. Then you may begin upstairs. Take these from me. Yes, take them, Beth, and get Gladys to help if you need. There must be one in each. Make certain there's enough oil to last the night."

My slow steps slowed even more. Mrs. Westcliffe turned and spied me.

"Miss Jones. May I assist you with something?"

"No, ma'am. I was just going up to bed."

"Well. Good night."

"Good night. That's . . . that's an awful lot of light in the windows, isn't it, ma'am?"

The maid ducked her head and bobbed awkwardly at us both, then shuffled on. Mrs. Westcliffe watched her go. She was so distracted she didn't even reprimand me for using the word *awful*, which she considered uncouth.

"His Grace has requested that a lighted lamp be placed in every window of the castle for the next fortnight. In honor of his son."

I knew it wasn't my place to question the mighty, and deeply bereaved, duke. But the words escaped me, anyway.

"Is that wise? Er, that is, in London we papered the windows. To hide the light."

I had gained her full focus. Her chin lifted. "Miss Jones, as you have undoubtedly noticed, this is not London. We are not any-where in the vicinity of London. The Duke of Idylling has made a very simple, very heartfelt request, and I will honor it. That is all you need know. Good night."

She stalked down the hall, ebony skirts flaring.

"Good night," I called, because I knew that, even with her chin like that, she would still be listening to make sure my manners were intact.

. . .

The duke's fortnight began. Every night, as soon as the sun sank past the horizon, Iverson glowed like a Christmas tree, merry lights dancing in each and every window.

Every window but one. I might live in their bubble now, but I hadn't always. I'd seen firsthand what a bomb could do to flesh and stone.

The nights ticked on. The moon got thinner and thinner.

Chapter 27

Letter from Major Bernard C. R. Sumner, War Propaganda Bureau, London Headquarters

To: His Grace the Duke of Idylling
Re: Marquess of Sherborne

March 15, 1915

Reg,

You'll be pleased to know your concerns regarding the marquess have been noted and all matters I assume sorted to your satisfaction. Paperwork regarding Sherborne's transfer from the Royal Flying Corps to this office as a liaison officer have been signed and filed. He should be notified of his reassignment any day. Expect to see him around end of April. RFC isn't fond of releasing trained pilots. Took a bit of harrying to get them to agree! Will send you his itinerary as soon as all is arranged.

On a more personal note, can't tell you how happy we are to soon welcome a hero into our midst. Langley's been saying for months

we could use a man here at HQ who's done some real fighting, been to the front, so to speak. The marquess's record of twelve confirmed air combat victories [and I believe another five unconfirmed behind enemy lines] has everyone's rapt attention.

Hope all is well. Margie sends her best. We'll pop by for a spot of hunting before long, I'm sure.

—Bernie

Chapter 28

"Reginald?"

Armand poked his head past the doorway of the study, glancing about.

Empty. Lights left burning. Curtains left open to show the night. A crushed cigarette and a china cup in its saucer on the desk.

He walked to the desk, lifted the cup to his nose. Coffee. *Coffee.* Black, unadulterated, a few good inches of it still sloshing around the bottom, gone cold..

Mandy dropped into his father's chair behind the desk and thought about that. He hadn't seen Reginald sober in days. Actually, he hadn't seen Reginald sober *or* drunk in days. His Grace had been distinctly absent from manor life, and damned inconvenient it'd been, too, leaving his remaining son to deal with all the endless details of managing an estate he'd never been trained to inherit.

But nothing dislodged Reginald from his mourning. Armand had asked the chatelaine to keep an eye on him as discreetly as she could; he couldn't forget those Vickers, despite what he'd said to Eleanore. The chatelaine's reports to him had all been of the same flavor: Reg was locked in his room or locked in his study. He ate very little; he drank a great deal. He shifted from one chamber to the other, back and forth, but tonight he was in neither.

Mandy had already picked the lock on the duke's bedroom door to be sure.

Something had changed. Something felt *not right,* and if he was going to be completely honest with himself, that same *not right* had been hounding him all day.

His fingers drummed a tattoo atop the leather blotter.

He glanced down. There was a crack in the line of the desk's edge that meant the drawer hadn't been properly closed.

The hairs on the back of his neck stood up.

That voice that lived within, that sly dragonish-thing, warned, *Don't do it. You won't like it; you can't change it. Don't look.*

The bracket clock counted out, *seven, eight, nine . . .*

No one would ever know how close Armand came to obeying that foreboding command, to just getting up and walking away and letting the world sort itself out as it would. He was seventeen years old and weary to the bone. If it were up to him, he'd abandon his entire family's legacy, his mother's lost magic, his father's insanity. What good had ever come of any of it?

But he had to look, didn't he? Drunk or sober, crazy or sane, Reg was all he had left. So he had to.

With a drowning sense of déjà vu, Armand Louis opened the drawer. He reached inside until his hand discovered papers.

He unfolded the top sheet, a letter. Official-looking, government letterhead.

> *You'll be pleased to know your concerns regarding the marquess have been noted and all matters I assume sorted to your satisfaction. . . .*

It took no time at all to understand the grisly enormity of what Reggie had done.

. . .

In the darkness of his bedroom, amid the mess of his sheets and all the golden songs he'd made and shaped just for her, Jesse Holms opened his eyes.

awaken! awake! the stars were crying, piercing with urgency. *your time is now!*

"Lora," Jesse said, into the sightless dark.

. . .

I opened my eyes, startled. Was someone in the room with me?

I sat up, rose to my knees in the bed. No one else was here, no Jesse, no Sophia. Nothing but me moved, yet something wasn't right.

The tower was gripped in shadows, a flat tintype of a small round room frozen in time, forever on edge. If armoires and bu-' reaus could respire, these were holding their breath. Even the sky beyond the window hung ominously still.

And purple. Amethyst. That rare, uncanny dark.

My nightgown had twisted into a tourniquet around my waist and thighs. I must have been tossing in my sleep. I plucked at it, walking on my knees to the end of the bed. My feet hit the floor and absorbed its unyielding cold.

Beloved, rose Jesse's song, strong and clear at once, shattering the calm. *Armand is in danger. He needs you.*

I didn't think. I just reacted. I opened the window and Turned to smoke and raced over the green and the water. Toward Tranquility.

The road to the plowed fields, farmhouses to the woods. Purple land, purple sky. I was a hazy streak sandwiched between them, more than halfway there before a new, heavy sensation settled over me, dragging me down to a crawl.

Armand wasn't inside Tranquility any longer.

I wasn't certain how I knew that, but it was so. None of his energy—his trail? his scent?—waited ahead of me. I felt the pull of him *behind* me. Back toward the coast.

Damn it.

I drew myself up into the stillness, condensing into a sphere above a rye field. A cloud of magpies exploded into flight from a thicket nearby, rushing frenzied wings carrying them away from me, inland.

The beast in me registered that. Hungered for pursuit. I quelled it.

Armand. Armand. The only other living being in the world with blood linked to mine.

I floated in place and tried to let my senses drift free, feeling for him, reaching. It would have been helpful to have Jesse sing me the way, but Jesse was silent.

The castle. Armand had gone there. He was in trouble and he had gone there, maybe even to find me.

I curled about, briefly assuming the shape of a fishhook—*don't think about the shark!*—and tore back the way I had come.

Iverson beckoned me home. Tiers of stone, arches and windows and towers and a hundred radiant eyes, all of them lit windows. Burning gold against amethyst, a target of such easy and immense proportions that it probably cast its glow all the way to France.

An automobile had been parked askew beneath a beech just past the island bridge, the grass behind it torn to shreds by the tyres. He must have driven here in a hurry but slammed to a stop there, far enough away that the engine wouldn't wake anyone. If that had worked, he'd have been able to creep inside the castle unnoticed. After all, Lord Armand knew his way around his former home, and the doors were never locked.

My mind put the pieces together. He didn't want to be seen or heard. He didn't want anyone else to know where he was. Was he hurt? Bleeding? Had the duke's sanity completely deserted him? Had he done something dire to his son?

Was he in pursuit?

Armand would expect to find me in my room. It would be the first place he'd look. I funneled back up to my window and poured inside, but the room was empty. No echoes of him. Nothing.

Jesse, I thought, slightly panicked. *Jesse, where is he?*

But, of course, Jesse couldn't hear me. I could only hear him.

I Turned, scrambled back into my nightgown, opened my door and paused, listening with dragon ears, tasting the air with a dragon tongue—or as close as I could get to either in my human shape. I detected limestone and cologne and furniture polish. The usual nighttime noises of a mass of sleeping girls; shifts and sighs, some snoring. The same from even farther away, perhaps the teachers' floors. The servants in their dungeon cells.

Then, from the far end of the castle, something very different: panting. A heartbeat so fast it sounded like nothing but an unbroken convulsion of muscle and blood, pumping louder and louder.

A teeny tiny metallic series of clinks echoed above that, but so dim compared to that heartbeat that I wasn't sure what it was or where it had come from.

Armand was in the eastern portion. I was in the west.

And Jesse, I realized, as his music lifted back to me in a full, imperative refrain. He was near Armand, as well.

There was no time to agonize over going to smoke or staying in this shape. If I met up with any firmly sealed windows or doors, I'd waste time Turning to open them. My feet flew down the stairs, the gown a white whip behind me. I might have made noise. Possibly not. I don't know that the soles of my feet had much contact with the floor.

In any case, I was in too much of a hurry to worry about it. If anyone did wake up, all they'd discover was an empty hallway.

Impressions flitted by me, the long corridors, sharp turns, unlit corners. I didn't recognize most of where I ran; I was just going. Going and going until suddenly I was in familiar surroundings again. I was at the base of the corkscrew stairwell that led to the roof of the castle.

Jesse and Armand were beyond them.

I grabbed the folds of the nightgown and sprinted up the stairs. The door at the top was closed but not bolted. I wrenched it open—now I was the panting one—stumbling out into a night that had shifted abruptly from stillness to chaos.

Everything after that happened rather quickly.

Wind howled, pushing me aside a step.

Jesse called, "Lora, no!"

Armand shouted, "No!"

And the duke fired his gun at me, the bullet tearing a path along the outside of my left arm.

I was tackled around the legs and slammed down hard against the limestone, pain a bright light cleaving through me. Jesse and I rolled together as another bullet ricocheted close by, close enough

that chips of rock stung my hands and face. Then he and Armand
were hauling me around the curve of the tower behind us. Another
bullet exploded past our heads.

"You're hit." Jesse was kneeling before me, protecting me from
the shots. "Let me see."

"Where?" Armand was beside him, grabbing at my arm.

"What . . ." My tongue felt too fat. I tasted copper and salt; I'd
bitten it in the fall. The words I wanted were jumbled around inside
my head, all mixed up. I spat out a mouthful of blood and tried
again. "What's happening?"

"My father," Armand said, clenched desolation and fury.

"He's got an arsenal over there." Jesse was much cooler; he had
his fingers at my face, tilting my head to the purple light. "We can't
get near."

"Right." I knew what to do. I would just Turn to smoke. He
couldn't shoot that. The world would stop slurring around me, and
I would Turn.

"No, Lora, we—" Jesse began, but too late.

It seemed like a good idea. It really did.

I surged past both of them. Armand actually thrust out his
hands, trying to grab me to hold me back, but I sieved through his
fingers and left him clutching air. Even as smoke, I still felt woozy—
strange, because I had no body any longer, so all the physical pain
was gone—but I knew I didn't have much time. If either of them
tried to follow me, they'd easily take a bullet. I wouldn't.

The duke never saw what was speeding toward him. He was
crouched at the edge of the battlement with the merlons behind
him, blockaded behind an improvised fort of crates. I could see his
hair puffed with the wind. His eyes gleaming. He had his arms

braced atop one of the boxes so his hands would be steady for the next shot.

He was so close to the end of the roof that I couldn't Turn behind him. So I did the only other thing that occurred to me.

I Turned back into a girl right above him.

We both went down hard this time, me on top and him too stunned to make more than a high, gargled sound in his throat. As soon as we hit the stone, I wrapped my arms around his head and held on tight, ready to fight him if he tried to roll, but His Grace wasn't moving. His body had gone completely slack.

Armand towed me up and Jesse hustled me away. I staggered against him, looking past his shoulder just in time to see my nightgown dance over the rim of the roof, a twirling, empty ballerina blowing away to the stars.

"That was stupid," I said loudly.

"Too right it was." None of Armand's fury had left him.

"No, I mean *you. Both* of you. Following me like that. You could have been killed!"

"*We* were doing well enough until you—did that! Went to smoke like that."

"He couldn't shoot smoke!"

"He could have shot the half-wit on *top* of him!"

"But he didn't!" I swallowed, a lump of something sick rising in my throat. "I didn't kill him, did I?"

Armand seemed to shrink a little. He looked back at the duke and shook his head. "No. I think you knocked him out. He's breathing."

"Has anyone a coat?" I asked, and found myself crumpling down to the roof, a leisurely sort of collapse. Armand grabbed me by the arm again and I managed to remain seated instead of prone.

"Dragon-girl." Jesse was stripping off his shirt. "Bravest girl. I keep telling you to eat more."

"Jesse!"

He was bleeding. The entire lower half of his left leg was covered in blood, wet and glistening.

"Clean shot," he said, his weight on his other leg as he bent to hand me the shirt. "Went all the way through. Might not even leave a scar."

Why hadn't I noticed it before? Why hadn't I smelled the blood? It was everywhere. All over him. All over me. I clambered to my feet.

He stopped my desperate groping of his thigh by cupping my face in his hands. "Truly, Lora. It's fine. My fault. I should have spoken to him through the door before opening it."

"I don't understand." I clutched his shirt to my chest, dazed. "What happened to him? Why was he shooting at us at all?" I noticed then that many of the crates were opened, shredded paper frothing over the edges of the wood, tumbling about. "What is all this?"

"The Vickers," said Armand. He lifted his hand and pointed at a pair of large, evil-looking guns set out past the crates. They'd been attached to legs of some sort, narrow muzzles, round drums, lots and lots of bullets. Just like he'd described before. "If he'd aimed those at us, we wouldn't be around to chat about it now."

"But why?"

His voice began to climb. "Oh, well, it turns out he's to blame for Aubrey's death. He wasn't able to leave well enough alone, to leave Aubrey to his goddamned glory in the goddamned war. He had gotten him reassigned back to England, even though Aubrey'd never have wanted that. Never would have agreed to that, so they must have forced him. But he was coming home. When his plane was shot down in that dogfight, he was on his way home. Because of Reginald."

He threaded both hands through his hair, staring at his father; I could see the fury draining away. When he spoke again, he sounded just . . . confounded. Disbelieving.

"So he's lured them here. The Germans. He managed—oh, God, he managed to somehow start a rumor that Iverson's been turned into a secret munitions factory. That we're building explosives or something out here. I found cables and cables about it, and everyone knows how—how easy they are to intercept. He wanted the Germans to come to blow it up, don't you see? And he meant . . . I think he meant to shoot them first. With the Vickers."

"I thought that ground fire couldn't reach the zeppelins," I said. "I thought that guns on the ground didn't have the range."

"Eleanore. Do you imagine for one particle of one second that he was thinking clearly enough to fathom that?"

"He was thinking clearly enough to fathom all of *this*," I retorted, my hand flung out to encompass the roof. Blood stained my palm. "Clearly enough to have men haul all these crates into the castle in broad daylight all week long, so that everyone could see them and wonder what was actually inside!"

"I know!" Armand's voice broke. He walked back to his father, going to his knees beside him. He placed his hands upon the unconscious man's chest. "I know," he repeated, beneath the screech of the wind.

Jesse left me to limp to them. The backs of his fingers grazed the top of Armand's head, not quite a caress. "Grief can break a mind. He loved and loved, your father, because that's his way. He couldn't turn it off."

"He *shot* at Armand," I felt compelled to point out. I wasn't in a forgiving mood; the duke certainly hadn't minded risking me and everyone inside the castle getting blasted into oblivion to gain his revenge. And the smell of Jesse's blood was becoming overwhelming. "He might have *killed* you."

"Yet he didn't. He had the opportunity to kill both of us when we first made it up the stairs, but once he saw he'd wounded me, he simply shot around us. I suspect the bullet that got you, Lora, was more of an accident than not. All he wanted was for us to go, so that he could finish his plan. Burn away his grief."

Armand was shaking his head. "I don't know what to do now. He's the duke of all this. The duke of everything. If people find out . . . I don't know what to do." He rubbed at his eyes. "God, Dad."

I had managed to get myself into the shirt, even past the throbbing ache of my arm.

"Right," I said once more, because it sounded firm, and because Armand's brittle desolation was beginning to eat at me. None of this, after all, was his fault. "We get him downstairs. We sneak him out of the castle, back to your motorcar. You take Jesse to a doctor and take your father home. Lock him in a room, pour some wine down his throat. Laudanum. Whatever you have to do to keep him out while I get rid of the guns. None of this ever happened." I looked at Jesse. "Are there hidden tunnels to use? So no one sees?"

"I'm sorry," said Jesse. "It's too late for that."

"No, we can at least get him to—"

"Too late, Lora. Listen."

I did, cocking my head to the wind. But I didn't hear any voices. I didn't hear people on the stairs. It was mostly schoolrooms over here; we were far from the populated part of the castle.

I held back my hair and shrugged at him.

Jesse glanced upward. Toward the eastern stars.

Thup-thup-thup-thup. It was hardly a sound at all, it came so faint.

"What is that?" I asked sharply, but I knew. Oh, I knew.

The Germans had believed the mad duke's cables. The airships were coming.

Chapter 29

"What is what?" asked Armand. "I don't hear anything."

I hadn't taken my eyes from Jesse. "There's more than one. Two at least, right?"

"Two," he said. "I hear two."

Armand stood. "Two *what*?"

I sent him a look. "Zeppelins. Headed this way."

He stared at us, silent. And, really, what could he say? *Sorry my father doomed us all? Nice knowing you?*

"All right, all right." I chafed my hands nervously up and down my sides, rumpling the shirt. "I can—I can fly up there. Turn to dragon. Claw them open, make them crash." Instinctively, I turned to Jesse, almost plaintive. "Can't I?"

He took up my hand. I swear I saw the stars brighten around him, a sparkling, silvered nimbus. "Perhaps."

"Well, I have to. That's all there is to it. I have to."

"No," burst out Armand. "They have guns! Bombs! They'll fill you with holes before you can blink!"

"Not if I'm smoke."

"*Smoke* can't tear apart a dirigible! We need to wake the others and evacuate the castle. Get everyone out before they make it here."

"No time," said Jesse. "We've only a few minutes. Look."

And, yes, I could see them now in the distance, two round, dark blots against the purple sky, steadily enlarging.

Thup-thup-thup-thup-thup . . .

. . . *shoom-shoom-shoom* . . .

"Hold up, what's that?" I ran to a merlon, tilting past it to scan the empty sea. The wind snapped my hair into a banner, a cheerful long flutter beyond my face. "Do you hear that, too? That swooshing sound? Is it a ship?"

"A submarine," replied Jesse, matter-of-fact. "A U-boat sent ahead. They do that with the airships when they can. It's about ten leagues out. Headed this way."

I think the word *despair* is much too small to encompass the magnitude of all it defines. For me, right then, *despair* meant that everything within me—my organs, my spirit, my hope—plunged down into a place of utter density, of blackness so heavy and bleak I had no idea how to lift any of it up again.

I can't do this. I'm just Lora Jones. I can't even remember how to tell a shrimp fork from an oyster fork. I can barely find middle C. I can't save Jesse and Armand and the castle. I can't defeat them all.

But I had to. We were going to die unless I did.

I pulled back from the merlon. I stood with my hands at my sides and made certain my face was scrubbed clean of any expression before I turned around to them again.

Jesse had decided to sit. The darkened figure of the duke stretched out flat behind him; the ruby from his ring was making a warbling noise, small and sorrowful.

"Is the tide high enough right now for a torpedo to make it inside the grotto?"

"Aye. I think so."

"But they won't know about the grotto," protested Armand. "How could they know?"

"It's been there for ages, Mandy. Longer than the castle, even. It's part of the geography of the island. How difficult could it be to find out about it?"

One strike. I'd bet that was all it would take. One lucky strike, and the grotto, the columns, the foundation of the castle itself, would shatter. And down we'd all go.

My heart was thudding so loudly I thought I might retch. Armand had taken my hand and was crushing it in his. His heartbeat nearly as frantic as mine.

Blood and muscle. Muscle and blood.

Jesse only watched us both from the limestone as his leg leaked a slow, slick puddle along the fitted grooves. I freed my hand and dragged off the shirt.

"I'll start in the air," I said, far more steadily than I thought I could, considering. I knelt to tie the shirt around his thigh, cinching it tight above the wound; he stiffened but let me finish the knot. "The air first, the airships, and then—then I'll dive."

"You can't swim," broke in Armand. "You told me that you can't."

"Maybe I can now. If I'm a dragon."

"Don't be an idiot! If you can't swim, you can't *swim,* Eleanore! You'll drown out there, and what the bloody hell do you think you're going to do anyway to a *U-boat*? *Bite* it open?"

I stood again. "Yes! If I must! I don't hear you coming up with a better—"

"You'll *die* out there!"

"Or we'll all die here!"

"We're going to find another way!"

"You two work on that. I'm off." I fixed them both with one last, vehement look, the Turn rising inside me.

Remember this. Remember them, this moment, this heartbreak, these two boys. Remember that they loved you.

Armand had reached for my shoulders. "I forbid—Eleanore, please, no—"

"No," echoed Jesse, speaking at last. "You're not going after the submarine, Lora. You won't need to."

Armand and I paused together, glancing down at him. I stood practically on tiptoe, so ready to become my other self.

Jesse climbed clumsily to his feet. When he swayed, we both lunged to catch him.

"Armand will take me to the shore. I'll handle the U-boat."

"How?" demanded Armand at once.

But I understood. I could read him so well now, Jesse-of-the-stars. I understood what he meant to do, and what it would cost him.

I felt myself shaking my head. Above us, the airship propellers thumped louder and louder.

"Yes," said Jesse, smiling his lovely smile at me. "I already sense your agreement. Death and the Elemental were stronger joined than apart, remember? This is our joining. Don't waste any more time quarreling with me about it. That's not your way." He leaned down to me, a hand tangled in my hair. His mouth pressed to mine, and for the first time ever I didn't feel bliss at his touch.

I felt misery.

"Go on, Lora-of-the-moon," he murmured against my lips. "You're going to save us. I know you will."

I glared past him to the harsh, baffled face of Armand. "Will you help him? Do you swear it?"

"I—yes, I will. I do."

I disentangled Jesse's hand, kissed it, stepped back, and let the Turn consume me, smoke rising and rising, leaving the castle and all I loved behind me for the wild open sky.

. . .

Airships aren't actually powered by air. They have propellers and engines that run on fuel, much like a water-bound ship, and they stay aloft by means of the hydrogen gas trapped inside the cells of their great elongated balloons.

I knew that much from the reports in the London papers, but what I recalled most about them, watching them float over St. Giles to let loose their unholy fire, were the windowed gondolas that hung beneath the balloon part, filled with crew. And the bomb bays positioned behind those, filled with death. When the ground-defense searchlights landed on them just so, you could clearly see the figures of the men behind the glass.

I remember thinking that the Germans must have had a very fine view of all the neighborhoods they were obliterating.

In every raid, I witnessed the return fire from the rifles and pistols of the watchmen stationed atop the buildings. A short-lived torrent of lights, insignificant as matches lit and dying. If any of them had managed a hit, I'd never been able to tell.

The zeppelins simply flew too high. If there weren't enough aeroplanes assembled nearby to dog them back to sea, they wiped out everything in their paths until they ran out of bombs.

No aeroplanes were coming to our rescue tonight.

Only me. A thing of smoke and tentative skills. I wasn't even certain if my wings were meant for flight. I hadn't exactly had any luck with it the one time I'd tried.

I could glide, though. Probably.

Maybe.

Should worse come to worst, I could smoke up to them, Turn to dragon right there, dig my claws in, and hang on. That might do it.

Looked like I was about to find out.

What I hadn't thought about, what I'd completely managed to forget about, was that I wasn't exactly skilled at maintaining my transformed shape, either. The reminder came to me rather forcibly as I was streaming my way east, over the channel, and felt myself beginning to solidify.

No. No!

Yes.

Several thousand feet up in the air, I Turned back into a girl. Screaming, cartwheeling, everything topsy-turvy purple as gravity reclaimed me and I plummeted down to the water.

fly! sang the stars, weighing in past my screams. *fly, beast!*

It was a damned near save. I was a girl and then I wasn't, managing the Turn so close to the sea that the foam from the cresting waves splashed up through the smoke of me.

Good thing I didn't have a real heart just then. It would have stopped entirely.

I bobbled there, terror-riven, until the sounds of the airships drew me upward again.

Smoke, smoke, I thought fiercely. *Just—keep—going—*

Above me, still so far above, the dirigibles grew larger. And larger.

And even larger. I'd seen them only from a distance; I'd never gotten any closer to one than the top floor of Blisshaven. It'd been obvious to me then that they were huge, but I hadn't comprehended *how* huge they were, how chillingly titanic, until I was a wisp alongside one of the balloons, barely as wide as a seam, trying my best to slink up the curving surface of its fabric so that I could Turn on its top.

Bigger than buildings. Bigger than cathedrals. Bigger than anything.

Don't look down. Dear God, whatever you do, don't . . .

Contact with its skin nearly undid me. It felt *alive* with the resonance of the engines, alive and cold, reptilian. I couldn't believe how quiet they were from below. From here, spread thin like wrapping paper against the monster machine, it seemed the noise would gel me back into a girl and shatter me into pieces.

It took an eternity to reach the top of the balloon, and once there, it was practically all I could see. Still arched above me was a bowl of amethyst, but below me there was only zeppelin. The other airship thumped to my left; I heard it, but again, couldn't see it.

All right. I was ready.

I Turned—into a *girl,* not a dragon—and was immediately knocked backward by the wind. I tried to scream once more, but my lungs got no air, and my fingers had no purchase along a material that felt more like solid steel than fabric. I was rolled toward the tail fins in seconds. A few seconds more and I would fall again, this time maybe into one of the propellers.

At the narrowed stern of the balloon, I Turned back to smoke and got sucked instantly into the ship's wake.

I tore apart. It was like when I had flown to the stars and been caught in the high winds, but much, much worse. No matter how

I tried, I couldn't right myself. I felt sick and dizzy and, in the end, had to give up. As the airship receded, the wake grew weaker, finally enough that I could rip myself free and drift.

The Germans were getting away. Both of them, both dirigibles, flying away from me utterly unscathed, closing in steadily on the castle. I hadn't managed to stop even one.

I fervently hoped Jesse was having better luck than I.

. . .

It would have been so much simpler if he could have walked, or run, by himself. If he could have sent Armand on his way with the duke, instead of leaving the duke insensible on the rooftop and relying upon his son for steady steps and eyes that saw clearly.

But that wasn't his fate, so Jesse told himself he should just stop wishing for it. Facts were facts. His left leg was useless. His sight was dimming. He could tell by the smell and the black guttering spots in his vision that they were leaving a trail of blood all along Iverson's pristine floors.

He didn't think Armand had taken note of that. Perhaps his sense of smell wasn't as keen. Not yet.

No one else awoke. There was that slim blessing, at least. With Jesse's arm slung around the other boy's shoulders, they made it all the way to the main doors without rousing a peep from anyone. Just the two of them, and the castle allowing their passage, and the blood-smeared footprints seeping into runners and following them down the corridors.

That was good. That was better than if there'd been a fuss. He wasn't certain his head was straight enough any longer to come up with even feeble lies to explain this.

Tomorrow morning, Jesse knew, was going to bring enough truth for everyone.

. . .

I was smoke atop a dirigible again, this time the one farther out from the shore, as if that might make a difference. I centered myself on its field of gray skin, fighting to stay apace with it. Fighting my revulsion of its living, pulsating power beneath me.

I Turned to dragon and dug in.

Dragon claws. As it happened, even though they looked like gold, they weren't gold. Not the actual metal. Gold was soft, and my claws were anything but. I learned that as soon as I began to back up: My front talons sliced through the fabric of the balloon as if it were lukewarm butter, leaving a series of black, gaping slits.

Gas gushed past me, unscented and colorless, but I could still see it, how it bent the purple air and then began to suffocate me, flooding my nose and throat and lungs.

I flapped my wings and tried to pull free. One talon was caught and I yanked and yanked, choking, enlarging the gash.

The dirigible began a mild descent.

At last I got loose, shredded fabric rippling up to the stars. I skidded awkwardly to my right, wings outstretched, landing again, digging in again. The hydrogen was stored in separate gas bags. I wasn't sure if emptying only one of them would be enough to fully bring the ship down.

The second set of slits was even longer than the first. Two of them combined in a sudden rupturing of material. The black maw of it gaped beneath me; when the ship listed hard aside, I nearly tumbled in.

Something zinged by me. With the gas in my face, I thought at first it was a gull or a gannet, but it wasn't. It was a bullet.

It was followed by a volley of about a million more.

. . .

"Why—the beach?"

Armand was out of breath. They were outside, nearly to the motorcar. By now he was carrying practically all of Jesse's weight, and even though he was strong—much stronger than he should have been, than a human boy his age would have been—Jesse weighed almost fourteen stone. He was heavy, and he wasn't helping. His legs at this point were just meat.

"Grotto's closer," Armand noted, still gasping.

"The water," Jesse said. His mouth felt so dry. He knew it was the blood loss parching him. That thinking about water or ale or tea or anything wasn't going to help, but it did seem to sharpen his mind some. "Water," he said again thickly, trying to clarify. "Distance. Must see it."

"Care to let"—they stumbled over a groove in the path; Armand heaved them both back up—"let me in on—whatever the hell it is you're—planning, Holms?"

"No," said Jesse.

Armand only grunted, pulling them on.

. . .

The other airship had machine guns. They had veered in close and were firing them at me. Perhaps I'd panicked them enough that they weren't even thinking about the fact that they were helping to annihilate their comrades.

The zeppelin I had wounded—like an animal, like a vicious

keening animal—kept listing. That's all that saved me. I was too slow to duck a bullet; they pocked into the skin of the balloon and left fresh new holes for the hydrogen to escape, and I was rolled out of range. By now I could hear the shouting of the crew in the gondola far below, trying to understand what was happening. For all they knew, their allies had turned on them. Perhaps even some of the gunfire was striking them, although, as far as I could tell, none of the men in their ship were firing back.

The night sky was diminishing. The writhing sea rushed to meet us. I withdrew my claws and opened my wings and let the channel winds have me, jerking me away from both ships, and the wounded one sank and sank.

I wanted to watch it go all the way down. But the men in the other ship had spotted me, had trained their weapons back on me. I had to dive fast away from them and then up, up, because I thought—I hoped—they wouldn't have the means to fire at me once I crested the side of their balloon.

I heard the first zeppelin smashing into the water behind us and couldn't help but glance back. Their bombs began to explode, one after another after another, deafening, and then everything was blue fire, white fire, and I was blinded.

I flapped around like a bat amid a stream of bullets, graceless, falling.

My front right leg was struck. My left wing.

smoke! shrilled the stars.

Of course. That worked.

As smoke, I was able to get my bearings again. I had ended up somewhere between the sinking wreckage of the first ship and the slipstream of the second. I narrowed into a dart and raced toward the untouched ship, something livid and pitiless waking within me.

I don't think I'd felt much of anything beyond desperation up until then. There had been no time. But as I sped toward that second dirigible, I realized I was more than desperate.

I was enraged. I'd been shot three times tonight, and I was going to make these men pay for that. For what they planned to do to the castle and to my country. For St. Giles and London and the orphanage. Everything.

They imagined themselves the dragon-slayers, but the dragon was going to slay them instead.

The zeppelin in the water had nearly finished its burn. By its dying light I could see the airmen in the second gondola with their guns poking out, more shouting, everyone searching the skies around them for the mythical beast that was no longer visible. I smoked up to them, right up to one of the windows, and examined the face of the man staring straight through the mist of me.

Youngish, square-jawed. Attractive. Navy-blue uniform with loops of brassy braid. White hat. Brows knit with worry.

Yes, do worry, I thought, and boiled up to the top of the balloon.

Same plan, same results—at least at first. I Turned to dragon in the exact center of the fabric field and jabbed my talons deep. The hydrogen surged out; the ship began to descend. I shifted over, ready to do it again, when the zeppelin made an abrupt left turn, throwing me free.

No doubt they'd seen everything I'd done to the first ship. They'd figured out how to counter.

I used my wings, but it hurt where the bullet had pierced me. Hurt like someone was twisting a dagger into my flesh. So I Turned to smoke to find a new place to dig in . . .

Only I didn't. I Turned to a girl again instead.

. . .

The Atalanta couldn't make it all the way to the water. The slope accessing the shore was too steep, and Jesse found himself remotely grateful that Armand had sense enough to pull the brake before they rolled. It left them to slide down the scrub and rocks themselves, which actually meant Jesse sliding and Armand attempting to keep them both upright.

The beach was wet pebbles and seaweed. The pebbles clicked and clacked as Armand dragged Jesse to the breaking surf.

There were things he wanted to say, Jesse realized. Important things. Things that seemed to matter. But it was too difficult to keep them in his head; the black dots in his eyes from before had engorged into tunnels, and all he could see now was a small wavering window directly before him. He might have been in pain. He should have been. But mostly what he felt were the pebbles beneath his body, cool and smooth.

"Leave me," he was able to say.

Armand's face filled the narrow window of his vision.

"Not bloody likely."

He felt it now, Jesse knew. Whether Lord Armand wanted to or not, he felt their bond. Dragon protects star. Nothing to be done about it.

Almost nothing.

"Get back," Jesse said, making it a command. He had life enough for that. "Get back into the auto, Armand."

"No—I . . ."

But it worked, as Jesse had known it would. The other boy's face left his view. His footsteps ground into the pebbles, halting, retreating.

It filled Jesse with an unexpected warmth. And hope. Things might . . . things might work out, after all. . . .

He focused upon the lip of seawater in front of him. He focused on moving his arm. His hand.

. . .

The second airship careened drunkenly from side to side. I bounced off its unbroken skin, into the air, then the skin again. The curve of the balloon was so immense that I slid down its side, trying to Turn to smoke or dragon or anything but a girl who could not hold on to a dirigible.

I managed smoke, but only long enough to find myself back down at the gondola. Then I was me again, a girl again, pressed naked and bloody against the glass, dropping. My right hand hooked the rim of an open window. Pain knifed through my arm, and I screamed.

My fingers released—and then a hand smacked around my wrist. I dangled in place, my legs kicking out to the infinite distance below, and when I looked wildly up I saw the German officer of before, the attractive one, leaning out the gondola window to hold on to me. Staring dumbfounded back at me.

His eyes were brown.

He shouted something, lost to the wind.

I snarled at him and Turned to smoke, flinging myself just high enough to Turn back to dragon and slice a long, vertical slit down the side of the balloon.

I met a girder beneath the fabric. I assumed it was a girder; as my claws raked its length, it squealed like steel and sparks leapt from our union, dazzling my eyes.

Sparks. Hydrogen.

I pushed off with all my might just as the balloon combusted, but the fire still got me.

I curled away from the airship—singed, falling—Turning and Turning. Within seconds I couldn't tell what I was. There was only the wind rushing past me and the fireball descending next to me, fabric in flames and red-hot steel.

And the brown-eyed man tumbled from the gondola. Three others like him, all of them shrieking as they hurtled to their deaths in the waiting sea.

I swooped toward him. I reached out for him.

Shiny talons curved around his wrist; I was pulled sideways from his sudden weight.

It seemed I was a dragon, after all.

. . .

Below us, all the sea flashed bright. Brief as a comet, glittering light spreading out miles in a fantastical, brilliant bloom. Night turned by Jesse into golden day.

Then it was over. The channel plunged to purple-black again.

Chapter 30

He lifted his face from the crook of his arm. He wiped the sand from his lids and allowed himself to breathe again, taking in the charred air, salt spray, and diesel smoke blowing over him in gusts. The smoke was especially foul, caustic stinking grease that seared his eyes and made him wipe at them again.

Armand climbed out of the Atalanta. Whatever had compelled him to fall back here in the first place—that infuriating, unbreakable command from Holms—no longer held him. He leapt down the slope, skidding through an avalanche of dirt and rocks, and bounded across the beach to the other boy.

Holms had collapsed on his side, one arm still stretched out to the channel. Mandy took him by the shoulders and rolled him to his back. It was dark out here, ruddy dark. Or maybe it was just that his eyes hadn't adjusted yet from staring at Holms when he'd detonated without warning into solid light.

"Holms. Holms! Jesse, wake up!"

Water shifted and sighed over the pebbles. Jesse was getting wet. Armand's knees were getting wet.

"Holms, did you see it?" he persisted. He tore out of his coat and lifted Jesse enough to spread it beneath him; the wool went damp right away. "She did it! She brought them both down—bloody, bloody amazing. Holms! Did you get the sub?"

There—the smallest thing: Jesse swallowing, his eyes still closed. Mandy felt hope ignite inside him, hard and glittering as the cast of golden fire.

"You did, didn't you? Come on, old chap. Tell me you did."

"Did."

"Excellent! Excellent! So let's get up, then, eh, and go find her. Go tell her, together."

Jesse smiled. His eyes never opened. The sea sifted nearer, pulled back. The pebbles all around them shone glassy with water.

"Jesse," Mandy said.

The wind fell calm. The diesel smoke wafted gently away.

"Jesse."

The sea drew back. Nothing else moved.

Mandy bent double, lowering his forehead to Jesse Holms's shoulder. His fingers felt like rusted iron against the coat. He could not get his fingers to unlock.

"I'll tell her," he whispered. "I'll tell her all that you did."

Chapter 31

The funeral for a hired hand is not the same as one for a marquess.

Mrs. Westcliffe was there for both. I guess that was the same.

Armand was there for both.

I attended only Jesse's. It probably would have been politic of me to also go to the marquess's; I had been summoned, but I didn't care. I didn't want to go anywhere, really. I wanted only to stay in my tower, in my bed, and spend the rest of my life doing nothing more than staring up at the ceiling, watching the spiders wending around on spindly legs, weaving their opal webs.

I roused myself for Jesse. That was all.

I stood between Mrs. Westcliffe and someone else. I think it was Professor Tilbury. Most of the teachers had shown up, which vaguely surprised me. Quite a few of the villagers, as well, along with all the other Iverson employees.

I was the only student. Even Malinda hadn't come.

Lord Armand—now the new Marquess of Sherborne—was the highest-ranking person in attendance, so he'd been given a place of honor right by the pit dug for the grave. He stood a solemn figure in stylish black, almost directly across from me. Whenever I glanced his way, he was staring at me. Lots of people were staring at me, frankly, but his was the only gaze that stung. So I tried not to look at him.

I also could not look at Hastings. If I looked at Hastings, stooped over his cane, I began drowning in a shame so deep and profound it made me tremble, and Tilbury would eye me uneasily and pat me on the arm.

It was my injured arm, too. It was bandaged up, but you couldn't see the bandages beneath the peacoat, so he didn't know.

Mrs. Westcliffe wouldn't glance at me at all. I think she no longer knew quite what to make of me. Was I an accidental heroine, as Armand had publically insisted, or was I something much different: a conniving slum girl who had taken advantage of her beloved Reginald's weakness and largesse?

There had been no disguising what the duke had done that night, or what he'd meant to do. Despite our initial intent to spirit him away and cover the whole thing over with darkness and lies, two burning dirigibles—visible for miles along the coast, I'd heard—were impossible to disguise. They'd woken everyone in the castle, everyone in the village, likely every single person all the way to Bournemouth. Woken them right up to the war.

And then we had been found, Armand and Jesse and me, there on that beach of broken stones.

And the duke had been found, because two minor children suffering bullet wounds, one of them dead, could not be explained away with any of the dubious, unsteady excuses that had come to me at the time.

Eventually, even the German I'd saved had been found. I'd left him in a cove of brutal surf and steep cliffs on every side. I suppose he could have tried to swim for it—I would have—but he didn't. By the next afternoon, a shepherd boy had heard his shouts and he'd been hauled up the cliffs and confined to an empty pigeon house, the sole survivor of his doomed mission.

Gone cracked, though, from the ordeal. Ranting in perfect English about dragons and a young woman who could fly.

No one believed him. A few people swore the airships had suffered lightning strikes, although the night had seemed so clear. A few more vowed they'd spotted them off the bluffs and fired at them, and that had brought them down.

Whatever it had been, everyone seemed certain of two things. It had not been a dragon, and it had not been the poor, tormented Duke of Idylling.

We'd had to give him up. To his credit, Armand had led the authorities straight to him, and apparently in the nick of time, too, as he'd been coming 'round. So no one else got shot.

I was in the hands of the local physician by then, who turned out to be the bespectacled man from the birthday party, the one chatting up Miss Swanston. He didn't seem to mind that I'd fallen mute, just like I'd been as a child. Other people talked and talked at me, but I had nothing to say.

Let silver-tongued Mandy come up with his crafty mesh of facts and fabrications. I couldn't speak. I couldn't react, not even when the bullet was fished from my arm.

I was still back on that beach, you see. I couldn't leave it. I couldn't leave Jesse.

Over the next few days, Sophia had visited enough times that I knew all the school gossip, which included a variety of tales: That

Jesse and I had been lovers, and the duke had discovered us on the roof. That Armand and Jesse had been lovers, and I had been jealous enough to inform the duke. That Jesse and Armand and I had been lovers, and the duke had tried to murder us all. . . .

Armand's official story was this:

He had discovered what his father intended that night and had raced to the castle to stop him. By pure chance he'd come across Jesse walking the grounds and had enlisted his help. He'd thought, Armand had explained bleakly to Mrs. Westcliffe when they were alone, that he could trust Holms. That perhaps there'd be a chance to hush it all up still, allow the family to deal with the situation privately. And that—although he was deeply mortified to admit it now—even if Holms had wanted to tell, he would be unable. Mute, you know. Simple.

But Holms had proven stalwart and valiant. When Miss Jones had shown up to discover them in the castle hallway, because she'd heard a suspicious noise and had feared for her schoolchums' safety, they'd had to bring her along. She'd wanted to run straight to the headmistress, of course, but Armand had persuaded her not to. How he regretted that decision now!

The duke had fired his guns at them all. They'd retreated, thought to go to the automobile to fetch a doctor and the sheriff, but they'd stumbled the wrong way and fallen down the slope to the beach instead. All three of them. And there, noble Jesse had died.

Fact. Fiction. Likely because so much of it *had* happened, and because Armand's red-eyed, stoic distress seemed so genuine, the adults around us had accepted it as truth.

Mostly.

I think if I hadn't been discovered wearing only Armand's coat as I knelt next to Jesse's body, Mrs. Westcliffe might have found the whole thing easier to swallow.

Yet the official version ruled the day. And here we all were basking in it, breathing fresh sea air, warmed by the generous spring sun. Burying a hero. A far, far greater hero than anyone standing around me at his funeral would ever suspect.

Somewhere in deep-blue briny waters, a U-boat rested, filled with live torpedoes and solid-gold men.

I thought I better understood Rue's letters now. I understood her warnings about the pain that would come with my Gifts.

I understood my sacrifice.

I listened to the vicar speak. I listened to the breeze. The birds. The sea. I watched the first handful of dirt land on Jesse's coffin and thought with absolute sincerity, *Wish it were me.*

. . .

I waited until Aubrey's funeral to steal away. It wasn't long to wait, only a week, so I made myself tolerate it.

I paid attention to my spiders. Their remarkable webs.

Due to a loss of blood, I'd been excused from attending classes, although the professors had made an effort to extend their best wishes for my recovery, mostly by assigning me homework. It'd been piling up on the bureau. I knew I should at least inspect it, but it bored me. Everything bored me.

Let them kick me out of Iverson if they wanted. Perhaps I'd fly to the moon to live.

Lora-of-the-moon. That would be me.

I itched where I was healing. The wound to my wing was a phantom itch somewhere in the vicinity of my shoulder blade; unlike my arm, no bullet hole showed there in my human form. But that particular itch was especially maddening, because I could not scratch at it. It was always present.

The following Saturday morning, the castle emptied. I got up to watch them all go, all the ebony girls, all the teachers, most of the help. Sophia had told me the formal ceremony was to be held at Tranquility, which had a completed chapel and nice, virgin grounds for its first grave. They would be burying an empty casket.

The duke, regretfully, would be unable to attend.

I wondered briefly if his madhouse was anything like mine had been, and found that I couldn't wish Moor Gate even on the man who had killed my true love.

I dressed—Blisshaven's clothes, not Iverson's. I walked like I knew what I was doing and where I was going, which was true, and I left the fortress.

It was an easy journey through the forest. The day was sublime, the kind of day reverently described in those sweeping, romantic histories of England that populated the castle library. Shafts of sunlight broke through the green canopy of trees, daubing yellow along wildflowers and butterflies and once even a rabbit, half a primrose in his mouth, staring at me with his ears high and straight.

I could smell the coming summer still, just as I had my first evening here, as I'd stepped from the train. It was warmer and lusher now, less a tinge in the air than a sultry blossoming. It traveled across the sea and laced through these woods. It slipped up my arms and neck and face and kissed me with the faintest hint of bitter salt.

Summer in the woods. Summer on the isle. I imagined it all so . . . full of life.

Jesse's cottage stood deserted. I'd wondered if Hastings had come by yet—surely he had—or had thought to maybe move into it now himself from his loft above the stables. Seemed like it would be nicer than living over horses.

I knocked on the door, in case. No one answered.

The latch gave at my touch. The cat's-eye knot watched me go in.

A shadowed place. A place of shadows. I had the feeling all the lamps in the world wouldn't illuminate the cottage again. Jesse had been its light, the heart of these woods.

Pine, soap, coffee. Cinnamon, vanilla, rain. Scents that wrapped around me as I walked in, a last trace of him. It was awful comfort.

I drew my fingers along the tabletop, remembering the buttercup turned to gold set there on that wood, how it had sung and gleamed. But then, Jesse's home had always sounded like song to me. Even at night, in our sweetest dark as I'd lain in his arms, golden songs had drifted over me.

Like now. Right now.

I glanced around and saw nothing but the expected. The table and chairs and stove and plates. The rug and fireplace. His closed bedroom door.

Ah. The bedroom. It was coming from in there.

I rested my hand on the knob and knew that I had to go in, that he had wanted me to go in. That's why there were songs resonating from inside. It was a message just for me. A message from dead Jesse.

But . . . the bedroom. The bed. Quilts we'd slept under. Sheets. His drowsy smile, half tucked against a pillow. The glass vase on his windowsill, pinkish-green with the first flush of dawn.

I hadn't come out here for his bedroom. I hadn't planned on being strong enough for that.

My hand pushed open the door.

I stood fixed in place, not breathing. I had no breath left in me. All the gold in the room had stolen it, and I might not ever breathe again.

I'd dreamed once of a forest of gold, and Jesse had done what he could to give it to me. His bedroom had been transformed into a wonderland of leaves and flowers, pinecones and branches of birch and oak, all of it glimmering, all of it singing. The bed was covered, his chest of drawers, the sill.

Much of it was jumbled together, beautiful for what it was if not its presentation. Jesse had last left this room on the night of his death, right after he'd called to me, right before he'd gone to the castle. So he would have been scattering his final gift in haste, knowing he worked against the clock.

Knowing, somehow, what was to come.

Which meant he'd been making gold for weeks. When I'd seen him so tired, when he'd told me all those nights that we should rest apart . . . he had been doing this.

For me.

A folded note had been set upon the bed. My name had been scrawled upon it.

I love you was all it said inside.

I sank to the floor. I looked up and all around as the sun danced through the window and turned Jesse's room into an ambered heaven of song and shimmer and sparks.

That was how Armand found me, hours later. That was what he saw, as well, what he heard, as he walked slowly into the chamber and eased down beside me to rest his back against the bed.

We sat there together, listening, marveling.

In time, his hand reached out and took firm hold of mine.

Epilogue

So now you know the beginning of her story, and the ending of mine. The end of my mortal time with her, at least.

But I'm not really gone. I'll never really leave her. How could I? She had been carved from the mud of the world just for me. I had fallen from the stars for her.

I told you before: Once a *drákon* holds your eyes and touches your flesh, you belong to them. And, believe me, when that happens, you're glad for it. You lay your heart at their feet and hope for their favor, knowing its true worth.

Our time together had been so short. Every turn of the planet, every hour and minute and second, I had loved her and celebrated her. And I considered myself blessed, even unto death, to have known her smile. The rapture of Eleanore.

Blessed to offer myself up for her.

Lora-of-the-moon. She'll fly my way again. I know it.

I dwell high above her now, back with my first family. The path of my dragon's earthly life shines before me like a skein of glittering crimson thread. It crisscrosses the mortal plane, tracing its way from the Atlantic, where she took her first breath, east to Europe, where she will take her last. Armand's thread glitters, too, plaited through hers.

The war will entangle them even more. The war will do its best to snip both threads short.

It is a thing of gore and violence. War cannot abide magic of any sort, much less a magic as brilliant as theirs.

I'll be the star above them both, watching. Singing.

I'd waited for her nearly all my life. I can wait a while longer, until she turns her ear up to the night skies, ready to hear my ballad once more.

Acknowledgments

I have been blessed with the best people: Annelise Robey and Andrea Cirillo, and everyone at the fabulous Jane Rotrosen Agency. Shauna Summers and all the brilliant folks at Random House who work so hard to make me shine. Sean, of the steady hand and kind soul. And, of course, all of you reading this now. Thank you.

About the Author

SHANA ABÉ is the bestselling author of thirteen novels, including the acclaimed Drákon Series. She lives in Colorado in a happy house with a good many pets.

www.shanaabe.com

About the Type

This book was set in Stone, a typeface designed by the teacher, lecturer, and author Sumner Stone in 1988. This typeface was designed to satisfy the requirements of low-resolution laser printing. Its traditional design blends harmoniously with many typefaces, making it appropriate for a variety of applications.